"This novel really does sparkle. It is witty and clever, and packs a very well-aimed punch."

RODDY DOYLE

"This book made me want to run away and join the circus. A delightful read about accepting and embracing the qualities that make us unique; Kelly McCaughrain is one to watch."

SUSIN NIELSEN, AUTHOR OF
WE ARE ALL MADE OF MOLECULES

"A quirky and complex story, told with an elegant simplicity that hooks you from the first few pages… Vibrant, funny, moving and thought-provoking."

THE BOOKBAG

FLYING TIPS FOR FLIGHTLESS BIRDS

KELLY McCAUGHRAIN

WALKER
BOOKS

First published in Great Britain 2018 by Walker Books Ltd
87 Vauxhall Walk, London SE11 5HJ

2 4 6 8 10 9 7 5 3 1

Text © 2018 Kelly McCaughrain
Cover illustration © 2018 Anna Rebecca Morrison

This book has been typeset in Bembo, Ubuntu, Rosewood, Open Sans, PT Serif

Printed and bound by CPI Group (UK) Ltd, Croydon CR0 4YY

British Library Cataloguing in Publication Data:
a catalogue record for this book is available from the British Library

ISBN 978-1-4063-7565-7

www.walker.co.uk

With love and applause,
to the stars of my own
personal three-ring circus –

Mum, Dad and Michael

Flying tips for flightless birds

Posted by Birdie

There's a moment during every trick. Circus people call it the crowd-pleaser. Or the ticket-seller. Or sometimes, among ourselves, the widow-maker. It's the drum-roll moment, the spotlight moment, the moment that makes an audience hold its breath. It's different for every act, but on the flying trapeze it always involves a lycra-clad lunatic leaping into space while dangling from a bar high above the ground, and then letting go.

But we'll get to flying later. The first thing you need to learn is how to introduce your act.

My name – drum roll, please – is Birdie Franconi and I am one half (the pretty half) of the famous Flying Franconis!

Well, so far we're only famous in our street. And it's not a very long street. In fact, it's more of a country lane in a minuscule village close to a tiny town on the outskirts of the outskirts of the outskirts of Belfast. But Franconis' Circus School is the biggest circus in Little Murragh and we're starting this blog because we want you to be part of it.

The other half of the Flying Franconis is throwing juggling balls at my head and telling me to hurry up and introduce him. Ladies and gentlemen, boys and girls, allow me to present the boy who puts the "double" into "double act", my partner, brother and *practically* identical (apart from the gender thing) twin, Finch Franconi! (Crowd goes wild as Finch bows from his perch on my bedroom windowsill.)

Flying Tips for Flightless Birds is our brand-new blog of all things Franconi, written by the newest generation of the Franconi circus family! Here you'll learn to juggle, ride a unicycle, tame a lion, walk a high wire and turn somersaults on horseback. Stick around, we'll even teach you how to fly.

"Finch, it's finished. Come take a look." Birdie waves me over and nods at her computer screen. "What do you think?"

I lean on the back of her chair, resting my chin on her shoulder as I read the blog post. In the screen reflection our two heads emerge from her neck like something from a cheap sci-fi movie.

"It's great, but you didn't mention the show; I thought that was the whole point."

"Yes, but there isn't going to *be* a show unless we drum up some interest in the circus school. I can only dangle from my ankles for so long; we need more performers." She grabs her school bag, which today is a vintage leather camera case, and says, "It'll do. Come on, we're late."

We're always late. You would be stunned at how long it takes Birdie to get dressed in the morning. Almost as long as me, in fact.

As we run down the lane, skidding on ice puddles and leaping over potholes, I adjust the length of the orange braces holding up my waistband, straighten my skinny tie and hold on to my pork-pie hat. My school bag, which today is a 1930s doctor's bag, bashes against my blue checked shorts. The doctor's bag makes my books smell a bit chemically, but I reckon anything that stops teachers scrutinizing my homework too closely can only be a good thing.

We make it to first period with thirty seconds to spare. Which is thirty seconds too long.

The secret to surviving high school is this: minimize corridor time.

Every boy in our class (except me) is already there, playing football on the two-metre-wide "pitch" of the maths corridor. As we pick our way through, I manage to get kicked in the ankle twice and then score an own goal.

"Out of the way, Freak Show!"

And with that, the week has officially begun.

Birdie kicks the ball down the corridor and they go chasing after it, allowing us to make it to the classroom door, where Kitty Bond takes a break from cackling at something on her phone to glance pointedly at me and say, "Look, girls, it's the gorgeous *Miss* Franconi and her sister, Birdie."

The Bond Girls laugh, one of the footballers wolf-whistles, and Kitty's boyfriend, James, "accidentally" boots the ball at the backs of my knees.

I'm not bothered. *Miss. Her.* This is standard Monday-morning stuff. Miss Allen is on her way down the corridor already; it's *so* not worth starting anything. But suddenly Birdie, who is usually pretty good at not rising to this crap, is stepping between me and Kitty, tiny fists on her hips, going, "Oh, look, it's the hideous Miss Bond and her soon-to-be *black eye*."

"Ooooooh, is that a threat, Birdbrain? Any day – you *and* your pretty sister. Unless she's worried she'll break a nail?" She arches an eyebrow at my fingernails, which are actually the same colour as hers today – bright green. Birdie was right about this town being small. It's everyone-knows-everyone-else's-business small. It's every-little-thing-you-do-becomes-gossip small. And it's *especially* boys-in-nail-polish-really-stand-out small.

I roll my eyes and take a step forward. I wouldn't

usually bother but Kitty knows getting Birdie involved is a sure-fire way to draw me in; we're kind of a package deal. I put a hand on Birdie's trembling shoulder, which in twin-speak means *I've got this*, and say, "The colour looks better on you, Kitty. What shade is that, 'Wicked Witch of the West' or 'Hulk'?"

"I don't care what's going on here, it stops right now," Miss Allen says in her sternest teacher voice, which isn't very stern at all, but it's Monday morning and no one has the energy anyway. She unlocks the door and waves the class in. Kitty barges past us, leading the Bond Girls and making sure Birdie and I are last. On our way through the door, Miss Allen mutters, "Ignore her, Finch. Anyone who uses their own gender as an insult has issues." I grin at her and hope her sympathy lasts until she's seen my half-finished homework.

Two buckets and a barrel (or one way to start your own circus family)

Posted by Birdie

The famous Franconis began with our great-great-granny, Alouette Franconi, and our great-great-grandfather, Ennis Mullins.

Alouette was half French, half Italian, orphaned young, and given away by her remaining relatives to a passing circus, where she grew up sewing costumes for the horse acrobats (that's acrobats on horses, not horses doing headstands).

She soon got bored with washing sweaty tights and began learning the tightrope instead, and by the time she was sixteen she was so good she was the star of the show. She travelled all over Europe and America with the Rossetti Brothers travelling circus, making her act more and more daring all the time. She didn't just *walk* the tightrope, she danced on it, rode a bike across it, stopped to fry eggs in the middle of it, carried children across it, did acrobatics on it – and she did it all without a safety net.

In 1899, aged seventeen, she walked across Niagara Falls; a thousand metres from one cliff edge to the other, in high winds, sixty metres above the raging river below.

And then she did it again with buckets strapped to her feet, just to make things interesting.

There's a photo of her, about to step off the wire onto Canadian soil, hanging in an American museum dedicated to the Heroes of Niagara (Headcases of Niagara, Dad calls them, but he's always been a feet-firmly-on-solid-ground type).

Back in 1902, this photo was hanging on the wall of a restaurant at the Falls, and that's where Ennis Mullins first saw Alouette.

Ennis was born right here in Little Murragh but, being a sensible lad, he ran away at the first opportunity, determined to have some fun. I guess he knew that someday he'd have to come back and run his dad's farm, so he decided that first he'd go and find the maddest thing he could possibly do and get it out of his system. He ended up at Niagara, which seemed to attract ~~nutters~~ thrill-seekers, and there he heard about barrel riding.

Barrel riding involves sealing yourself inside a wooden barrel and being hurled into the river to be swept along and over the Falls. Probably to your death. Success rates were not encouraging.

Ennis decided to go for it, but on the morning of the stunt, maybe he was feeling nervous; maybe he wanted some sort of insurance policy. That's when he spotted the photograph of Alouette – it was on the wall of the restaurant where he was having breakfast. I have to admit, she looks incredible in that photograph; calm and triumphant, knowing she's beaten Niagara.

Ennis swore on a Bible that if he survived the Falls, he would find the girl in the picture and marry her.

This idea was madder than the barrel riding, if you ask me. But if Ennis thought that making that promise would ensure his survival, maybe he was right, because when they hauled his bashed and waterlogged barrel out of the river, he was only half-drowned. And as soon as the majority of his shattered bones had healed, he set out to find this complete stranger and ask her to marry him.

I guess I'm telling you this story because it's always helped me to be brave on the trapeze. It reminds me that the best way to tackle something scary is to have something even scarier lined up for tomorrow.

<< Previous Post

"You're such a romantic, Birdie." I'm reading today's blog post on my phone as we cross the empty school playground, which everyone just calls "the yard". Birdie's wearing a blue polka-dot Lindy Hop dress, black-and-white brogues, and a Muppets backpack that *strictly* doesn't go with the outfit at all, but I forgive her because she's ingeniously added a pair of scarlet trapeze tights to the look. Which is awesome, but doesn't make it easy for us to slip unnoticed into class twenty minutes late.

"How are our stats?" I whisper as Ms Hatch glares at us.

Birdie winces. "One page view."

"I'm not sure a blog was the best idea."

"Don't worry. I'll keep posting – someone has to see it, and then maybe they'll want to join."

"We should put up more posters."

"Everyone here already knows about the circus school. They could hardly miss us, could they?" she says.

This is true, since several of Franconis' performers (i.e. me, Birdie, our big sister, Wren, and little brother, Jay) can be seen juggling, doing somersaults or riding unicycles in the yard every day. Birdie and I juggle without realizing we're doing it; we just start tossing the contents of our pencil cases to each other while we talk.

Besides us, Franconis' also has the Juggulars (our Friday-night juggling club), a class of little kids called the Tots Acrobats, the Tuesday Night Acrobats (who meet on Thursdays) and a couple of solo performers. Two of the Juggulars are in Jay's class and one of the

Tuesday Night Acrobats is in Wren's, but all the other circus kids go to different schools.

The whole point of the blog is to recruit new members since we don't have enough performers to put on a big show at the end of the school year. And if it doesn't work, it won't just be the end of the year, it'll be the End of Everything. Mum and Dad can't afford to keep the place open with so few students.

The thing is, Franconis' is the *only* thing in my life besides high school. And my high school resembles a post-apocalyptic wasteland where only the morons have survived, so Franconis' is pretty important. The blog *has* to work. Because I can't even think about the circus school closing.

So I think about the show instead, which is what I do in most of my classes. My schoolbooks are full of scribbled notes like *Tots Acrobats + vertical trampoline = human catapult?*, diagrams of trapeze routines and sketches of show-posters. Miss Allen gives me extra marks if I make her laugh, but the other teachers complain about the waste of paper.

If we can pull it off, the show will go down in Little Murragh history. We'll have a circus ring and spotlights and everything choreographed to really cool music, and Birdie and I will be the headline act – performing our craziest trapeze stunts with no safety net ("No chance," Mum said) – and the posters will read:

FRANCONIS' CIRCUS PROUDLY PRESENTS:

THE FABULOUS ...
FANTASTIC ...
FAMOUS ...
FLYING FRANCONIS!

"Finchley Sullivan, are you paying attention?"

My real name brings me down to earth quicker than sweaty palms on a greased trapeze bar.

"Yeah, I definitely was, Ms Hatch." I nod reassuringly. She gives me a warning look and goes back to whatever it is she's doing on the whiteboard.

Well, you couldn't name a circus school "Sullivans'", could you? Even Ennis Mullins reinvented himself as Ennesto Franconi after he married Alouette. Eventually he became a flyer, but he started out as a freak show act because, since his Niagara barrel-riding adventure, he could pop his left shoulder in and out of its socket like a Lego man.

3

"What are you reading?" I ask, sitting down beside Birdie at breaktime on the low wall that runs all the way round the school yard. Before the school was a school, it was a farm, and the wall was to keep the sheep in. Now it's to keep the sheep out. One day a whole herd of them got in from a nearby field and caused havoc in the corridors for an entire afternoon. If you live in the country, this is about as exciting as life gets.

Birdie holds up her book, *Freaks: We Who Are Not as Others*. "Circus research," she says. "For the blog."

"That's really going to encourage people: 'You too can be a freak!'"

"Or 'If you're already a freak, you belong with us!'" She grins. "It's pretty cool actually. The 'freaks' were superstars. They were the reason people came to the circus. The other performers treated them like royalty."

"Yeah, but that was like a hundred years ago. There aren't any freak shows any more."

"That's not true, there's one on Coney Island, New York," a voice behind us says. "I read about it."

Startled, we turn to find a boy reading the book over Birdie's shoulder. He's pale and has bright white hair sprouting in disorganized clumps all over his head, held down over his ears by a pair of earmuffs that look like someone scalped a teddy bear to make them. Thick, black-rimmed glasses. Train tracks on his teeth, Doctor Who scarf, mittens on a string. A Star Trek backpack is slung over both shoulders and a rolled comic book pokes out of one pocket. His school trousers are a few centimetres too short and he's wearing black shoes with orange socks and a school blazer that looks like it will fit him in about four years. I'm hardly in a position to criticise people for standing out, but even I cringe.

"But that's the only one left in the world," he adds.

He climbs over the wall (to be completely accurate, he's unbalanced by the weight of his backpack and almost *falls* over the wall) and sits down beside Birdie. We stare at him. Not because he's new, not because he's a bit strange-looking, but because no one *ever* sits with us. We just blink at him, which I guess must seem unwelcoming because after a moment he shrugs, gets up and starts the perilous climb back over the metre-high wall. But, seeing the disappointment on his face, Birdie calls him back.

"Hey … who are you? Are you new?"

I roll my eyes but say nothing. Birdie is *always* picking up strays. Usually they're farm cats that have no intention of living indoors.

"I started today. Moved here from Belfast," he says.

"Aw, bad luck. I'm Birdie, and this is Finch."

"Hi," he says. "What's with the freak-show book? I know a bit about circuses if you're interested."

"Thanks, we're set," I say drily. I don't need to be lectured about the circus, especially by Trekkie types who beam down out of nowhere and tell me I'm wrong about stuff. "What's your name anyway?"

The boy's face is so pale he's practically blue, but he goes a bit pinker as he says, "Hector. Hector Hazzard."

Even Birdie can't suppress a smile.

"Yeah, I know," he sighs. "It's like a lame Marvel character. *Before* they get bitten by something radio-active and develop superpowers."

"It's not so bad," Birdie says, but he just looks at her like she must be mad.

Then, changing the subject, he says, "How do you do that?"

I wonder what he's talking about until I follow his gaze and realize I'm spinning my pen across the fingers of my left hand, over and under each finger in turn. It's an exercise to keep your hands flexible. And it can while away a whole maths class when you're doing algebra.

I shrug and shove the pen back in my pocket, but Birdie takes a biro from her bag and hands it to him. "It's easy. Here, I'll teach you." She pulls one of his mittens off and manoeuvres the pen around his fingers, showing him the pattern. "Repeat until your arm falls off."

He laughs and gives it a try but he doesn't seem able to move one finger without moving all of them, and he can't get the pen past his second finger without dropping it.

Ten minutes later they're still giggling at each other and it's like I've ceased to exist. "I'm cold," I say pointedly, standing up.

No response.

"And hungry. I'm going to the vending machine. Coming, Birdie?"

She doesn't look up. "I'll see you in there," she says. "Get me a yogurt." She's demonstrating in slo-mo with her own pen and Hector's trying to follow. After a moment I walk away, their giggling following me across the yard.

"I guess you haven't heard, but making friends is generally considered a *good* thing," Birdie says at lunchtime. "You should google it."

"Ha ha."

"He might want to join the circus school. Wasn't that the point of the blog and everything? We need people. Which involves *talking* to people."

"Yeah, I know. I'm just super impressed that when you decide to pick a new best friend, you manage to find the only person in school destined to be less popular than us. Did you *see* him? And having him at Franconis' is a terrible idea. I don't think our insurance will cover a guy who walks with both feet turned in and can't open a door without injuring himself." It's true, I've seen him trip over his own shoelaces and whack himself in the face with the chemistry lab door already and we're only halfway through the day. "I don't think he'd fit in. Unless we used him as a juggling club."

"Finchley Sullivan, you are being mean," Birdie says. "I like him, he's nice."

"He's just another Gingham. Or he will be, give him five minutes. As soon as he makes some normal friends, he'll start ignoring us like everyone else."

"I don't think he is a Gingham, Finch. Bet you my glow-in-the-dark beanbags."

I stick my hand out to shake. "You're on."

After lunch I'm standing outside physics with half the class, waiting for Birdie, who's probably in the loos with a can of hairspray (she has an obsession with beehives at the minute), when I notice Hector looking hopefully at me as he comes up the corridor. I stare firmly out of the window.

Birdie thinks I'm being harsh about Hector but I have my reasons. The most (possibly *only*) useful thing I've ever learned at high school is *never* to leap into random friendships. People always turn out to be jerks or morons or just generally disappointing, so you might as well save yourself the hassle. Anyway, I already have a lab partner, if she ever gets here, and I don't need a new one, especially one who's likely to electrocute me.

Hector stands at the window to my right, reading a book and glancing at me every few seconds. A clatter of heels announces Kitty, the Bond Girls and a few of the lads approaching from my left, sniffing the air like they've caught a whiff of fresh meat. But for a change, they're not looking at me.

"You're new," Kitty says. Kitty doesn't ask questions, she decrees things. Everyone in the corridor turns to look at Hector, who quickly stuffs the paperback in his blazer pocket.

"Yep," he says brightly, but I can hear the nerves in his voice. "Brand new. Just out of the shrink-wrap this morning!"

No one laughs, until Kitty says, "Guess that's why he's so short," and then *everyone* laughs.

The whole group starts firing questions at him like one of those tennis machines that serves balls at you as if it wants to take your head off. Hector does his best to answer, but they're so quick he can't even keep track of who's speaking.

"Why'd you move here?"

"My dad got moved here for his job."

"What job?"

"He's the new minister in Little Murragh."

"So, are you like a religious nut or something?"

"Not really."

"Is your hair bleached?"

"No."

"Are you an albino?"

"No, I'm just pale."

"You look anaemic. You should eat more meat. Do you eat meat?"

"Yeah."

"Why are you wearing a blazer? You don't have to wear the uniform, you know."

"I know, but it's my first week. My dad thought—"

"Do you have a girlfriend?"

"I just got here."

"Do you play football?"

"Not really."

"Do you support Northern Ireland?"

"Um … yeah."

I wonder if Hector knows this is the most important conversation he will ever have at Murragh High. They're deciding what box to put him in. Everyone has a box; Kitty likes things neat and tidy. Hector is about to be packed, stacked and labelled, and the box system is a one-way process.

I have zero credit with these guys so there's nothing I can do for him, but I wince every time he opens his mouth.

"Why were you talking to Miss Allen in the corridor?" Kitty finally says, cutting off everyone else's questions.

Hector shrugs. "I was in an advanced class at my last school. She was giving me some extra work to do."

"What, are you like a brainiac or something?" she says.

"No, I'm just good at maths."

"How thick are your glasses?" Sinead, one of Kitty's Bond Girls, says. "Can I try them on?"

"Um ... sure." He hands the glasses to Sinead, who puts them on and stands, hands on hips, like a scary librarian. Hector laughs along uneasily. But she doesn't give them back, she hands them to Marie, who passes them to Adi. They go around the whole group while the interrogation resumes and Hector squints after them.

"What are you reading?" Marie says.

"It's about J.R.R. Tolkien."

"Are you one of those sci-fi losers?" Adi looks like he just smelled something unpleasant.

"Tolkien isn't sci-fi, it's fantasy. But I do like sci-fi," Hector says.

"Do you have Star Trek costumes?" Kitty smirks.

"No, although… No."

"Do you have brothers and sisters?" Sinead says, finally handing back the glasses.

"No, it's just me."

"What do you think of Murragh?" she adds.

"It's … small?"

"And the school?"

He hesitates. There is no right answer to this question, even he must know that.

"It seems OK."

"Just OK?" Kitty says. "I suppose your last school was fricking Hogwarts?"

"I mean, it seems great."

"Wrong, it's a dump. But you love school, don't you?"

He sighs like he knows he might as well give up. "Not really." But he decides to go for broke and, looking Kitty in the eye, he says, "It depends on the people."

Kitty smiles slowly, like a cat who's just spotted live prey. Miss Deshpande comes jogging up the corridor then, arms full of files and hair escaping from her bun. "Sorry I'm late, everyone. Go on in, go on in. What are you all standing out here for?"

As the class shuffles through the door, Hector calls

after them with as much sarcasm as he dares, "My name's Hector, by the way."

Kitty turns back, one eyebrow eloquently raised, and says, "We'll see."

Sure enough, somewhere between us sitting down to learn how to wire a plug and running for the door forty minutes later, there's been some sort of committee meeting to decide Hector's name, rank and status in the Murragh High food chain, and by the end of class they've rechristened him Hector the Holy Ghost. And of *course* Birdie, dashing in ten seconds after Miss Deshpande, invited him to sit with us.

"Leave him alone, Kitty," she says, when the Bond Girls start crossing themselves every time he walks past.

"Mind your own, Birdbrain," Kitty sneers.

Birdie leans over our mess of wires and says, "Ignore them, Hector."

"I've been called worse," he says.

"And you will be again, just stick around five minutes," Kitty says, knocking Hector's plug onto the floor with her elbow as she passes by our desk.

"She seems nice," he says with a grin.

"Did she give you the eyebrow?" Birdie whispers.

"Yeah!"

"Then congratulations, you are officially one of us!"

He looks pleased. Can't be *that* smart then.

How to make a spectacle of yourself

Posted by Birdie

You're in a *ginormous* scarlet-and-yellow canvas tent. There's jangling music playing at a billion decibels, the lights are dim, the four-hundred-strong crowd are still cheering for the last act – a guy who juggles cactus plants while wearing a mankini and balancing on a tightrope – and there are clowns running through the audience chucking buckets of confetti. Half the kids are throwing up candyfloss and the other half are screaming because they're afraid of clowns.

How do you get their attention?

Well, you have to want it. Think about the last time you did something massively embarrassing in public. Skirt tucked into your knickers? Called your head teacher "Mum"? If your reaction was, "Oh my God, hide!" then maybe the circus isn't for you.

My latest malfunction involved a little-known position called the Inverted Mermaid.

Literally.

We were on a geography field trip at the beach, clambering over rocks on the shoreline searching for creatures in rock pools. A bunch of us had gone quite far out, where there were still big rocks to walk across but the water around them was deeper.

Our instructions for the day clearly stated that we were to wear "trousers" and "appropriate footwear". I couldn't resist the pair of purple flared cords I'd just got on eBay, teamed with a flowery shirt and a purple suede bag with fringing, and my hair held in a high ponytail by a pink hairband – perfect for a day on the beach, if you ask me.

"And the shoes?" said Mr Brown, who did ask me, peering over the tops of his glasses while everyone else piled onto the bus that morning.

I frowned at my feet. "I did consider the black ones," I admitted, "but it's so summery. You think pink was a mistake?"

"I was referring to the three-inch heels. The instructions clearly said 'appropriate footwear'."

"Exactly! That's why I went for platform wedges."

Mr Brown seemed confused.

"Well, what would *you* wear with purple flares, Sir?"

His eyes closed briefly. "Just get on the bus, Bridget. You can go barefoot."

OK, it's not easy walking on sand in three-inch wedges, but if Mr Brown thought I, Birdie Franconi, trapeze artist extraordinaire, would have a problem balancing on a few rocks above some limp waves, he'd obviously never watched my YouTube channel.

When the rocks got further apart, I leaped from one to the next with all my Nike-clad classmates. Right behind me was Finch, who'd escaped Mr Brown's attentions by wearing leather brogues and pink socks with his skinny jeans.

Unfortunately he was a little *too* close behind me.

Just as I was about to jump off one big rock and onto the next, I spotted a huge starfish in a rock pool at my feet. I halted, pre-leap, and Finch didn't.

Flying Trapeze Rules Number One, Two and Three: Communication is *everything*.

Finch slammed into my back and instead of springing, gazelle-like, over the little stretch of water between me and the next rock, I flailed, lemming-like, right into it.

A lesser artist might have panicked. But I'm a professional. I sank for a few moments and then started to rise, exactly like falling into a safety net and gently bouncing back up again, and the whole time all I was thinking about was my next move.

I surfaced, spouting salty water and half-blinded by mascara, to a dozen faces peering down at me (no one had leaped in to save me, I noted), and the sound of Mr Brown racing across the rocks screaming, *"Pull her out, for God's sake!"*

I looked up at Finch, who looked down at me, and, as if on cue, the two of us flung our arms in the air and yelled, *"Ta-dah!"*

But even if your natural disposition is *not* being the world's biggest attention-seeking show-off, there are ways to get noticed:

1. Be nice to the spotlight guy.

2. Add two million sequins to your costume.

3. Wear eye make-up so thick, your lashes start to inhibit your aerodynamics.

4. Turn the music up loud and, if at all possible, set something on fire.

5. Always pronounce your name as if there's an exclamation mark at the end (and in an American accent).

6. Find a partner who's as bonkers as you are (probably no one else will want to know you after the field trip gets cut short because you're in danger of hypothermia).

< < Previous Post

_____

"You *were* pretty unpopular on the bus," I remind Birdie, reading the blog post over breakfast.

"I smelled of seaweed. You can't take that person-ally; even *you* didn't want to sit with me." Birdie grins and steals a piece of toast from my plate, then we juggle butter knives while we talk. "Anyway, we're used to being unpopular," she adds.

"True."

She throws two forks into the mix and says, "Doesn't that ever annoy you?"

"Doesn't what annoy me?" I'm not really listening; I'm wondering if we could get Jay to join in and make a comedy juggling routine with chef outfits for the show.

"All that *Freaky Franconis* stuff," she says. "The fact that no one likes us."

"Rubbish!" I scoff. "We are adored by legions of internet fans."

"We've had *one* page view."

"It's a start."

"I mean *real* people," she says.

"Real people?" I collect the cutlery as she throws it, set it on the table and nick my cold toast back. "You mean the Drones? The Normals? The *Ginghams*?" I give her a meaningful look. "You can start hanging out with them if you want, but do me a favour and wear a name tag so I can tell which one you are."

She shrugs and goes to make more toast, and I go upstairs to get dressed. Since we're publicly recommending being gawped at, I decide to go for flip-flops and my Indian shawl with the hood. That always gets a reaction.

★ ★ ★

If Birdie and I have thick skins, it's because we've earned them.

One of the reasons I'm not about to pledge undying friendship to Hector is that I already loathe everyone at my school. And, OK, Hector hasn't done anything too loathsome *yet*, but pre-emptive loathing just saves time.

My classmates are probably no worse than your average high-school clones, but I don't hate them for being completely average. I have much more specific reasons.

The specific stuff all happened a while back, but in high school, time is meaningless. The same faces, day in, day out, year in, year out, the same cliques and feuds dragging on and on; the only difference between a playground punch-up in Year Eight and one in Year Eleven is that everyone's a bit taller and has better hair. So the fact that this particular nuclear explosion in my life happened three years ago doesn't matter at all, because the fallout just keeps coming. Making me the social equivalent of radioactive waste.

Back when Birdie and I started high school, we were quite shy. We'd come from a primary school that had thirty-seven pupils. In *total*. Our high school is in the town of Murragh, which is next to our village, Little Murragh. It's not a big town, and it's so close we can walk there, but kids from other small towns come to it as well, so we went from thirty-seven to three hundred schoolmates just like that, and we weren't used to it. We'd always spent most of our time juggling with Jay and Wren in the garden, or practising on the trapeze, or doing tiny shows for the parents of the circus school kids. Other than that, we'd kept our heads down. And I guess we'd have stayed that way if it hadn't been for James Keane.

James Keane: football captain, class rep, most popular guy in our year, voted Hottest Male in the Girls' Annual Elections last term, and my best friend for a whole three months when we were eleven.

With Birdie around I'd never felt the need for a proper best friend (it's hard to be lonely when you were assigned a human shadow at birth) but I liked James right away. He chose a seat next to me in our first class and just started talking. As a shy person, I found that pretty impressive. He turned out to be impressive in lots of ways. He was six and a half inches taller than me, he was smarter than me, he made everyone in class laugh twice before the period was over, he already had a girl-friend (Kitty Bond – Hottest Female award three years running now), and he had such a good singing voice (which probably broke when he was like *five*) that they gave him the lead in the school musical, *Oklahoma*. By the time we got to chemistry that afternoon, I was fol-lowing him around like a lapdog.

The weird thing was he liked me too. Everyone

wanted to be his mate, but he sat with *me* at lunch, came to my house after school, kicked the ball to me during PE, and then didn't laugh when I kicked it in the wrong direction. Since the only thing I could do that he couldn't was juggle, I went a bit crazy trying to impress him. I broke so many eggs over myself that every time I took a hot shower there was a smell of omelette.

"You need to calm down, bro," Birdie said. "You spend all day sitting on his desk chucking the contents of his pockets about. You look like a trained monkey."

I reckoned she was just jealous. She'd never had a real best friend either, and I *was* spending a lot of time with James instead of her.

Sometime just before Christmas I noticed he hadn't replied to a text message I'd sent. Or an email. And when I called, it went to voicemail. He never said anything, but he wasn't coming round to my house as often, and sometimes I'd spot him in town at the weekend with the guys from the football team. Rehearsals for the leads in *Oklahoma* were practically every day so I put it down to that, but then he started eating lunch at another table and sitting with someone else in the library. It was as if I were contagious. Every time I tried to broach the subject, he'd brush it off while backing away from me down the corridor.

I got sick of it. And Birdie got sick of me moaning

about it. "Just forget it, Finch; he's a jerk, that's all."

But he wasn't a jerk, I knew that. So I must have done something wrong and I couldn't let it go until I found out what.

I cornered him at the *Oklahoma* dress rehearsal. I was in the chorus (I can't sing; I only signed up because he was in it) and the costume department had gone overboard with the gingham, so even the boys were in gingham shirts under their waistcoats and most of the girls were in flounced gingham dresses. If you looked at everyone up on-stage together, it made your eyes cross. James had managed to wangle a plain blue shirt, so he was the only one who didn't resemble a picnic blanket.

After he and Kitty, who was playing the female lead of course, had gone off on their honeymoon and the rest of the cast were done pretending to be overjoyed for them, I followed him off-stage to where everyone was milling about, waiting for instructions from Mrs McDonagh, who was arguing with the music teacher. James was sitting alone at the edge of the crowd, checking his phone.

"Nice shirt," I said, sitting next to him. "Don't suppose you want to swap?"

"I don't do gingham," he said.

"Do you want to come over tonight? I could help with your art homework." Art was the only subject

I was better at than him. I sucked at it, but less than he sucked.

"Nah, that's OK, I have a lot of stuff to catch up on with all these rehearsals," he said.

"Sure."

He stood up to go.

"I mean, unless you need some help?" I stood too and tugged his elbow and he turned back, glancing down at my hand on his arm but not at my face. "If you're behind with stuff I could, I don't know, I could … help." I shrugged.

He took a step away, then paused. His lips tightened and he stepped back close to me, hissing, "I don't need any help. Stop crowding me, Finch."

"I'm not!" I tried to laugh it off but he didn't laugh back. "I just…" I took a deep breath. "Why don't you want to be friends any more? What did I do?"

By now people were starting to notice us. A couple of James's friends had wandered over and were watching. When he saw them, he stepped away from me again. "Get a grip, Finch," he said, louder. "You're clingier than my bloody girlfriend."

They laughed. *He* laughed.

I don't know what I was thinking. I *wasn't* thinking, I suppose. I put my hand out to get his attention, stop him walking away, I don't know… I just laid my hand on his shoulder and said, "Don't be like that."

A jeer went up from the boys behind him. "You've upset her now, Jamie, better buy her some flowers!" someone called.

James looked me in the eye. I think it was the last time he ever looked me in the eye. And then he punched me in the gut.

Thanks to all the juggling, I have lightning reflexes. I managed to hit him once, square in the jaw, before everyone piled on. Mrs McDonagh was on her way before I even hit the gym floor, but there were still a good thirty seconds when I was being shoved, punched and kicked by a mass of eleven-year-old boys in gingham, while Kitty Bond led the girls up on-stage for a better view.

It was Birdie who picked me up. She'd been waiting outside for rehearsal to finish and rushed in when she saw what was going on. While Mrs McDonagh handed out detentions to everyone within shouting distance, Birdie got me out of there.

I suppose you can't go around doing backflips and cartwheels with your pink-tutu-clad sister without attracting a few comments, but I never thought James would be like that.

"You *have* been pretty obsessed with him," Birdie said as she helped me out of school that day. "Even I wondered. Do you...?"

"What? No!"

"All right, all right, just asking."

"I just thought he was a nice guy," I said through the blood running out of some unidentified place in my mouth. "I thought we were friends. I guess I was wrong."

Unfortunately, we ran (or limped) straight into Little Murragh's resident maniac.

"Hi, Lou," I said.

"Christ almighty, child, you look like you've been

trampled," she said, handing Birdie her handbag to carry and me a greying hankie, which I reluctantly used to wipe the blood off my chin. "What happened?"

"Long story," I muttered. "Can we just get out of here?"

Lou had been walking past the school on her way to our house, probably out on one of her phone-box change-slot raids around town, so we couldn't avoid walking home with her. Her battered tartan trolley bounced along behind her as if trying its hardest to get away, and occasionally she'd turn and curse violently at it.

Lou is our granny, but "granny" has never seemed the right word. "Granny" suggests someone with kind eyes and sweets in her pockets. Lou has the bloodshot eyes of a 3 a.m. drinker and her pockets are full of pipe tobacco and scratchcards.

For some reason she seems to like me and Birdie, not that you'd know it from her behaviour. In fact I thought she hated us until I saw how she treated other kids, or "parasitic little cretins", as she calls them. We always get her least horrific hand-knitted jumpers for Christmas, for example; completely unwearable of course, but usually with the right number of sleeves. And she's less likely to hit us round the head with her handbag for no reason.

Mum is forever getting phone calls complaining about her. The manager at Tesco rings all the time because she steals the pick 'n' mix; she's had to be collected from O'Brien's pub on more than one occasion because she's "lost the use of her legs", as Edna O'Brien politely puts it; and she's been banned from the park for life for "wilful intoxication of wildlife" (she was feeding the squirrels Christmas pudding soaked in rum).

By the time we reached our house, I was battling with the tartan trolley myself because I was sick of apologizing to people she'd bashed with it, but since I was still spitting blood and Lou was just spitting, people were giving us a wide berth anyway.

"God, I've desperate gas," she moaned, rubbing her stomach with the palms of both hands as we came through the front door, where Jay appeared to be building the world's longest car track in the hall. "I'm like an oxygen balloon."

"Helium," Jay said, ducking automatically as one of her hands swung at his head.

"They're both gases, aren't they, you little—"

I pushed Jay through the kitchen door and stepped over the complicated motorway system to get into the living room. Lou followed me, flattening a bypass like Godzilla.

"Do you want tea?" I asked.

She made a face. "Gives me palpitations. Any whiskey in the house? A wee nip would do me the power of good."

"Mum says you're not—"

"God almighty, will you do as you're bid! If I needed your mother to nursemaid me twenty-four hours a day, I'd ask. I don't know how you lot were brought up, but in my day…"

I didn't hear any more because I was halfway down the hall in search of whiskey, while Birdie absorbed the impact and tried to calm her down. Jay was hiding in the kitchen.

"Dare you to put laxatives in it," he whispered as I poured a small glug of Dad's whiskey into a glass.

I considered it. "Nah, she'd only be here all day and then describe the results to us in graphic detail."

"Ugh." Jay made a face and went back to the car track, now stretching across the kitchen counters since the floor wasn't safe.

I took the whiskey to Lou, wondering how to get rid of her so I could run upstairs, die of humiliation and then convince Birdie to run away and join the Ringling Brothers circus with me.

"There's a good lad," Lou said, downing the lot.

"There isn't any more," I said, before she could ask.

"Well, you'd better get some in from O'Brien's. If anyone's ever been in need of a drink, it's your father, poor man."

I blinked. I'd never heard her say a nice word about Dad in my life. When she's talking to Mum, she calls him "that killjoy you married". But I suppose her main concern was the whiskey.

"They wouldn't sell me it, would they," I pointed out.

"Could you not get one of them fake IDs? All the kids on telly have them."

"I could, but since Edna O'Brien sends me and Birdie a birthday card every year, I doubt she'd fall for it."

"Busybody," she muttered. "So what's wrong with you anyway?"

"You mean in general?" It was possible she meant in general.

"You've a face like a busted sausage. What happened?"

I don't know why I told her; she's the last person on earth you'd confide in. But I burst into tears at that point (I was only eleven) and had to tell her something.

"Well, for God's sake, no one died, did they?" she said when I'd finished hiccuping out the whole story.

I glared at her. When she was my age, she could walk a twelve-metre-high wire with a tiger prowling the ground beneath her, but sympathy has never been one of her skills.

"We're talking *social* death here," I explained. "Which is worse than *actual* death because you have to go on living after it."

"What do you care what that lot think?" she said.

"I have to spend every day for the next seven years with 'that lot'. I care a fair bit what they think."

"Then more fool you." She raised her whiskey glass as if to have another swig, remembered it was empty and tutted at it. "Listen, pet," (*Pet!* I was so surprised I stopped sniffling) "you're not bawling because they laughed at you, you're bawling because you *care* that they laughed at you. And that's easy fixed." She got up then and put on her cardigan. I noticed she was already wearing two, and one of them was Dad's.

"You're a Franconi, Finch," she said as she left. I waited for her to elaborate on that, but instead she farted loudly. "God, that's better!" she called on her way through the door.

Parlari, you rokker?

Posted by Birdie

Every tribe has its own language. That's why when you say, "Mum, did you see Finch wipe-out at training? It was sick! Hashtag *legend*! He was, like, *twerking* in mid-air!" and your little brother says, "Burn, brah!" and your twin says, "And your face, douche," your parents look blankly at you, and you say, "What? It's just bantz."

Circus people have their own language too. It's a way of talking in secret, a way of saying who belongs and who doesn't. It's called Parlari, and it's a mixture of slang, jargon and foreign words collected from their travels around the world.

To the beginner it can be a bit confusing, so here's a handy glossary to circus lingo that will let you pass for a pro in any big top:

Barney – an argument or punch-up, as in "Mum, the police called, Lou's had another barney in the veg aisle at Tesco."

Bats – shoes, as in "Get your bats off the furniture, Lou."

Buffer – a performing dog, as in "You want to borrow my bats? Sit up and beg, buffer."

Chapiteau – the big top, as in "Is that a dress you're wearing or a chapiteau?"

Chovey – a cheap clothes shop, good for clown outfits, as in "Where did you get that chapiteau, a chovey?"

Dekko – look at, as in "Take a dekko at that chovey!"

Dinari – money, as in "You paid dinari for those bats?"

Flick-flack – a backward handspring, as in "I'll give you all the dinari in my pocket if you can do a flick-flack."

Gaffer – the boss, as in "You're not the gaffer of me!"

Gardy loo! – watch out, as in "Gardy loo, the gaffer's coming!"

Kativa – bad, as in "That flick-flack was kativa. I've seen better buffers."

Manjaree – food, as in "I'm starving, is there any manjaree?"

Mr and Mrs Wood and All the Little Woods – empty seats in the audience, as in "Please come to our show so Mr and Mrs Wood and All the Little Woods won't be there on their own!"

Nantee – no or none, as in "I need to buy a ticket for the show but I've nantee dinari!"

Omee – a man, as in "Be an omee and join the circus!"

Panatrope – recorded music, as in "Omee, your panatrope sounds like someone drowning a bag of buffers."

Polony – a young woman, as in "Polonys can out-juggle omees any day."

Ring-door curtains – the artists' entrance to the ring, as in "My dressing room is through the ring-door curtains with a big star on the door."

Rokker – to understand, as in "No, the *big* dressing room is mine, you rokker?"

Shush – to steal, as in "Finch, stop shushing my manjaree!"

Slap – make-up, as in "He's just doing his slap, he'll be ready in about four hours."

Tawni – small, as in "This was a tawni introduction to Parlari!"

< < Previous Post

Every circus also has a word for non-circus folk. Officially they're called "jossers", but the particular breed of non-circus folk roaming the corridors of Murragh High are known to Birdie and me as "the Ginghams".

Me caring that every person in our year seemed to suddenly know who I was (and not in a good way) was not, as Lou reckoned, "easy fixed". But on the Friday after *Oklahoma* Monday, as it was forever after known, when I was sick of being sniggered at in class, shoved in the corridors, evil-eyed by Kitty and the Bond Girls (who'd decided it was my fault James was kicked out of the musical), and having *Finch and James 4eva* scrawled on the toilet walls, I decided Lou might have a point.

All week I'd been having the same sweaty nightmare about that crowd of people about to lay into me, that mass of gingham on the stage looking down and laughing. But it was only when I went to circus school on Friday night that I realized what was most horrible about it.

When I walked in, Birdie was already on the trapeze practising with Mum.

"Finch!" she called, swinging upside down above me. "I did it! The double! I did it twice in a row!"

We'd been working on double somersaults for two weeks and neither of us had managed it yet. I immediately started stripping down to my workout gear, ignoring the bruised ribs I knew were going to hurt like hell as soon as I stepped off the platform. "Don't get too smug!" I called back.

As I climbed the ladder, looking down at Dad and Jay and the Juggulars watching from below, I figured out what was wrong in the nightmare.

When stuff goes wrong in a performance – and stuff goes wrong all the time – it's salvageable, because *you're* in charge. The person on the trapeze, the person in the centre of the ring, the person on the stage – they're in control. You can make a joke, you can pretend it was deliberate, you can get the crowd to go "Awwww!", and if all else fails you can fall hilariously on your face and start again. The crowd are always right behind you, and they only get to laugh when you allow them to.

If I'd been the one on the stage and all the Ginghams had been looking up at me, somehow I think I could have salvaged it. Somehow it would have been all right.

I nailed the double first time, and decided that from then on the Finch Franconi Show was going to be choreographed exclusively by me.

Birdie let me exhaust my rage on the trapeze that night, and then the two of us sat at the top of the rigging watching the Juggulars brain each other with juggling clubs far below.

"Lou's right," I told her. "Trying to fit in is pointless; you just end up getting squished. Who wants to be a Normal anyway? It's duller than plate spinning."

"*Lou's right?* It's my responsibility as your sister to remind you that Lou is madder than a bag of cats. You're not going to get a tartan shopping trolley and start stealing cardigans, are you?"

"No, but from now on, when I want to do something, the first question I ask myself will not be 'What would James Keane think?' or 'Would Kitty Bond laugh at me?'"

"You ask yourself that?" she said.

"Don't you?"

She looked guilty. "Maybe. Sometimes."

"From now on, the only opinion I care about is mine," I said defiantly. "And yours," I added. "Stuff the Ginghams. We don't need them, we don't want them, we aren't friends with them, we don't date them, we're —" I looked down the length of the ladder to the ground below us — "ten metres better than them."

"Right!" Birdie said firmly. Supportively. But I'm not sure she knew then exactly what she was supporting.

That weekend, Mum took us to the city and I dragged Birdie around The Rusty Zip vintage clothes shop while I bought all the brightly coloured, crazy-patterned, downright weird clothes I'd always loved the look of but had never had the nerve to even try on. I was still getting the hang of putting outfits together, so the stunned silence we got when we walked into first period on Monday morning was fully justified, but I'd decided turning up to maths in a tweed jacket, knitted yellow waistcoat and deerstalker hat (pink tea-dress and head-scarf for Birdie) was probably good practice for the next seven years of our life.

Ta-dah!

Three years later, the Ginghams *still* treat us like a source of entertainment, but since that's what we're aiming for, I don't think they get a lot of satisfaction from it.

Not leaping into random friendships is a lot easier when you're not being stalked.

At lunchtime Hector is perched on the yard wall, head ducked down and collar up, like a scraggly sparrow sheltering from a storm, face in a book as usual. I can't find Birdie anywhere, but these days it seems like everywhere I look, Hector's there. He's even started walking home with me, telling me random facts about the circus that invariably start with the words "Did you know..." (Yes, I did) and end with "I read about it."

He notices me and waves so I give up on Birdie, climb onto the wall and sit beside him.

"Do you never get sick of reading, Hector?"

"Yeah," he says, turning a page of the enormous book cradled in his lap.

"Oh." What do you say to that?

After a moment he adds, "It's just a habit I've got into."

"What, like smoking? You want to quit but you get the shakes?" I laugh.

He lifts his head at last and screws his face up, trying to think of a way to explain it to me. "You know how if you're supposed to meet someone somewhere public and they're late, you get out your phone and start messing about with Instagram and stuff? Just so you won't look like you're standing there with nothing to do and no one to talk to?"

"Totally, Birdie's late for *everything*." Which is kind of why I'm sitting here.

"Well, I didn't get my own phone till this summer." He goes back to his book like this should clear things up for me.

"Hector, I feel like we're having two different conversations. What has all that got to do with –" I wave my hands in his general, hunched direction – "all this?"

He rolls his eyes like I'm the one being dense. "OK, imagine you're in the middle of the playground at lunchtime and you have –" he counts off on his fingers – "no mates, no girlfriend, no sister, no football buddies, no juggling team, not even a study partner."

"Yeah?"

"And no phone. Where do you go?"

"The nearest cliff?"

"Or the library," he says.

"Ah."

"Libraries have lots of benefits they don't put on the posters." He's counting on his fingers again. "They're quiet, so no one can yell insults at you. They're staffed by adults, so no one can ram your face into a desk or shut your head inside a book. They're unlikely to be populated by the people who most hate your guts because *they're* outside slamming people's faces into things. *And*," he finishes in mock triumph, "they're full of books you can read, which makes you look like you have better things to do than care that you have no mates and no phone."

"That's kind of tragic, Hec." I must look sorry for him because his expression lightens.

"It's not so bad," he says. "If you carry a paperback in your pocket at all times, you can avoid any nightmare situation. Unattended classroom? Left on the subs bench for the entire football game? Valentine's Day classroom post comes round? Get a book out and look busy. Parents want you to chat to the missionary exchange group that's descended on your house and taken over your flipping bedroom?" He scowls for a moment at the imaginary missionaries. "Stick a desk in the attic and tell them you have an essay on the Industrial Revolution due on Monday. Eventually people start to forget you're there." He grins unconvincingly. "And you do learn the odd interesting fact." He hesitates, then shrugs and ploughs on, a pink blush rising up his cheeks. "For example, when you google the new town you're moving to and discover the circus blog of some people who go to your new school, you can read books on circuses so you have something to say to them."

"You *cyber*stalked us?" I'm more bemused than freaked out.

"I wanted to make some friends when I got here."

"And you picked us?" Again – bemused.

He shrugs. "I thought you seemed pretty cool."

"That says a lot about you, Hector. Now you know better, don't feel you have to hang around with us to be polite."

He looks surprised. "I think you guys are great," he says. Then he dives back into his book. There's an awkward few seconds before he adds, "I suppose after a while it becomes your thing. That you read a lot and you're smart, I mean. And if that's the *only* interesting thing about you, maybe you start to take it too seriously. I dunno…" He waves away the conversation with a flick of his fringe and dives back into his book again. "Reading's just my thing."

His cheeks fade back to their usual pasty shade. It seems rude to just get up and walk away, but I don't know what to say either. I notice the way he clutches the book cover, the uncomfortable curve of his spine folded around it, as if he'd like to absorb the book whole, or fall head first into it and disappear.

"OK, so tell me something about –" I glance at the page he's reading – "Vincent van Gogh."

He looks suspicious, but when he realizes I'm serious, he straightens slightly and says, "Did you know he had an older brother, also called Vincent?"

"No! Two Vincents in one family? That's a serious lack of imagination."

"The first one died at birth. But the weird thing is he was born and died *exactly* a year before the second Vincent was born. On the *exact same date*. And because their father was a minister—"

"Like yours!"

"Like mine – they lived right next to the church-yard where the baby was buried. So our Vincent, the artist, had to grow up looking at a headstone with his own name and birth date on it."

"Creepy."

Hector nods. "It's no wonder he went mad and chopped off his ear."

I'm lost in thought for a few moments, imagining this little kid playing in a graveyard, finding a grave marked with his name like it was waiting for him. Eventually I notice Hector grinning at me. "OK, I take it back; read whatever you like and tell me the cool bits."

"Deal," he says.

"Nothing about the Industrial Revolution though, yeah?"

"Are you sure? There's some bizarre stuff about train timetabling."

I give him a deadpan blink and gather my bags.

"They had to standardize the clocks!" he says as I walk off, but we're both laughing now. "Did you know Oxford time used to be five minutes behind London time?" he shouts after me.

People in the yard are staring at us but I just turn and wave, walking backwards. "Later, loser." And he waves back.

Sometimes Lou waits outside school for us, like we're six and need walking home. Mum says we can't tell her not to, and I don't think this is so we don't hurt her feelings, I think it's for our own safety. Lou has quite the temper.

"Hiya, Lou," I say as we reach the gates and find her sitting on the yard wall with her trolley, eating grapes and spitting the seeds a *little* too close to the feet of the teachers organizing the bus queues to be completely accidental. No one says anything. Lou thinks it's brilliant that old people can do anything they like and get away with it. "I'd have got old a long time ago if I'd known," she says.

The buses for the out-of-town kids are pulling up and we're being swarmed by people, but it's taking her ages to get off the wall and put her grapes away and button her cardigans and swear at all the kids jostling past. I think she knows it's embarrassing for us. I think that's why she does it.

She takes so long our head teacher, Mr Cooper, comes over on his way out and says, "Mrs Franconi, lovely to see you."

"Miss," she says, sticking her chest out, sucking her stomach in and batting her eyelashes.

Coop coughs. *"Miss* Franconi. While I have you here, I think I should mention that Finch and Birdie were late today."

"Yes?" she snaps, putting the lashes away.

"Again."

"Well, I'm sure they had a good reason."

"I don't doubt it. I'd be interested to know what it was, though." He folds his arms and waits. The three of us glance shiftily at each other.

"Er... Women's Troubles," Lou says. "That was it, wasn't it, Birdie?"

"Lou!" Birdie hisses. The surrounding bus queues give a collective snigger.

"Finch had to wait for her; she couldn't walk by herself." Lou looks around conspiratorially and whispers the next word at exactly the same volume as her speaking voice. *"Cramps."*

"Yes, well, perhaps a note to that effect next time?" Coop says, not that he believes a word of it. He walks off down the road and when he's *almost* out of earshot,

Lou yells, "Josser!" after him. At least, I *think* she said josser.

The bus queue begins to move and Kitty Bond sweeps past, her eyes gleaming evilly. "Sorry to hear about your Women's Troubles, Finch," she says.

I imagine I'll be hearing a lot about my Women's Troubles from now on, thanks, Lou.

Lou eyes Kitty up and down, slowly, and Kitty looks grateful that the queue is still moving. I know who I'd put my money on.

"Friend of yours?" Lou says.

"Kitty Bond," I tell her as we start walking. "And, no."

"Bond? Well, what do you expect from a family like that? I knew her granny, bitter old hag. Used to cross the street to avoid me when I was pregnant with your mother, just because I wasn't married! She was only jealous because she had to tie a man to her apron strings."

To be fair, a lot of people cross the street to avoid Lou.

"Why *weren't* you married?" I ask, since dying now will at least save me hearing about my Women's Troubles tomorrow.

She glares at me. "You can put a lion on a leash," she says, "but don't expect to keep your hand."

★ ★ ★

I guess it was around the time James Keane, Kitty Bond and the Bond Girls shoved me up against a wall, jammed a tiara on my head and stapled a *Miss Murragh High* sash to my tank top that I started freeze-framing episodes of *The Vampire Diaries* every time Damon took his top off. Unless Birdie was there, and then I had to listen to her drool over Damon with his top off.

At first I wondered if it was a phase. Adults are always going on about teenagers being confused; it was pretty much *all* they told us in sex ed, which wasn't much help. If they'd given us some actual facts, we might have been less confused.

Actually, I soon realized I wasn't confused at all. And I was only bothered because I couldn't stand the thought that those morons at school had been right. And that they'd known before me! I'd spent years denying and retaliating and ignoring and not sinking to their level, etc. I wasn't going to just turn up one day and say, "Actually, yeah, you were all right about me."

No way.

Because they were also totally wrong about me, but in ways I couldn't really put into words.

So I decided to keep things strictly between me and Damon. It's none of their business anyway. They don't go around making a big deal of the fact that they happen to fancy the opposite sex; they just go ahead and date someone when they feel like it. Well, there are exactly zero guys at Murragh High I would *ever* date, so there's no need to tick the box that says *Torture me, please!* on my school records. If Damon decides to drop by, I'll reconsider the matter.

I haven't even told Birdie. She would be totally cool about it, but Birdie's the sort of person who tells her life story to people at bus stops. She'd want me to dye my hair rainbow colours and stage a one-man Gay Pride march down the high street (well, one-man, one-slightly-insane-sister) and I am so not doing that.

I'm pretty sure my parents would be fine about it too. They're not exactly conventional themselves. I found out two years ago that Lou isn't the only one who never got married. I was filling in a family tree for our school's "Tracing the History of our Town" project. The town is so small the project didn't take long, and it basically proved that half of my schoolmates are inbred mutants. Which came as no surprise to me.

"What date did you get married?" I asked Mum and Dad over breakfast.

They looked at each other and Dad slapped his forehead. "Ah, crap, I knew there was something we forgot to do."

"Do you think we should return all those gifts?" Mum said.

"You're not married?!"

"We had a handfasting ceremony."

"A what?"

"We made up some vows and held hands in the forest. It was very romantic." They gazed at each other over their cereal and then reached out to hold hands over the top of mine. I rapped their knuckles with my spoon until they let go.

"Have you ever done anything *normal* in your lives?"

"Oh yes. Wren and Jay were both home births. They were born in our living room, in a paddling pool!" Mum said. "No drugs, no machines, just the way nature intended. They came out like little sea creatures!"

"Ugh! I'm *eating*!"

"Couldn't with you two, though; twins are tricky." She said this like we spoiled her weirdo fish birth on purpose.

"That doesn't help me with this." I stabbed my family tree with the end of my spoon. "I'm supposed to put 'M' for married, with the date."

Mum sighed. "So conventional. Put 'F.I.L.' 18 March 1994."

"What's F.I.L.?"

"Fell in love." She grinned at Dad and he winked back.

"You two are gross."

"Love is not gross, sweetheart. And you don't have to be married to be a proper couple. You tell Mr

History −" (Mum never knows the names of our teachers, she just calls them Mr History, Miss Chemistry, etc.) − "that your parents abstained from marriage on feminist grounds. Or was it religious grounds? I can't remember. Anyway, we were staunchly anti or pro whatever it was."

So I doubt they'll have a problem with me and Damon announcing our engagement, as long as we get married underwater, or up a tree, or while parachuting, or something else bizarre. In fact they'll probably join the one-man, one-slightly-insane-sister Gay Pride march, along with Jay and Wren and Lou, and basically turn the whole thing into a circus.

Literally.

---- MONDAY 26 JANUARY ----

Roll up! Roll up!

Posted by Birdie

Since our granny, Lou, was once a travelling circus star, you might be wondering why Little Murragh has been ~~inflicted~~ blessed with her non-travelling presence for so many years.

Her mother, Evelyn (Alouette and Ennis's daughter), and father, Carlo, retired their act when Lou was a teenager and they all moved back to Little Murragh, where Ennis Mullins came from, because, even though they'd never been there, it was the closest thing to a permanent home they had.

Lou often says she misses performing, and when she was younger she used to freak out the neighbours by walking the ridge pole of the roof of her house. She still threatens to do this every New Year's Eve but we keep a close eye on her.

Lou taught her daughter, Robyn (aka Mum), to juggle and tightrope walk, and made her love the circus so much she just had to start her own, and that's how Franconis' Circus School began.

So, in the industrial estate just outside Murragh town, next to the noisy building site and across the road from the derelict biscuit factory with all the graffiti, we have a very big warehouse and a very small circus school, and we need you to come and join us! Don't be shy – we're so small you have a pretty good chance of being the star of the show!

< < Previous Post

"Did you read the blog today?" Birdie asks.

"Um … yeah."

She gives me her X-ray-vision look. "What?"

I frown. "It's just … I don't think you should mention Evelyn and Carlo. We're trying to attract students, not put them off."

We're sitting on Birdie's bed while I sketch out a new trick diagram and she sews black sequins in the shape of skulls and crossbones onto a shiny red silk skirt. I have this idea for rockabilly-style trapeze costumes — fake tattoos, blue stripy boat-neck T-shirts, and red braces holding up her short red skirt and my blue jeans. The Flying Fifties Franconis! All timed to the song "Mama Don't Allow No Boppin'" by Vern Pullens. If we can perfect the routine by the end of next term, it'll be killer.

"I couldn't *not* mention them – they were the stars," Birdie says through a mouthful of pins. "Anyway, they're interesting."

"Yes, interesting from a historical point of view. But if your point of view is from ten metres up, you'd probably rather not know."

"Don't be grisly."

"Where did you go after school today?" I ask.

"Sew and Sew, for sequins. They had a sale."

"You should have said – I would have gone with you." She tuts. "We don't have to go *everywhere* together."

I look up from the trapeze diagram, a little stung. It's not that we never snipe at each other, it's just that usually I can tell a mile off if she's in a mood. "I didn't say that; I just meant I could have got the elastic for the braces while we were there."

"We'll get it tomorrow."

We go on with the sequins and the map of arrows that traces the choreography of the new routine, not speaking. In the background Vern Pullens is slapping his guitar around like a lunatic. It's getting irritating.

"Anyway, I only said they retired," Birdie says eventually.

"What?"

"The Franconis. I said they retired. I didn't say why."

Strictly for the birds

Posted by Birdie

Considering how much time our great-great-granny, Alouette, spent in the air, it's a funny coincidence that her name is the French word for "skylark". But it's no coincidence that the rest of the family have been named after birds.

Alouette and her husband, Ennis, had twin daughters, Evelyn (French for "little bird") and Avis (Latin for "bird"). Together they formed the Flying Franconis' Trapeze Act and travelled the world with the Rossetti Brothers circus.

Evelyn married Carlo and had a bunch of kids, including our granny, Lou (named after Alouette). Lou had our mum, Robyn (father unknown and we've learned not to ask Lou questions), and Robyn married the very un-bird-like Diarmuid Sullivan and called us Wren, Bridget (Birdie), Finchley (Finch) and Jay.

But don't worry if you weren't born with a ready-made stage name. We encourage everyone at Franconis' Circus School to choose their own performance name, and not just because it looks good on the posters.

Your stage name is like a costume – something you put on that transforms you. I *never* let Bridget Sullivan climb the rigging to the flying trapeze. She'd be nervous and whiny, and she'd fumble every catch. But Birdie Franconi? She can do anything. She's fearless, with a capital "Let Me At It".

Most things in life you're just stuck with – frizzy hair, little brothers, dads who dance at weddings, a complete inability to understand physics. Tough luck. But in the circus you can leave all that behind, invent a new personality and be whoever you want.

And not only are you transformed, you're also protected, because if anything goes wrong, it happens to the Great Ennesto or the Amazing Alouette, not plain old Ennis or Lou.

Try it. Pick your act. Pick your costume. Pick your name.

I bet you feel braver.

< < Previous Post

Our school does have a uniform but you don't have to wear it, so practically no one does. Except Hector.

The day Birdie showed up in a pink tutu edged with fairy lights around the hem, a few teachers complained and Mum got called in to see Mr Cooper. She insisted we come with her.

"This is your fight," she said. "You tell him why it's important."

But in the end we barely got a word in.

"So, you're saying they don't have to wear the school uniform?" Mum said, sitting across the desk from Mr Cooper, the picture of parental cooperation.

"Correct."

"But they can't wear ordinary clothes?"

"No, no, they *can* wear ordinary clothes, that's what we *want* them to wear."

Mum looked at us, sitting on either side of her. I was wearing a tartan blazer, red skinny jeans, a bow tie and a straw boater, and Birdie was in the pink tutu and a purple jumper.

"These *are* their ordinary clothes," Mum said.

"All right, let me put it another way." Cooper rubbed his eyes and leaned his elbows on the desk. You could tell his heart wasn't in it; he'd basically been forced into this by the Vice Squad (our vice principals), who would kill for a stricter uniform policy and were using the tutu as an excuse. But the reason we don't have a strict uniform policy is that Coop doesn't see the point in rules he will have to spend time and effort enforcing. He told us this once in assembly. He said it wasn't for our benefit; it just left him plenty of time to chase up truants, smokers, bullies and foul-mouthed little miscreants, so we should all be very careful.

"It's just that it reflects on the school," he said to Mum. "We want our students to appear neat, clean and respectable. When I say ordinary clothes, I mean nothing … outlandish."

"Outlandish." Mum mused on this for a moment, nodding as if she was trying to see the argument from Mr Cooper's side. Birdie and I shared a grin and sat back to enjoy the show.

"That's a subjective term, though, isn't it?" she began. "I mean, if I'm to decide every morning which of their outfits is outlandish and which is ordinary, I might need a more specific definition." She took out a notebook and pen. "Maybe we could put together a list? But you'll have to be quite detailed. I mean, does colour and print come into it? Is a plain yellow bow tie better than a tartan one? Or are bow ties out altogether? Birdie, do you have any tutus in more muted tones?"

Birdie shook her head. "But I could dress it down with boots."

"Finch has a lot of hats too," Mum continued. "Could you specify which are outlandish and which are ordinary? I've noticed a lot of the kids wear woolly hats in the winter. Finch, do you have any woolly hats?"

"I have a tweed flat cap, but it only goes with shorts."

Mum jotted this down and then turned back to

Cooper, looking completely earnest. "Would that be OK?"

Coop's head slumped into his hand, probably imagining spending the next six months listening to the Vice Squad debate the precise diameter at which an ordinary boot-cut becomes an outlandish flare. Mum smiled over the desk at him. "Should we move on to hem length?"

Coop knows when he's beaten. He sighed, giving Mum a weary look. "Can we lose the tutu?" he asked without lifting his chin out of his palm.

Mum grinned and stuck her hand across the width of the desk. "Done."

So Birdie's tutu was put back in the warehouse costume box, our one and only concession to Murragh High's uniform policy.

It's not as though Mum even likes our dress sense, so we were sort of surprised that she stuck up for us. "You can't please everyone," she said, when we stopped for celebratory ice cream on the way home. "Uniforms are proof of that. No one can agree on what to wear, so the solution is always to come up with something that absolutely *no one* likes. If you wear whatever you want, at least one person likes it, even if it's only you."

She eyed the ice-cream menu. "Hmm, do you think a pistachio fudge nut sundae would be too outlandish?"

11

It takes a lot of work to fail this bad

Posted by Birdie

Did you know it was statistically harder to get into the Ringling Brothers' Clown College than it is to get into Harvard Law School?

You don't just roll out of bed one morning and decide "Today I'm a clown". Or a juggler, or a trapeze artist. It takes time. Lots of it. It takes effort. Lots of it. It takes practice and practice and practice.

And it takes focus. You have to focus on ONE thing. You will not have time for ANYTHING else. Believe me, I know.

I'm just saying, Mum and Dad, when you get my exam results this week, please remember that physics is not the whole picture. Seriously, you should see my double back somersault with half twist these days. It's an A+.

< < Previous Post

My maths exam comes back with red pen scrawled across the front. *Finch!* it says. *27%!!!* it says. Then, *Did you revise for this?*

I foolishly decide a straight question deserves a straight answer and write *TBH, no* below the red pen before handing it back.

After class, Miss Allen calls me up to her desk.

"Finch, what am I going to do with you?" she says. She looks so genuinely worried I stop feeling defensive and start trying to reassure her.

"Hey, it's not that bad, Miss," I say. "Twenty-seven per cent isn't terrible, it's almost a quarter of the marks!"

She closes her eyes briefly. "I don't know. Either you're not putting in the effort or I'm failing you in some way," she says.

Miss Allen is new. She's young and smiley, and encourages you to talk about your feelings. She's the kind of teacher who *would* think she's failing you. She probably lies awake at night thinking about it, unlike all the teachers who actually *are* rubbish and never think about it at all. I feel bad.

"It's not your fault, Miss, I was just really busy this weekend. Plus me and Jay were doing unicycle jousting and he won, and I might have had a slight concussion on Saturday. I don't really remember. I think all that stuff about gradients just literally *fell out* of my head. I'll do better in the next exam, promise. We'll aim for a *fifth* of the marks, how's that?"

She sighs. "Maybe you should get a study buddy, Finch. And work on your fractions."

"Birdie helps me – she's really smart."

Miss Allen raises one eyebrow almost imperceptibly.

"Relatively speaking," I add.

"The trouble is, when you two get together I've a suspicion not much work gets done."

"Hey, that's not fair, me and Birdie work really, really— Oh. You mean at *maths*."

"I think you should try studying with someone else."

"Yeah, I'm sure they'll be queueing up," I say, glancing around the empty classroom.

She gives me a sympathetic head tilt. "Ignore them, Finch, it's better to be yourself than be popular." Obviously in my case it's one or the other; I'm never going to be both.

"Or perhaps you should work on your own," she goes on, handing the exam paper back to me. "I want you to redo this before next week. I think Birdie distracts you, or vice versa. Either way, you could both do with buckling down."

We're into the "buckling down" section of this lecture. All I have to do now is nod contritely for a couple of minutes, looking resolved to turn over a new leaf, pull my socks up, get my brain in gear, etc., and then it'll be over and I can forget the whole conversation. Sure enough, two minutes later I'm backing towards the door. But then Miss Allen gives me a cereal bar out of her sad yellow plastic lunch box, "for studying energy", and a pat on the shoulder before I leave and I'm back to feeling bad.

After school I wait for the yard to clear and then I settle on the front steps of the building and get out the maths exam. Miss Allen has a point; there are too many distractions at home. There's an unfinished trick diagram on my dresser, a book about the Ringling Brothers on my bedside table and a mustard-coloured blazer arriving from eBay, for example. If I go home I'll never get anything done, so I decide to sit right here and work.

But an hour later I realize I'm not getting anything done here, either, and it's not because there's anything to distract me, it's because I have no idea what I'm doing.

I'm about to rip the paper up in frustration when the door opens behind me and a voice says, "You know school's over, right?"

"*I* do, do you?"

Hector manages to trip over his shoelaces coming down the two front steps and I grab the hem of his blazer just in time to stop him face-planting onto the tarmac.

"Thanks." He sits next to me to tie his shoes and

I tuck the red *27%!!!* under my textbook.

"I was at the library," he says.

"No kidding."

"Is this an average Grumpy Finch Day or is something wrong?"

"Flipping *maths*. What is Pythagosaurus's Theorum anyway?"

He smothers a grin. "I don't know but it couldn't have been that good since all the Pythagosauruses are extinct now. Maybe you should look at *Pythagoras's* Theorum instead."

"What?"

"Do you need some help?"

I remember Miss Allen's suggestion about getting a study partner. Hector would be good at that. Hector would be perfect, in fact, but I can't bring myself to ask. The thought of spending hours and hours with Hector while he goes on about gradients and intercepts and axes… Ugh.

"It's up to you but if you want a study partner or something…" He gives a *whatever* shrug and fidgets with his blazer cuffs.

But I can't say yes even if I wanted to. Because study partners help *each other*. And there's nothing Hector needs help with. Even if there was, I wouldn't be much use. I'd be sponging off him, and I refuse to do that.

"I'll manage," I say, gritting my teeth and opening

my textbook again. "I'm sure you have better things to do."

He stands up, and I'm sort of glad he's leaving and sort of not, because it means it's just me and the Pythagosauruses again, but then he says, "Not really."

"Hmm?"

"I don't have much else to do. I thought maybe, if you had time, maybe you could teach *me* some stuff."

Like what, how to make your teachers cry? "What stuff? I'm not bad at art but I'm not great at it."

"No, I mean circus skills," he mutters, his face the colour of Miss Allen's marking pen.

I burst out laughing.

"Forget it," he says.

"Hey, no, come back. I'm sorry," I call as he turns away. "That was harsh, I didn't mean to laugh." I laugh. "It's just that I didn't think the circus would be your scene."

"Why not?"

"Well, you're so … shy. And so quiet. And so… How can I put this?"

"Uncoordinated?"

"I was going to say 'like a puppy on roller skates' but we can use your word."

"But that's why I want to learn!" he says. "I thought it might help with all that stuff."

"You don't need help, Hector. There's nothing

wrong with just being yourself." Classic Miss Allen line.

"Yeah, right." He looks me up and down. "You don't believe that for a second. No one does. You're just saying it because you don't want to teach me." He whips the exam paper out from under my textbook and looks at it while I try to grab it back. He has a surprisingly strong grip for someone that pale.

"You need help as much as I do," he says. "Come on, deal?"

I hesitate, but the thought of going back to the textbook alone is just too depressing. I stick my hand out. "Ugh. *Fine.*"

12

"Really? Hector?" Birdie says when I tell her about the plan to teach Hector circus skills.

"I know. It'll be hell, but I'm not going to survive this year at school otherwise."

We're in the back garden. I'm on a pair of stilts and Birdie is measuring me for new trousers; they don't come ready-made in Primark for people nine feet tall.

"But will Hector survive *you* teaching *him*, that's the question," she says, handing me one end of the tape measure.

I glare down at her. "I'll be nice. If he doesn't force me to murder him."

"I think it's great he wants to learn," she says. "I could teach him some stuff too."

"Nah, he won't want to embarrass himself in front of a girl. I mean any more than usual."

She looks thoughtful. "Maybe you're right. I suppose

he'll show me when he gets good at it."

"Don't hold your breath."

She jots down some numbers, snaps her notebook shut and leaves me to walk up and down the garden path on my stilts, looking over the neighbours' hedges and freaking Dad out as my top hat bobs past the window of his study upstairs.

"Getting a new perspective on life, Finch?" he calls after me, which is his standard stilts joke. I give him my standard *very funny* look and keep going.

Stilts are pretty basic circus stuff, but I can just imagine the carnage if I let Hector loose with a pair. I wouldn't have to murder him – he'd break his own neck. What on earth am I going to teach him? I probably should have let Birdie take over; she's a lot more patient than me. But I don't like the idea of her teaching him, and it isn't because I care about Hector being embarrassed.

The truth is, I have this sneaking suspicion that Hector and Birdie like each other, and the last thing I need is those two pairing up. You see it at school all the time: someone gets a girlfriend or a boyfriend and it's like they become this two-headed monster. Like James and Kitty; even when we were best friends, it was difficult to get him on his own, and you couldn't say anything to him without it being passed on to her. Couples are designed to make you feel like you're in the way.

I walk the stilts down the driveway and try balancing along the length of the low wall at the bottom of the front garden. Some passing kids stop to watch.

Anyway, for now we have to concentrate on the show, and that means I need Birdie here, not mooching about behind the bike sheds with Hector the Walking Outtake Video.

As I negotiate a step up halfway along the wall, the kids start chucking pens and rubbers at me, like I'm a human coconut shy. That's the thing about audiences: some part of them that they'd never admit to really wants to see you plummet to your death. Just so they can scream and cover their eyes, and then repeat the gory details to their friends. If circus people are weird, flirting with death on a nightly basis for kicks, what does that say about the candyfloss-munching crowd who come to watch?

Half a dozen felt tips whizz past my nose like coloured bullets and I wobble as I dodge them, but that only distracts my attention from a larger missile in the shape of a homework diary flapping tattered wings in the direction of my ear. Direct hit. I reel sideways, ending up in a heap of tangled legs, arms, rose bushes and stilts as a triumphant cheer goes up from the kids.

I don't even bother to get up. "Thanks, guys," I call over the wall, but they're laughing too hard to hear.

Just to make things worse, there's a squeal of metal

as Lou and her trolley round the gateposts.

"Leave him alone, you little weasels, or I'll have your hides!" she shouts and they laugh even louder. She bends towards me and I hold a hand out, expecting her to help me up. Instead, she twangs one of my elastic braces and, while I grab my nipple in agony, says, "Good grief, boy, all you need is the big red shoes."

I glance over *her* outfit, which looks like a floral duvet cover with lace in odd places. "You're one to talk," I say. Then she and the trolley squeal on up the driveway.

One of the kids peeks over the wall. I'd like to think it's to see if I'm alive, but the sight of me just makes him snort Coke out of his nostrils.

I have one thought as I lie there, settling into the soil and putting off the moment I have to get up and count the bruises: I'm glad Hector wasn't here to see this. After all my ribbing about him being uncoordinated! Although if he *had* been here, he might have stopped the kids chucking stuff, or at least drawn their fire. Would Hector take a bullet for me? I doubt it. And the chances of him catching the homework diary mid-flight would be approximately nil, so he'd probably be lying next to me right now.

And then I realize what I can teach Hector.

I can teach him to look like an idiot. I mean, he's halfway there already. He can be a clown!

In reality, clowns only *look* uncoordinated, but if we can harness the inner bouncy ball that is Hector's sense of balance, maybe we can do something with it. He can learn basic juggling, pratfalls, getting whacked in the face by cream pies, toppling from stilts. As my friendly neighbourhood kids have just demonstrated, people love that stuff.

It could be good for Franconis' too. We've never had an official Circus Fool before; it's not a popular job. Mainly because (and this, I realize, thinking about Hector and Birdie again, is the best part) the clowns never *ever* get the girls.

13

It's derelict chic

Posted by Birdie

Obviously by now you're all dying to join the circus, but you should know what you're letting yourselves in for.

When Mum and Dad started Franconis', before Finch and I were even born, it was just one big room that they hired at a community centre in the city, and they taught juggling and high-wire walking on a wire half a metre from the ground, because that's all they had space for. Eventually they started looking for more permanent premises and Finch and I, though we were only six years old, flatly rejected anywhere that didn't have space for a flying trapeze.

Which is how we ended up here, in an old, freezing, dilapidated warehouse at the edge of an industrial estate. It has no spectator seating and no changing rooms; in fact certain parts of it (in a back corner which we're choosing to ignore) have no actual roof. But what it does have is space. We've laid out sponge mats on the floor for the acrobats, rigged up spotlights and a sound system, constructed curtained-off changing areas, and shoved in old sofas, kitchen cupboards, a microwave, a fridge and a big, battered dining table where we have regular meetings to discuss how we can't afford to keep the place on unless we get more students.

And rising above all this, way up in the shadowy heights of the corrugated ceiling, is the rigging for our flying trapeze. Just below it is the high wire, which we take down when we're practising, and below that the safety net Is stretched between us and a dusty concrete floor.

At Franconis' we provide the equipment, but you have to bring your own glamour.

< < Previous Post

I like Py because he gets it. Circus school isn't something he does on Saturday afternoons because his mum wants him out of the house, it's the reason he breathes in and out. I met him two years ago when he joined Franconis'. Didn't ask if he *could* join, just walked in and informed me that he *would*, as if we'd sent him a written invitation.

Mum was busy with the Tots Acrobats so I was filling in his enrolment form, which was a Post-it with the phone number of his next of kin. Just in case.

"Freddie Carson," he told me.

"Welcome to the circus, Freddie. Do you have any circus skills already?"

He flashed me a grin, like *Please.* "Guess," he said, then stood back to let me look him over.

Scuffed red Doc Martens, black combats, slashed black T-shirt, leather jacket with small holes speckled over the front. Chain belt with a heavy brass lighter hanging off it. Piercings, lots of. The lips grinning at me were chapped and the hands he took out of his jacket pockets were filthy – blunt nails, calloused fingertips and black stains worked deep into the lines on his palms. I noticed a plaster sticking out the neck of his T-shirt, the skin around it pink and shiny.

Above all this, though, two things stood out: a smell that wafted from his clothes, not unpleasant but heady, the way markers or aerosols are heady; and the brick-red hair shaved close on the sides of his head, but longer on the top and styled into a sort of wavy Mohican.

No, not brick-red. *Flame*-red.

My eyes widened. "You're a fire eater!"

He gave a little half nod, half bow. "Fire eater, fire dancer, fire juggler – you name it, I'll pour lighter fluid on it. Call me Pyro – the police do."

I could just imagine Dad's face at the thought of the extra insurance we'd have to get if Pyro joined our circus, but I didn't care; a fire eater would be a big attraction and so far we didn't have one.

"Are you any good?" I asked.

He fingered the plaster absently. "I'm dedicated," he said. That was good enough for me.

And actually, he *was* good. He could already juggle three burning torches, swallowing them at the end, and knew enough fire-poi moves to put together a five-minute fire-dancing routine. But it wasn't his skills that made me like him. I think it was the moment he drew his soot-blackened hands out of his singed jacket, held them out and spun around, all swagger, so I could examine him. He was one of us. Born to perform.

That was two years ago. These days Py has red dreadlocks, he can handle five torches and he's teaching Jay to work with fire so they can do team juggling. The result of this is that Jay is losing his fingerprints and Dad is losing his hair.

I'm sitting in the middle of the safety net, bobbing gently and watching everyone practise while I wait for Birdie to arrive. The Juggulars are playing Combat Juggling below me, which is a game where everyone starts out juggling three clubs and then they all try to keep going while sabotaging each other. The winner, usually Jay, is the last one still juggling.

Mainly I'm watching Py work on his poi routine. He's holding the ends of two metal chains, one in each hand, each about half a metre long and each with a heavy ball on the end. During a show we turn the lights down and he sets the balls on fire, but for now he's just working on the routine. He starts the chains spinning and soon they're whirling over his head, under his arms, crossing and uncrossing in front of him and behind, all in time to a selection of Seventies punk classics pumping out of the sound system. He looks like a ninja at a nightclub.

Fire poi are very technical, and very dangerous. If he misjudges anything, he'll get a face full of burning lighter fluid. I've tried it with practice poi, and even with the plastic versions you end up covered in bruises. Jay has already chipped a tooth but at least the ball wasn't on fire at the time.

Py is good because he makes everything look so effortless. Every move segues seamlessly into the next, as if he's dancing in the dark and there just happen to be fireballs strobing in orbits around him. I watch him make giant wing shapes appear in the air above him as he bends so far backwards, his chest is almost parallel to the ground. For a guy with arms like a body builder, he's impressively flexible. And far more graceful than anyone dancing to Seventies punk is supposed to be.

"Saw Birdie's blog the other day," Py says, hauling himself onto the net beside me and collapsing, out of breath. He makes it look so easy you forget he's been in constant motion for the last two hours. "When's she going to get to the good stuff?"

"I assume you mean *you*?"

"Natch. I want a whole post to myself. My fifteen minutes of fame or whatever."

"You realize no one reads our blog?" I say. "Except you, apparently."

"That's because you haven't had anyone good on it yet! Who wants to read about you sparkly pigeons flapping away up there –" he gestures at the air above us – "when they could be reading about—"

"A guy giving himself third-degree burns?"

"Exactly."

"You may have a point. I'll get Birdie to interview you."

"She'll have to clear it with my agent; I'm a busy man. Hey, how about a black-and-white photo – me, in the dark, swallowing a torch? Topless, obvs."

"Obvs," I say, rolling my eyes, though to be honest, that shot could double our membership overnight and I'm trying hard not to visualise it myself.

"We could do a video too!"

"Not sure my phone screen's big enough to capture your *entire* ego, but we'll give it a go."

He grins. "Good hat today." I'm wearing a grey flat cap with a yellow tee, skinny shorts and a suit jacket I got at Oxfam. Quite understated, for me. Py wears the same outfit every day – black tee, black combats or black jeans, boots, black leather jacket. Once he turned up in a grey tee and caused even more of a stir than the day Birdie wore a knee-length wedding dress to school (she wore a tight red jumper on top – she's not *insane*).

Py can't believe anyone would spend longer on their clothes than the time it takes to sniff the armpits of a black T-shirt. I'm a little afraid to tell him how much time we spend shopping.

He takes an apple out of one enormous combat pocket and devours it in three bites.

"How's school, Py?"

Py is the only person on the planet who hates school more than I do. This is partly because he's not allowed lighter fluid on the premises and partly because he's dyslexic and has to put in twice the effort everyone else does. I wish he went to our school but he lives too far away.

"Ugh," he says through the apple mush. He's two years older than us and he's counting the days until he can quit. That's another reason we want to make the circus school into a thriving business; if we could, we'd hire Pyro on the spot as a teacher, but so far we can't afford it and he's looking at a full-time job in the local KFC, which also has a No Lighter Fluid policy.

I consider suggesting he trade fire-poi lessons for

tutoring from Hector, but the thought of Hector let loose with a naked flame is downright terrifying. Besides, if the plan is to make him undateable, fire poi is not the way to go. Pyro is unquestionably the coolest person at Franconis', though I'd never tell him that.

14

In the end I get the juggling balls out because I cannot listen to Hector say the words "common denominator" one more time.

He stands there in the middle of his bedroom, hands out, palms up, in front of him. He looks like a novelty towel holder.

"Don't be so rigid! Relax your muscles – you have to be ready to move."

"Well, I'm tense! You're making me tense!"

I put both hands on his shoulders and push them down, away from his ears. "It's simple," I tell him, placing a single beanbag ball on one palm. He grips it like a hand grenade and I make a mental note to get him to practise holding eggs instead. Then I take his wrist and move his hand in the simple pattern the ball will follow.

"You're just tossing a ball from one hand to the

other. The ball goes up, then it comes down again, and you catch it with the other hand. Simple, yeah? Now you try."

He chucks the ball sideways and completely fails to catch it. I scratch out my mental "egg" note.

"No. That's not tossing, that's passing. The ball has to go up then down, not sideways. It should go past your nose."

"Kind of like a normal distribution curve! A parabola!"

I stare at him. "Whatever. Up then down. When you can get it to land in your other hand without reaching for it, then you know you're doing it right."

He tries. For two hours. The ball lands by his feet, under his bed, in his wastepaper basket, on his head and, once, out the window, but it seems to be repelled by a mysterious force field from going anywhere near his other hand. Every time he throws it, my muscles twitch instinctively, and by the time his mum calls him for dinner we're both exhausted.

"My back's killing me," he says.

"So stop dropping the ball," I growl.

"Can I keep this? I'll practise some more tonight."

"Really? You're not ready to quit?"

He looks surprised. "Of course not. I'm sure it takes everyone a while to get the hang of it, doesn't it?"

"Er, yeah." But usually hours, not *eons*.

"Will you come back tomorrow? We can work on your chemistry write-up." He says this like it's an incentive.

But the chemistry has to be done so I tell him I'll see him after lunch and then I leave, with the *thud-thud-thud* of falling beanbag balls echoing in my brain.

He must have stayed up all night because by Sunday he's got it. Sort of. One in three lands in the right place, anyway.

"Thank God," I say. "OK, now take a ball in each hand. Throw one, and when it gets to the top of its arc, throw the other one. And then catch them both. When you can do that, we'll add the third."

His delighted smile turns to dismay. "Maybe we should do the chemistry first."

15

Don't try this at home, kids. (Come to circus school and try it here!)

Posted by Birdie

Ladies and gentlemen! Introducing one of Franconis' most popular stars, our very own tame(ish) arsonist, Mr Freddie "Pyromaniac" Carson!

Pyro (16) has been with Franconis' for two years now and always lights up the show with his flaming poi, flaming torches and flaming hair! I've conducted a quick interview with him to show prospective students the kind of skills they can learn at Franconis'.

BF: Py, can you tell our readers what age you were when you started working with fire?

P: Hiya, Birdie. I suppose you could say my introduction to the business was when I made my first aerosol flame-thrower at the age of four.

BF: Riiiiight. But you probably wouldn't recommend that to our younger readers, yes? You'd probably say that was a mistake?

P: (Shrugs) It was a good laugh is all I remember. But, now you mention it, my sister does still have a very small bald patch, so yeah, in retrospect I should have done a bit of practice in direction control first.

BF: Um, OK. And why do you want to be a circus star?

P: It's not about the fame for me, Birdie. It's an art, what I do; and I'd do it whether anyone wanted to watch or not. In fact it's better if no one's watching because you're less likely to get in trouble. Basically I just like setting stuff on fire. At circus school you can do that and not get arrested, which is why I'd recommend it to all your readers.*

BF: Working with fire must be pretty dangerous. What's been your worst injury to date?

P: Hmm, I suppose the worst was a fractured leg. Whacked it with a fire staff. Those wooden staffs are pretty solid.

BF: Wow, I didn't know you'd fractured your leg, Py!

P: Oh no, it wasn't *my* leg.

BF: Ah.

P: I'm much better with the staff these days. And I haven't had a burn in ... (consults a Post-it note covered in scored-out numbers) six days! That's almost a record. I'm interested in teaching, too, so if people want to join Franconis', I'd be willing to teach them everything I know.

BF: What an offer. Any final advice for wannabe fire starters out there?

P: Yeah. Remember, kids, you'd be surprised how flammable household furnishings can be.

BF: So, "safety first", that's what you're saying?

P: No, I'm saying it pays to experiment.

BF: I think we should wrap this up now. Thanks for talking to us, Py, and we look forward to seeing you in Franconis' upcoming shows!

P: No problem, Birdie. Keep 'er lit, yeah?

*Disclaimer: Franconis' Circus School is fully stocked with fire extinguishers, first-aid professionals (Dad) and comprehensive insurance. What you get up to with Py outside class times is your own responsibility/fault.

< < Previous Post

It's two weeks before Hector can manage one complete cascade with three balls. I explain, I demonstrate, I draw diagrams, I make slo-mo videos, I yell, I coax, I move his arms around, but he's *hopeless*. My school work is improving so fast I'm approaching the class average in tests (and I now know how to work out the class average), so I feel bad that Hector still looks like a blindfolded beginner. Even clowns have to be able to manage basic juggling.

"Hector," I say gently one day as he rubs his fists into his aching back like a pregnant woman. "I don't know. Either you're not putting in the effort or I'm failing you in some way." I *totally* know how Miss Allen feels now.

He sits next to me on the yard wall and probes a couple of blue-and-yellow bruises on his forehead. He bruises like he has tissue paper for skin. "I'll get better, Finch, I promise. I'm way better than I was last week."

"Well, that's true; you haven't almost killed any wildlife this week."

"That pigeon came out of nowhere!"

"I imagine it's saying the same thing to its mates about you right now."

"Don't give up on me."

"I'm not giving up. But you know the basics now, you just need to practise, and I don't think my nerves can stand watching it."

"Oh. So you don't want to hang out any more?"

Is that what we've been doing? It occurs to me that I don't "hang out" with people. I spend time with Birdie, Wren, Jay, Py and all the classes at the circus school, but if you asked what we were doing, I'd say "working". We're either rehearsing routines, talking about routines, planning new routines, designing costumes for routines, or watching each other practise routines. I wonder what people do when they "hang out". Hector puts his chin in his hands and stares at the ground, dejected. *This* apparently.

"Of course I want to hang out," I say. "I just think we need to try a new skill. Can you ride a bike?"

He twists his lips non-committally. "I had one years ago."

"Great!"

"That's why one of my kneecaps is lumpier than the other."

"Oh. Do you still have the bike?"

He looks apologetic. "It had to be scrapped."

I join him with my chin in my hands.

16

Don't look down

Posted by Birdie

Janie Chang (15) has been with the circus school almost as long as I have. She can ride a unicycle, walk on stilts and she's a Tuesday Night Acrobat, but her main passion is aerial silks and she is usually to be found dangling from the ceiling down at Franconis'.

As well as looking stunning, aerial silks are impressive because there's exactly zero safety equipment involved. No wires, no nets, no harnesses, just a couple of lengths of material hanging in the air. Aerial-silks artists need serious arm muscles for climbing, doing fancy poses, swinging, spinning, spiralling, wrapping themselves up in the silks, and then unrolling suddenly, dropping like yo-yos and catching themselves before they hit the floor. It takes strength, flexibility and grace, and Janie's got all three. And today she's going to tell us a little bit about herself.

BF: What is it about circus skills that you love, Janie?

JC: I love the sense of achievement, how you get better and better every week. And it makes you stand out, you know?

BF: Tell me about it. I know you have *loads* of different skills, why do you love the silks in particular?

JC: I guess I especially like the silks because I'm in control. There's a bit of danger and you can make everyone gasp when you drop out of a wrap, but if you know your stuff you get to feel quite comfortable up there. Wrapped up in my silks is where I feel safest in the whole world.

BF: You were pretty young when you started here. Do you think that's important?

JC: I think you can start at any age. It was just luck that I found this place so young. I've lived in (calculates on her fingers) thirteen different houses with thirteen different families in the last nine years. The very first family, whose names I don't remember, brought me down here one Saturday because I wasn't very good at mixing with other kids and they thought this would help.

BF: Did it?

JC: On my first day Finch lost control of his diabolo and gave me a black eye.

BF: Ouch.

JC: He started teaching me the unicycle to make up for

it. Anyway, the foster families came and went, and I was sent to a bunch of different schools and got expelled from a few, but I kept coming back here every Saturday. It's the only thing that's stuck.

BF: You'd have to screw up pretty bad to get expelled from Franconis'.

JC: Yeah. It feels like home now.

< < Previous Post

I look around at the cold warehouse, with its salvaged kitchen furniture and charity-shop sofas. The roof is leaking, the industrial estate outside is dark, and our neighbours include a smelly animal feed factory, a noisy building site and an abandoned biscuit factory where the older kids from our school go to smoke and drink and snog in unhygienic conditions. If this is Janie's "home", I wonder what the rest of her life is like.

I'm sitting on the sofa watching her practise. Her waist-length black hair is as straight and smooth as her silks, and she ties it in a shiny knot while she's up there. When there's an audience, she puts on fast music and does all the dangerous stuff, showing off for the crowd, but when she's training she puts on her favourite tunes – nothing flashy – and zones out, just running through her poses, trying new ones, oblivious to everything, every muscle in her body standing taut as she changes positions. When she comes down, she seems peaceful.

Today she scooches in beside me on the sofa, tucking her bare feet into the warm spot beneath my legs.

"I liked your interview on the blog," I say. "Better than Py's, but don't tell him that. At least yours doesn't make us sound like a training ground for arsonists."

"I wouldn't normally talk about all that stuff. My foster families and everything."

I look at her, alarmed. "Do you want Birdie to take it down? I'm sure she didn't mean to post anything too personal. You know Birdie, she'll say anything to anyone, but if she'd known—"

"No, no, it's OK. I told her it was OK. If it'll help the school, I don't mind. This place is important to me; it *can't* close."

I wrap an arm around her knees and give them a squeeze.

"Anyway, not talking about stuff can be harder than talking about it," she says. "You get tired of being careful what you say, you know?"

I sketch a few more lines on the diagram of the new trapeze routine I'm working out. "The family you're with now, are they nice?"

"They're not bad. And I've been there two years, which is good. They remember how I take my tea and that I'm vegetarian. Life's OK!" She grins and holds her mug out for me to clink. "Here's to Franconis' continued success!"

I don't know about "continued success". At the moment, we'd settle for "survival", but I don't want to tell Janie that.

Py leans over the back of the sofa and drapes his arms round our shoulders. "Liked the blog today," he says. "Great photo of you, Janie, very pretty. I mean, it was artistic. Well lit, good contrast, yeah." He coughs because his voice is getting tight. "Are you *sure* you don't want me to get you a flaming hula hoop?"

I roll my eyes and rustle my papers like *I'm sitting right here, guys*. Janie just smiles. "Any chance of new members, Finch?" she says. "Anyone see the blog?"

"Hmm," I say reluctantly. "There's this one guy, but I really don't think he's circus material. And he definitely won't be ready in time for the show. He'd need about five years' solid practice before you'd let him loose with a bucket of confetti."

"Rubbish," Janie says. "Everyone's got potential."

"Potential he's got. Potential to harm himself and others."

"Bring him," she says firmly, getting up and going to the kitchen.

Py, watching her go, nudges me and says, "This new guy, is he good-looking?"

I laugh. "You've got *nothing* to worry about."

The unicycle turns out to be more of a success. Well, it's more of a success in the sense that it's entertaining to watch, not because Hector is any good at it.

I make a cycle lane down the length of the ware-house, lined with crash mats, and the whole circus school cheers as he wobbles along. We make a game of it by each picking a spot along the route where we expect him to fall. Whoever is closest wins a jelly baby. There's a bit of jostling for positions near the start line.

Hector's wearing all Jay's skateboarding safety gear: crash helmet, knee pads, elbow pads and wrist guards, plus a groin protector cup I found in the school PE cup-board, but I feel like it's not enough. We could encase him in rubber and it wouldn't be enough.

"Too slow, Hector, you can't balance at that speed!" I yell over the noise of the Juggulars chanting "*Hec*tor! *Hec*tor! *Hec*tor!"

"I can't balance at *any* speed!" he yells back.

"Stop waving your arms around, they're toppling you!"

Crash. Wren chooses a yellow jelly baby but gives it to Hector. "You need to keep your energy up," she tells him and he blinks gratefully up at her from the crash mat.

I sigh. "Take a break, Hector. Py's making pizza."

Birdie and I practise on the trapeze for a while. Well, it's practice for her; for me it's stress relief. Hector gets me so wound up.

"He can't do *anything*!" I tell Birdie as we sit on the platform looking down at everyone gathered around the big table below.

"Give him a break, Finch, he's new at this. And I think you make him nervous."

"Me?"

"You keep yelling at him. And you're usually such a great teacher. You've taught loads of people here and you're always so patient. Why can't you be like that with him?"

"Because he's impossible. Have you seen him juggle?"

She winces. "He showed us all in the kitchen earlier. We're down three mugs and the toaster's dented."

"Exactly."

"It *was* funny though," she says. "I thought that was what you were going for."

"But you have to be able to control it; there's a big difference between making people laugh and being laughed at. We can't just let him loose in front of an audience and hope he's funny in the right places and doesn't kill any spectators."

We swing out and flip over into backward somersaults, tumbling neatly into the safety net like two ripe apples. There's a smell of pizza and the sound of laughter from the kitchen area. Maybe Hector's juggling again.

"He *is* the worst I've ever seen," Birdie admits.

I know it's not meant to, but this makes me feel better. The Official Circus Fool idea may not be going exactly to plan, but my attempt to make Hector completely undateable seems to be right on track.

But then she says, "I think it's sweet that he doesn't mind people laughing at him. Like, he really doesn't seem to care. That's kind of cool."

Great. "You don't have to constantly stick up for him, you know."

"Someone has to. And I want you to like him."

"Why? Why is that so important?"

She puts her hands on her hips. "Because I'd like to hang out with him, and we do *everything* together. I can't even have thin-crust pizza because you like deep-pan!"

"What does pizza have to do with anything? Hang out with Hector if you want, you don't need my permission."

She cuts me a look. "Yeah, right. Just go easy on him, OK?"

Everyone's crowded around the table, snatching slices of pizza and discussing ways to improve Hector's unicycling (invisible wires? stabilizers?). Everyone except Hector, who's squashed onto half of Janie's chair and doing Py's homework. An awful thought occurs to me.

"Py! You haven't traded him fire-poi lessons for homework, have you?"

Py stops adding singe marks to his coat with his lighter long enough to say, "I'm not insane, Finch. He offered."

I drag a chair up beside Hector, who's doing some intense-looking maths. There are symbols I've never seen before.

"We haven't covered that yet, how do you know how to do it?"

"I took an advanced maths class at my last school. I might do the GCSE a year early."

"I might do mine a year late." Py laughs.

"But you've got brains in your hands and feet," Hector says. "I wish I had that."

Py looks pleased with this assessment. It's true too,

he can do anything with his body. I'm always trying to cheer him up about not being good at school work, but I never thought to point out all the things he *is* good at instead.

"This bit's quite simple," Hector says. Py looks dubious but Hector starts explaining it to him, slowly and patiently, getting Py to do each step. Soon both their pizzas are getting cold but Py seems to understand what Hector's saying. I notice Birdie smirking at me. I can practically hear her saying "Like *that*!"

So Hector's even a better *teacher* than me now. Why can't I walk him through some basic circus skills the way he's walking Py through his homework? The way he walks *me* through my homework. I nick Birdie's pizza slice and promise myself that tomorrow I'll be calmer. I'll be patient. I'll be methodical. I'll be kind.

"Hector, I am going to bloody well *throttle* you!"

"There's something uneven on the floor there!"

"There's something uneven in your *head*! Pick up the stilts and start again. And next time you fall, don't aim straight for the only bruise-able object in the room, i.e. *me*!"

We pick ourselves up off the floor and I brush the dust off my brand-new shirt and pop the dent out of my fedora.

"If I was capable of aiming my falls, I wouldn't have a problem, would I!"

Calm. Patient. Kind. I take a deep breath and lower my volume. "Never mind, you're doing fine. Let's just start again."

He looks suspicious but drags the stilts over to the wall, where there's a rail two metres up he can hold on to. He almost strangles me, leaning on my neck and shoulders to get himself up on the stilts, but I don't complain. When he's up and clutching the rail, I say, "Good! That's great. Now just stand there and get used to the stilts. You have a new body and it's eight feet tall with very long, skinny legs. Where's your centre of gravity?"

He wobbles experimentally back and forth. "Theoretically, it should be higher up. Practically, I'm not sure I have one."

"Course you do. And you want to keep your centre of gravity from going outside your base. How do you do that?"

"Widen the base."

"By?"

He moves his legs further apart.

"Good! You're more stable already." I'm so relieved I actually applaud.

"I am! And I'm impressed, by the way," he says.

"You're impressed?"

"That you remember all that centre-of-gravity stuff we did for physics last week."

It's true – the first time I've managed to teach Hector anything and it's only because he taught me something first.

We teeter along the wall for half an hour and he does seem to be getting better. He even takes a few steps without the handrail. I've never seen him so happy.

"I'm getting this, Finch! Maybe stilts are my thing! Do you think I could learn to juggle while I'm up here?"

"Um, sure. Someday. Hey, that was nice of you to help Py with his maths."

He shrugs, which is a mistake and he has to grab the rail again. "I don't mind. They're nice, aren't they?"

"Who?"

"The circus guys. They're friendly."

"I guess so."

"You're lucky," he says. "I've never had a big group of mates. Look, Janie gave me this." He holds out his wrist, at great personal risk, and I grab one of the stilts to stabilize him as I look up at what he's showing me. It's one of Janie's bracelets. She makes little plaited bands out of her old red silks when they're worn out. Like a little *Janie's Friends* badge. We've all got them: me, Birdie, Wren, Jay, Py. And now Hector. He looks thrilled to death with it. Over the last few weeks I've wondered why he's putting himself through all this. I thought it was to impress Birdie, but now I wonder if he's just so lonely, he'll take a few knocks to make some friends.

"Circus people are like that," I say.

"Like what?"

I'm not sure how to explain it. "They treat each other like family. I think it comes from being travelling people. They take their community with them and that's all they've got in the world, so they're important to each other. Like a tribe."

"But Franconis' doesn't travel."

"I know, but it's just part of the atmosphere. And maybe… Maybe it's because people in circuses are all a bit weird to start with. Like, they have that in common: being on the fringes of normal life. If you get a whole bunch of fringe-people together, you can make your own middle. Does that make sense?"

He nods. I guess people don't come much fringe-ier than Hector. He looks so pleased with his bracelet, I can't help adding, "They said you were great, Hector. You should come here more often and I'll teach you some new stuff."

His face lights up. My heart sinks.

Achieving stardom

Posted by Birdie

When they arrive at the circus school and see the trapeze bars hanging ten metres in the air, everyone wants to get up there and start swinging. Sometimes you have to let them, just so they can get it out of their system, otherwise they can't focus on anything else. But once they've leaped off the platform and screamed their way across the heights of the warehouse, they realize that, actually, they have no idea what to do up there and also, how do they get down, please?

Then Finch and I lead them to the static trapeze and start teaching them the basic positions.

Number one is Star on the Bar:

1. Sit on the bar with your hands holding the ropes.

2. Lean back so you're horizontal and the small of

your back is resting on the bar.

3. Lower your head and raise your legs, so they point straight up and your feet are on the outsides of the ropes.

4. Spread your legs wide and point your toes.

5. Smile like you're not terrified.

6. Let go.

If you end up doing a "Falling Star" by mistake, remember to make a wish! (Strangely, people always make the same one. It involves their necks.)

< < Previous Post

In the crush of people squeezing through the school's main entrance as the bell rings, my attention is drawn by someone ahead of me, and I find myself thinking something I never in my life thought I'd find myself thinking in a crowd of my classmates.

Hey, nice shirt.

It actually is. I can't see who's wearing it but it's purple paisley with a wing collar and it would go really well with my yellow cords. In fact, I can totally picture myself wearing it. And then I realize why.

I find Birdie at the lockers.

"Is Hector wearing my paisley shirt?"

"You were giving it away — you said it was too small."

"It is. That doesn't explain why Hector's wearing it!"

"I thought it would suit him. It does, doesn't it?"

"No! It's ridiculously geeky on him."

"It's *supposed* to be. Geek chic, that's what you said when you bought it. It looked so good with your Seventies newsreader glasses."

"Yes, on *me* it looked good. *I* was wearing it ironically. And *my* glasses were fake. Hector looks bizarre. You can't go around giving him makeovers; he's not a Barbie doll. I'm sure he has no desire to be dressed like a Seventies newsreader."

Birdie laughs. "I don't recall you ever asking me if I *wanted* to walk around in a puffball skirt and an orange tank top. Why does *he* get a choice?"

"You're never going to let me forget the orange tank top, are you?"

"*Matching* orange tank tops."

"The skirt wasn't that bad."

"It was hideous."

"Whatever. The point is, that's our thing. *Ours*, not his. And we only just get away with it."

She gives me a pitying look. "Oh, sweetie, you think we get away with it?"

"Whatever. *He* won't, and he'll take us down with him."

"Fine, so I won't make him wear an orange tank top. Anyway, I think he looks cute. And let's face it, he needed to do *something*; he was never going to get a date in that school uniform."

I frown. "What date? Why does he want a date?"

"Um, because he's *human*?"

"What did he say? What have you heard?"

"Oh, nothing." But she's grinning her *I'm not telling* grin. "I'm just trying to make him one of us. I thought you'd like that."

"Why does he have to be one of us? *Us* is just you and me. We don't need anyone else, do we? It's not like he's going to join the act — he's not exactly trapeze material."

She sighs and gathers up her books. "Don't you ever take a day off?"

"From what?"

"Franconis'. Does everything have to be about the circus?"

"I *am* a Franconi. You can't take a day off from who you are."

"Tell me about it," she mutters. "Hey, why don't *you* try and get a date so *I* don't have to listen to you 24/7!" Then she slams her locker and walks away.

I try to avoid Hector for the rest of the day but at lunchtime he corners me in the yard and starts planning this week's study schedule.

"Thanks for the shirt, by the way. I wasn't sure it

was me, but Birdie kind of insisted I wear it."

"It's a great shirt," I say through gritted teeth. And I'm not the only one who's noticed it. Kitty, the Bond Girls, James and the lads are walking this way, and I suddenly realize that hiding in a corner of the yard wasn't a good idea because now there's nowhere to run.

As they pass, Kitty turns towards us. I swear, it's like she's got heat seekers. Or geek seekers.

"Isn't that sweet!" she croons at Hector. "You swapped your clothes with a homeless person on the way to school! What a saint. Or did you two get confused when you were getting dressed in the dark this morning? *Sleep*over, was it?"

I do a deadpan laugh. "God, you're so *funny*, Kitty! You know, we're looking for clowns at Franconis' – you should audition. If you toned the make-up down a *little* bit, you'd be perfect."

"And would you lend me some of your pretty clothes for a costume? Or is it only His Holiness here you play dress-up with?"

"Kitty, as usual it's been a pleasure talking to you, but since I'm getting bored now I'm going to have to insist that you *bite me* and go away."

"Ooooh, the claws are out, girls," she says, and behind her someone shouts, "Handbags!"

With a quick glance around for teachers, Adi and

Chris step forward, grinning and backing me towards the wall. I tense up, fists clenched already and stomach braced for impact, but suddenly Hector is leaping between me and them, shouting, "Stop!"

They both stop, but only out of surprise as the diminutive, bespectacled Hector rams a restraining hand into Adi's chest and looks fiercely (for Hector) up at him. Adi laughs, shakes his head and says, "Far too easy." He and the rest of them saunter off, doing high-pitched, squealed impressions of Hector's "Stop!"

"For God's sake, Hec, did you have to do that! He wasn't going to hit me. Probably. And even if he was, I could have handled it. A lot better than you, in fact!" This is true. I may be Murragh High's biggest loser (well, second biggest since Hector arrived) but thanks to the trapeze, I have the upper-body strength of a JCB.

"From now on, Hector, can you just mind your own..." But he isn't even listening to me. He's bent over on the ground. "Hector?" Did Adi hit him and I blinked and missed it? I crouch beside him.

"He's not hurt," he says with relief. *He?* Who's he? I start to wonder if Adi hit him in the head.

"What are you doing?" I follow his gaze to the tarmac by my feet, but there's nothing there except a dead bee. No, it isn't dead; as I watch, it twitches its antennae, or whatever it is bees have, crawls a few millimetres and stops.

"He was about to stand on it," Hector says.

"A bee? You made all that fuss about a flipping half-dead bee?"

"He's just exhausted. Sometimes they run out of energy and you find them crawling along on the ground. If they can't fly to find food, they die. I read about it."

"Of course you did."

"But we can save him!" He looks up at me excitedly. "If we give him sugar dissolved in water, he'll get enough calories to fly away and find nectar."

I put my head in my hands. "You are unbelievable. It's just an insect!"

He frowns. "Bees are becoming endangered. Some people think that if they die out, it'll be catastrophic for the *whole planet*!"

"You've been reading too many sci-fi novels."

"It's very serious. They pollinate food crops; without them we can't grow food. Now you sit here and guard him, I'll get the sugar. Do you think they'd give me some in the canteen?"

"I'm sure if you explain the whole situation to them, they'll give you anything you want to get rid of you."

"Right, stay here then."

He runs off and I'm left sitting on the tarmac guarding a dying bee from four different games of playground football. There's a fair chance we'll *both* get trampled before Hector comes back. I tear a page out of my physics textbook and slide it underneath the bee in case I have to make a quick rescue.

"Good thinking," Hector says when he gets back. "Now lift him onto this saucer." I tip the bee off the page at the edge of the little sugary lake Hector's brought and, to my amazement, it pokes out a long tongue and starts slurping the stuff faster than Lou hoovers up whiskey. A few minutes later it's in the air, slow and woozy, but it's up there. Hector watches delightedly. "I wonder what it's like to be so small," he muses.

I shake my head at him. "I wonder what it's like to be so weird."

And then the bee's gone. Hector's so thrilled, I forgive him for being such a monumental twit.

"Well done, St Francis of Assisi. I suppose you didn't give a toss if Adi *was* about to lay into me then?"

He waves a hand at me. "As if! I'm not losing teeth for someone wearing tap shoes."

"They're spats! And thanks a lot!"

20

Falling in love with flying

Posted by Birdie

Everyone falls eventually. You're better getting it over with, because once it's done, you're never afraid to fall again. And you will. Over and over. Unfortunately, along with Star on the Bar, Mermaid and Half Angel, one of the basic positions you have to get used to is "Flailing Octopus".

You'll become fearless about pain, too. For example, Jay's greatest ambition is to be able to dislocate his shoulder like Ennis Mullins. Dad wants to take him to a child psychologist.

I was once almost dragged to social services by a visiting school doctor when I took my top off to let her listen to my heart, displaying the full extent of the bruise rainbow across my chest, neck and arms.

"Oh, dear God!" she said.

I grinned. "Good, aren't they?" It didn't occur to me that she might not guess the obvious explanation – we'd been learning to juggle with wooden clubs that week.

So you *will* fall, and you *will* get hurt. But don't be scared: Franconis' little family of performers will always be there to pick you up, make you tea and post the embarrassing video on YouTube.

< < Previous Post

It's true, you do get used to falling, but I still don't enjoy it.

I remember my first fall vividly.

I knew all the static trapeze positions and I was used to swinging on the flying trapeze, hanging by my hands, knees or ankles, and then letting go and enjoying the free-fall feeling on the way to the net. But this was my first grab. Mum was swinging upside down on the bar opposite me, in a strong Catcher's Lock position, ropes wound around her legs, waiting for me.

I stepped out into nothingness and swung back and forth, gaining height. I flipped into a knee hang, arms outstretched, hands free, and then I was hurtling towards her and she was hurtling towards me, and I knew this was the one. We would meet in exactly the right position; all I had to do was let go.

One moment she was there – I could have sworn she was close enough – and the next she was plummeting away from me. My fingertips brushed hers. Someone screamed.

I was still looking up at her in shock, so it came as a surprise when the safety net hit me in the back and I realized I'd fallen. And screamed like a little kid.

"Never mind, Finch," Mum called, swinging above me as I lay, panting, on the net. "Next time."

I guess remembering what it was like to be a beginner makes me more sympathetic towards Hector as we practise in the yard at lunchtime.

"Maybe it would be easier if you only had to think about one hand," I say as he dashes around after dropped beanbag balls.

"I can't juggle with *two* hands, never mind one."

"You'll *have* two hands, except one of them will be mine."

"That makes no sense whatsoever."

"It's called tandem juggling." I get up from the yard wall and stand next to him, close on his left, so we're both facing away from the school. "It's the same as two-handed juggling but you do the right hand and I do the left, like we're two halves of one person. Put your other hand behind you." We tuck our inside hands behind our backs and he takes two balls in his outside hand and I take one in mine.

"OK, go."

Predictably, it's a disaster. Hector can't stop his left hand twitching for the ball every time his right hand throws it, which means he keeps walloping me in the back, and he's concentrating so hard on not doing that, that he isn't placing this throws anywhere near where they're supposed to go. But we keep trying, and when he gets used to how weird it feels, he actually starts to improve.

"This is great!" he says. "I bet it looks dead impressive."

"Try to throw a bit higher. Past my forehead, remember."

"OK."

His next throw is almost perfect. He lobs it into the air and it rises in a beautiful arc over our heads. A perfect curve. A parabola Miss Allen would be proud of. Good speed, good height, maybe a *bit* off in terms of direction. We watch it descend gracefully, a metre behind us, where it lands neatly in the rat's nest of Kitty Bond's blonde hair.

Hector immediately starts to apologize, as though Kitty Bond is a reasonable person you can apologize to for a reasonable accident and who'll forgive you in a reasonable way.

She turns to glare at him, struggling to pick the ball out of her complicated knot of over-sprayed hair. She's wearing a T-shirt that says You Can't Sit With Us.

"That hurt!"

As usual, I pile in, which is just what she wants. "It's a beanbag ball! It couldn't have hurt." That's why Hector's using them, though I don't say that.

Hector tries to retrieve the ball for her, and Kitty thumps him in the chest and screams, "Keep your hands to yourself, perv!" She untangles it herself and chucks it at me, hard. Her aim is *much* better than Hector's. "And keep your stupid toys to yourself, Freak Show."

She's turning the glare back to Hector when I can't resist saying, "I think it's an improvement." I nod at the collapsed mess of hair. "Hides your face nicely."

Kitty's eyes narrow and her voice goes chillingly smooth. "You Franconis are a danger to yourselves and others," she says, folding her arms and jutting out one hip. The Bond Girls close in behind her, matching her pose. It's like being circled by extremely fashionable birds of prey. Hector and I each take an involuntary step closer together. "Maybe I'll talk to Mr Cooper about getting potential weapons banned from school grounds."

"Potential weapons! It's a beanbag ball!"

"You could have broken a window. Or your boyfriend's glasses." She gives Hector a nasty grin. "We can't have dangerous implements in the hands of unstable schoolboys now, can we?" she says in her best teacher voice. "They could be used to intimidate. They could be used for *bullying*."

"Yeah, and what would that look like?" I mutter.

They start to move off but I know better than to relax. Sure enough, there's a last raised eyebrow, a last slow scan of my clothes. "Did you lose a bet?" she says. "Hate it when that happens."

Finally she's gone. "Jeez, I thought she was going to shoot lasers out of her eyeballs or something," Hector says, collapsing on the wall. "Thanks for getting in the way."

"I'm used to it. You're new; she should give you a break."

He's thoughtful for a moment. "There was a girl like that at my last school," he says.

"There's always a girl like that."

"Did you used to date her or something?" he asks.

"What! Are you serious? She hates me."

"Yeah, I noticed. I wondered if that was why. The girl at my old school…"

I look up in surprise. "You dated her?"

"Don't look so stunned. We were only eleven and 'dating' meant holding hands in the canteen queue. I broke up with her and after that she always had it in for me. Unfortunately when puberty hit, it turned out she was pretty and I was *not*, which meant I'd pissed off the most popular girl at school. I think she was furious at me for ever going out with her, like I'd tricked her into dating some nobody when she was too young to know any better."

"Why did you dump her?"

He shrugs. "She wasn't very nice. I thought maybe you and Kitty had a history too."

"Nah. James and Kitty have been on-again-off-again since he sent her a Valentine's card in primary school."

I consider telling Hector about James, but I don't feel like going into it. And it was all so long ago, it couldn't matter to anyone any more, except losers like Kitty.

James has probably forgotten all about it by now. In fact, I hope he has, because I'd like to think he'd tell Kitty to lay off if he still remembered we were ever friends.

Kitty doesn't make empty threats, and before the week is out, Hector, Wren, Jay, Birdie and I have been hauled into Mr Cooper's office.

Wren reasons with him, Jay argues, Hector pleads and we all stage demonstrations of our ability not to lose control of the various objects from his desk whirling over our heads. I even stand against the wall and let the others fire juggling balls as hard as they can at my midnight-blue velvet tuxedo jacket and ruffled shirt, but Coop is unrelenting. Actually, I have a feeling he's on our side (and quite entertained by Jay's stapler and hole-punch juggling), but he's been backed into a corner by Kitty and her thorough knowledge of the school's "zero tolerance" bullying policy.

"Go on, Sir." I force a couple of balls into his hands and stand back against the wall. "As hard as you like, it won't hurt!"

"Finch."

"Come on, when do you get the opportunity to chuck stuff at students! It's not like the old days, is it?"

"Finch!"

"Remember the time I joined all the Bunsen burners together in chemistry?"

"Finchley!"

"And the fire brigade had to come?"

"*Mister* Sullivan!"

"One of the sinks cracked."

"Stop this."

"Miss O'Dowd was *crying.*"

For a moment he weighs one of the juggling balls in his hand thoughtfully, remembering the smoke damage, I guess. But then he sets it down on the desk. "I'm afraid the decision has been made, Finch. I'm sorry, you'll have to leave the equipment at home in future."

"I'm so sorry, guys, this is all my fault," Hector says as we trail outside.

"Don't be silly, Hector," Birdie says gently. Then, more harshly, "It's all Finch's fault."

"Me? I didn't throw a beanbag ball at Kitty Bond."

"You're his teacher! You're responsible. And you know better than to do *anything* to attract attention to yourself around her."

"Yes, I'm all about being low-key, aren't I?" I gesture at the velvet tux jacket.

"Well, it's too late now, you'll just have to teach him somewhere else. He can come to our house!" she adds, linking arms with Hector, who beams at her.

Even the ruffles on my shirt sag.

So when we're not at the warehouse, Hector starts hanging out at our house. In my room, to be precise, because Mum says if he breaks another plate in the kitchen, we won't have anything to eat off.

"Sorry, Mrs Franconi."

"That's all right, Hector, we all have to start somewhere. It's just that some of us should start somewhere with soft furnishings."

Birdie's started going to the library most days to write her blog posts because she can't stand listening to me yell at him, so it's just me and Hector and the *thud-thud-thud* of beanbags taking a serious beating.

"Jugglers the world over are weeping right now, Hec."

He sighs. "You think I should quit?"

I'm tempted to say yes. But he looks so dejected, I get up from the bed, where I've been lying on my back bouncing three rubber balls off the wall, and say, "Let's try the tandem thing again."

I stand next to him and put my right arm behind my back, but this time Hector wraps his left arm round my waist. Actually this is a much more natural way to stand because we're closer together, like conjoined twins, fused from shoulder to ankle. We're both more stable and it's how I'd do it with Birdie or Jay, but it feels a bit odd with Hector. He's just looking at me, though, waiting for me to start, so I put my right arm round him and say, "OK, go."

I fumble a few catches and Hector apologizes, even though it's not his fault. I'm too aware of his arm round me, that's the problem. Which is ridiculous, but it's the first time anyone I'm not related to has ever put their arm round me, and the last time a guy put his face this close to mine, he was calling me *gay boy* and stealing my crisps.

Eventually I get it together and we manage to get a rhythm going. We spend the rest of the afternoon like that, trying rings and clubs, bouncing balls off the floor instead of throwing them. It's fun, actually, and I forget his arm round my waist, his skinny ribcage under my fingers.

Until he moves away and says, "I'd better go or I'll be late home," and then suddenly I feel disappointed that he's leaving.

Which is my second brand-new experience today.

★ ★ ★

I walk Hector out and then sit on our front step and watch him trot down the lane, tossing a beanbag ball from hand to hand and tripping over potholes.

I tried to teach James to juggle once. He wasn't bad but he wouldn't practise enough to get good, so we could never do team stuff. In return he taught me to flick a football up behind me with my feet and make trick shots at pool, neither of which I was remotely interested in. But it didn't matter that we had nothing in common; we just laughed a lot and talked a lot and stayed over at each other's houses and had fun hanging out.

There's still a rumour that I tried to kiss him at a sleepover. *Not* true.

Friendships break up all the time. Kitty's always surrounded by the same Bond Girls, but her Best Friend seems to be decided by rota. Jay (the only Franconi who's ever been popular, mainly because everyone wants to see which bone he'll break next) brings home different friends all the time. And there's always some scandal at school about friends fighting, or making up or breaking up. It's normal and you're supposed to get over it. "I don't know why you care so much," Birdie said one day when I'd been moaning about James *again*. I shut up about him after that, but the whole thing irked me for months. Years. It still irks me. Why *did* I care so much?

I suppose it was the fact that it was so unfair. I didn't

do anything. I'd understand if I'd slagged him off on Facebook, or wrecked his bike or kissed his sister or stolen his position on the football team, but I didn't. I think that's why I can't let it go; he didn't ditch me because of something I did, he ditched me because of something I *am*. And that's a sucky thing to do to someone.

21

Spots and shadows

Posted by Birdie

Someone recently told me that you can't take a day off from who you are. I suppose that's true in a way: people expect certain behaviour from you and there are consequences if you don't deliver. But for circus people I think it's often the other way round: you can't take a day off from the person you're *pretending* to be.

Sometimes I think about being someone other than Birdie Franconi. Some kids run away to join the circus, but when you live there, it can be tempting to run away and join the real world. Being someone else, even boring old Bridget Sullivan, would be a kind of holiday. I am Birdie Franconi so often that I'm starting to think she's real.

But the person in the spotlight isn't real, that's what you have to remember. She or he is just a shiny surface, a collection of polished tricks designed to entertain. And where there's a spotlight, there's a shadow. Another self that the girl on the high wire or the boy on the trapeze is trying to distract you from. Few people notice. Even fewer think to ask why.

< < Previous Post

I read Birdie's latest blog on the way out of school. Weird one today. I don't know what she's on about sometimes. Not that it matters, since no one reads it.

She's already at the warehouse but I had to stay behind to study with Hector before going to meet her. Birdie and I try to keep at least one night of the week for just us. If Hector's around, I'm too distracted to practise. I've always got one eye on him so I can yell, "You're overreaching!" or "Drop your shoulders!" or "Look out for the Tots Acrobats!" When it's just me and Birdie, I can get some work done.

I decide to walk to the warehouse. It'll be a good warm-up, and anyway, I feel too bouncy to sit on the bus. I had a great day at school, and I never have great days at school. I got a B for my history assignment, sixty per cent in a maths test (Miss Allen did a victory dance – it was kind of embarrassing), double chips at the canteen because I was the last person served and they were left over, and sustained no bruises from team juggling practice with Hector (even though we were practising in the disabled loo, thanks to Kitty Bond's

War on Fun). *And* I've finally finished working out the new trapeze routine. It took me the whole of Spanish and I failed my vocab test, but it was totally worth it.

I'm playing out the routine in my mind as I walk, my muscles twitching with every turn and flip and grab, so I don't notice the figure walking towards me from the direction of the creepy old biscuit factory until he's quite close. It's getting dark and he's hunched over, chin tucked into his collar, and by the time I see who it is, it's too late to cross the street. I start my usual inner debate about whether or not to say hello.

On the one hand, we used to be best friends. And although his girlfriend is a happiness-sucking vampire, he doesn't go out of his way to torture me or Birdie personally. OK, he'll look me over and shake his head, but my own father does that. And we were close; I still have the Hard Rock Cafe T-shirt he brought me back from Paris.

But on the other hand, we used to be best friends. And he chose the happiness-leech over me. And he doesn't go out of his way to *stop* anyone who feels like torturing me or Birdie. *And* he gave away his Ringling Brothers pencil case the day after he punched me and then let his mates pile on.

You can't really say "Hi, James" in a tone of voice that encompasses all that.

He blanks me, as usual. But before he does, just as

he passes, he narrows his eyes, like he's daring me to even think about being friendly.

As if.

"*Hi*, James, good to see you too!" I shout after him, as sarcastically as I can. "Nice talking to you!"

I don't know why I do this to myself, but I'm annoyed that he's still being a josser three years on. We're on a deserted street and he's ashamed to say hello to me.

I expect him to keep walking but he stops, and after a second or two turns back. I can tell from the way his jaw is clenched that it's not to say hi.

"You're a jerk, Sullivan, you know that!"

"Me?" I look around like he might be referring to some other Sullivan. "I'm sorry, are you still sore from where I punched you in the gut? Oh no, hang on … *that was you*!"

He holds his hands out incredulously. I notice his T-shirt and coat are filthy and streaked with dust; I guess he's started hanging out in the biscuit factory with the Year Twelve wasters, breaking windows and drawing genitalia on the walls in spray paint. I wouldn't be surprised.

"That was three years ago!" he says. "Get over yourself!"

"Me!"

"You! You, you, you. You know, everyone's sick of hearing about you. Do you ever think about anyone else?" This from a guy I did nothing *but* think about for a *year* after he dropped me like one of Hector's beanbags.

"We can't all be as perfect as you, James. You attract such nice people. Where's Kitty, off looking for people to scratch? Didn't think you were allowed out by yourself."

He takes a step towards me. I'd forgotten how tall he is. "What's that supposed to mean?"

"Um, that your girlfriend's an evil cat? It's a metaphor. A play on her name? Too sophisticated for you?" I am pushing it now.

But he doesn't hit me. Instead he snorts down his nostrils, like I'm not even worth a proper laugh, shakes his head and looks disgusted. "You know, it *amazes* me that you don't have any friends," he says.

"Hey, I have friends," I say, but I instantly regret it because I know what's coming next.

"Oh, yeah, your little circus-freak shadow! Finch and the Holy Ghost! Bet Saturday nights are a riot with him. Bet the study fun just never stops!"

"Yeah, he's smart and he reads a lot. Is that the best you can do for an insult? You should take lessons from Kitty – *she'd* have managed to get his hair, clothes and face in there. He has a very slight squint if it helps. And his smile is crooked. And his teeth. His nose is all right though. In a certain light." James is looking at me like I'm cracked. He might be right. "But I'll tell *you* something," I go on, ignoring him, "he's a better friend than you ever were." I have no idea why I'm sticking up for Hector. If he'd heard what I just said, I'd have died of embarrassment.

"Yeah? Well, then the poor guy deserves better than you," James says. Then he walks off.

What a nutjob! I've had conversations with Lou that made more sense. What have I ever done to him? I stomp off towards the warehouse but I'm not thinking about the trapeze any more. Suddenly I'm wondering if we should introduce a knife-throwing act. I could have a big target with James's face on it and practise being a really, really bad shot.

The thought has almost cheered me up by the time I get to Franconis'. I run the last few metres, bursting to tell Birdie what a complete tool James Keane is, the words bubbling up already, but when I get inside she's not there. The lights are on, there's music playing, but she's nowhere in sight. I glance towards the kitchen area but she's not there, either. Or on any of the sofas, or at the big table. I even check the safety net to see if she's lying on it.

And then I realize I'm looking in the wrong places. As I shrug my bag off and bend to set it on the floor, I get a view under the net, to the space beyond it. Sometimes we stack the foam mats there but today they're elsewhere. There's just the floor. And a small figure in white leggings and a white top, her body crumpled like a scrunched paper ball, lying motionless on the concrete.

"Birdie!"

She's as white as her clothes. And cold from the floor. I want to move her somewhere warm but I've been told often enough never to move someone who's hurt. Dad gives us first-aid classes every year in case one of the students has an accident, but now all I can remember are the injuries, not how to deal with them. Words like "concussion", "spinal injury", "internal bleeding", "head trauma", "paralysis". As I take my hands away from her head to dig my phone out of my pocket, there's blood on my shaking fingers. When the emergency services answer, the words come out of me like machine-gun fire – no hesitation, no panic – and I wonder who's pulling the strings, because inside I feel like a rag doll. I give them the address, tell them how far she fell, that she's breathing and that her head's bleeding. I tell them to hurry.

I'm not sure I blink, never mind sleep, for the next three days. None of us do. Instead we sit on a row of plastic chairs in a corridor outside Intensive Care and flinch every time the door opens.

No one says much. No one wants to eat. Jay lies with his head in Wren's lap, watching the knees of the doctors and nurses whisk by his face, and Wren strokes his hair and tries not to cry on him too much.

I get obsessed with replaying it all in my head, trying to figure out what happened. A safety net doesn't mean you're safe: people have broken their necks falling *in* the net. You can fall awkwardly, get disoriented, you can miss the net, catch the edge. You can bounce out.

For three sleepless days I visualise every possible scenario over and over in my head. I'm exhausted, we're all exhausted, but sleep just doesn't come.

Because it's all in that little room. Every time the door opens, I can sense it, sleep, like a suffocating bird hovering over her. While we sit there, not talking, not eating, not sleeping, Birdie doesn't open her eyes once.

After three days, Dad drags me home and forces me to go to bed. And by then it's not sleep; it feels more like death.

22

At 9 a.m. on Monday, I'm woken by a *bing* on my phone.

"Sodding junk mail," I mutter, pulling the duvet over my head. I don't want to get out of bed. Because once I get out of bed, today is going to happen. And if it's anything like yesterday, I want nothing to do with it. Ideally I'd like to sleep through today – and tomorrow and every day until Birdie is finished sleeping through todays and tomorrows – but the internet has other ideas.

I snatch my phone from its charger and scan my emails. The last one, the one that woke me, is the automatic notification I get when Birdie puts a new post on the blog.

I sit up in bed, wide-eyed. Is she awake? I scrabble at the link until it takes me to Flying Tips.

There *is* a new post. But it doesn't say, "Hey, Finch, I'm awake, get out of bed and come visit me, waster," which is what I'm hoping for. It's just a standard blog post, something about the Franconi twins. It takes me a minute to realize what's going on, and then the disappointment hits me like a slushy snowball in the face. Automatic scheduling. She wrote this post days ago and set it to appear automatically today.

It's weird, seeing her words appear on the screen when she can't even open her eyes and speak to me. And it seems inappropriate to post stuff about trapeze artists, considering the accident. If there are more posts lined up, I should cancel them.

I try to log in to the blog account but it's password-protected. I'm pretty sure I know all Birdie's passwords and I try them one after the other – RinglingBros, BusterK, GetLostFinch – but none of them work and Mum's calling me to go to the hospital. I give up. Maybe there was just the one post anyway.

———————— MONDAY 16 MARCH ————————

Everyone makes mistakes
Posted by Birdie

The big acts at the circus are big precisely because they allow the least margin for error, and risk the biggest consequences. Lion tamers, high-wire walkers, human cannon balls, flying trapeze artists – they're the ones on the posters. Along with the words "death-defying!", because they are.

Circuses tend not to talk about their worst accidents – it's not exactly good for business. So I wasn't going to mention Franconis' most infamous act, but if you google "Franconi" you'll find it anyway, probably in a list of "Ten Worst Circus Disasters!" that includes an elephant being hanged for murder (seriously, google it, it's bizarre and horrible) and a fire that killed hundreds of spectators.

I've already written about our great-granny, Evelyn Franconi, and her twin sister, Avis, but I left out the bit about how their act came to an end.

They were performing with another trapeze artist, a man called Carlo Fellini. The details are sketchy; all we know is that they were performing without a net and at some point Avis fell and was killed instantly. This was in 1930 so there's no film of the event, no photographs, no CCTV, no YouTube video taken on someone's phone. Even though there were four hundred people watching that night, including a couple of journalists, we'll never know exactly what went wrong.

But that didn't stop people speculating.

It got around that Carlo was engaged to Evelyn but in love with Avis, and that was the birth of a dozen conspiracy theories. The newspapers, the spectators, the police, the circus owners, friends of the Franconis – everyone had a different take on it: Evelyn hated Avis; Avis felt guilty and jumped to her death; Avis was plotting to get Evelyn out of the way, and Evelyn knew it and took action first; Carlo wanted to get rid of Evelyn but dropped the wrong girl; Carlo had to get rid of Avis before Evelyn found out. It was murder. It was an accident. It was sabotage. It was suicide.

What *was* Avis's mistake? Letting go too soon? Trusting the wrong person? Falling for her sister's boyfriend? Did she make her mistake in the air, or on the ground, long before she even got up there?

Evelyn ended up marrying Carlo, and they performed for a while with their kids, including our granny, Lou. But the story followed them around and eventually they had to leave the circus to escape it.

Whatever happened, I think it was brave of Evelyn to get back up there after losing her partner, her twin. But I'm not surprised it became too much for her. I think you'd get very tired of instinctively reaching out for someone who's no longer there.

<< Previous Post

For the first few days, Birdie's room is chaos. Strangers race in and out – doctors, nurses, specialists, consultants – adjusting machines and scribbling on charts. Orderlies wheel Birdie up and down the long corridors, day and night, rushing her to different departments for scans, X-rays, blood tests. *Here we go again, Bridget!* The doctors are constantly frowning and shaking their heads, taking Mum and Dad aside, giving each other instructions, and I feel like crawling under the bed so I can stay close to Birdie but stop being in everyone's way. They all talk over my head as if I'm not there anyway.

One day they stop using the word "concussion" and start using the word "coma". It's a heavy word, and it falls at my feet like a bird shot from the sky.

And then, like a TV being switched off, one morning it all just stops. The doctors vanish and the machines settle into a slow, regular riff of beeps that I come to know so well I hear them in my sleep. The little room goes still and quiet, swallowed up by a fug of waiting. The doctors say there's nothing else we can do.

So I take two buses to the hospital every day and sit silently by her bed, waiting, doing my "shift" on the family visiting rota, like Birdie is our job now, and feeling useless.

One day a new nurse comes in and starts doing all the checks the nurses do.

"All right?" he says.

"Hi," I say. Then, "I'm her brother," as if I have to prove my right to be there.

"I know, I was talking to your dad. Twins, aren't you?"

"Yeah."

"I'm Tony."

"Finch."

He goes on taking readings from the machines and writing numbers on Birdie's chart. I've been tempted to look at that chart many times. It just hangs from the end of the bed. I could pick it up, but I haven't. I'm not sure I want to know what it says.

"It's OK to hold her hand," Tony says, and I realize I'm sitting with my hands through the metal rails around the bed, a few centimetres from Birdie's fingers.

"You won't hurt her, but stay clear of the wires and tubes. We put the rails up because people in comas sometimes move around and she could fall off the bed, but while you're here you can lower them."

He finishes his checks and looks like he's about to leave, but he's the first person I've met here who's talked to me like a human being, so I say, "Tony?"

"Yeah?"

"What's wrong with her?" He walks back into the room, slowly. "OK, I know what's wrong with her, she's in a coma. But what does that *mean*?"

He lowers the rails himself and sits on the end of the bed. "It means her brain is trying to fix itself. She's gone offline for a bit. That's normal for a serious head injury."

"Oh. How long will it take?"

He shrugs. "It varies. She's also got broken ribs and a shattered fibula. Calf bone," he adds. "But we're treating that and she's not in any pain. It's just like sleep. Deeper than sleep. We've taken the breathing tube away because she's stable now and breathing for herself. The machines tell us what's going on inside her body, and the tubes in her arm are feeding her because she can't eat or drink."

"Oh. I guess that makes sense."

"It *looks* scary, I know," he says. "But we're taking good care of her, I promise. I'm sure Birdie wouldn't want you to worry."

I do feel better. It feels good just to hear someone call her by her name. "Thanks, Tony."

He winks. "No problem. I'll be back in an hour, if you have any more questions, OK? And you should talk to her — she can hear you. Bye, Birdie, see you later!"

I get off the plastic chair, settle myself on the bed and hold Birdie's hand. "Well, he's nice, isn't he?" I say.

For the first two weeks it feels like everything's been freeze-framed. We don't go to school, Dad doesn't go to work, no one buys groceries or cooks or does house-work or homework, we don't watch TV or listen to music.

The only time I get out of the house, except to go to the hospital, is when Mum sends me to the ware-house to stick a note on the door. I tape it up and then stand there, staring at the words Birdie and I have been dreading for months.

FRANCONIS' CIRCUS SCHOOL
CLOSED UNTIL FURTHER NOTICE

The warehouse is dark and gloomy and even quieter than Birdie's hospital room, and I wonder if we'll ever open again. The longer we're closed, the more money we'll lose. How will we pay the rent? It feels like the end already. And it happened so fast; we thought we'd at least get time to put up a fight. I lock the doors and walk home.

Mostly we sit around Birdie's bedside or around our kitchen table. We don't talk or anything, but it somehow seems important that we're together all the time. Like more of us might start disappearing if we lose sight of each other.

They say all we can do is wait, so that's what we're doing.

But nothing happens. Birdie lies there on pause while the rest of us start to realize that the world has kept going without us, which seems shocking in a way, almost rude. We get emails from parents asking about circus classes. Lou gets a chest infection and has to be taken to the GP. Teachers send me notes for classes I've missed, and Hector, Py and Janie post YouTube videos on Facebook.

One night Jay taps Wren on the shoulder as we're all sitting silently around the bare kitchen table and whispers, "I'm hungry."

Mum blinks at us all, like someone coming out of a trance. Then she takes a deep breath and says, "Wren, take Jay and Finch to Tesco for groceries. I'll tidy up here and then we'll have dinner."

And life starts again, just like that. Mum and Dad

insist we go back to school and Dad starts working from his laptop at Birdie's bedside. I know we don't have a lot of choice, but somehow it feels like a betrayal; like we're not waiting any more, we're getting on with things.

On my first day back at school, Hector gives me a pile of papers and a hug.

"I'm sorry about Birdie. If there's anything I can do…" he says over the yells of "Get a room!" from across the yard.

"Erm … thanks. What's all this?"

"Your homework for the last ten days."

"Great, how am I going to get through this lot?"

"No, not the assignments," he says. "The answers. I've done it all for you – you just have to copy it out and hand it in."

"Seriously? Hector, that's pretty decent of you."

"Don't get too excited, I'm going to make you go over all this stuff when Birdie's better."

"Should have known. Did you see the blog post?"

"Yeah." He winces. "Seemed kind of inappropriate."

"I can't get into her account to delete it! I've spent hours trying to guess her password."

"You'll never guess it," Hector says. "That's the point of passwords."

"But Birdie's passwords are terrible. She always picks something obvious and personal, so she'll remember.

I can guess it, I know *everything* about Birdie."

Hector scoffs in disbelief. "You can't know *everything* about a person."

"Is that a challenge?"

"Yeah," he says.

"Bet I guess it before she wakes up."

"You're on. Movie tickets, loser pays."

"Deal."

Hector also starts calling for me every morning so we can walk to school together, like I might collapse if I have to spend five minutes alone.

My second morning back, I opened the front door and he was there, waiting for me.

"What are you doing here?" I asked him. But he just blinked at me.

"What are you *wearing*?" he said.

I looked down at myself. "What's wrong with it?"

"Nothing." He frowned. "*That's* what's wrong with it."

I was wearing jeans, a pale green T-shirt and black trainers. Hector couldn't seem to get himself off the doorstep. "What, no big collar?" he said. "No ruffles? No tassels, no garish orange print? No braces, no hat? Those aren't even bell-bottomed jeans." He put a hand to my forehead. "Are you feeling OK?"

I knocked his hand away and started down the

path. "I was in a rush this morning. I decided to go understated."

"You mean boring."

"I call it Hector-chic. I thought you hated my clothes anyway."

He shrugged. "Yeah, but this is worse. You should get up earlier."

Actually I lied about sleeping in. I'd been up at seven, standing in front of the mirror in a loud Hawaiian shirt and my "Rupert Bear trousers", as Mum calls them. Something wasn't working. I tried a leather jacket. No. Then a velvet jacket. Worse. Poncho. Sandals. Red belt. Braces. Even my goes-with-everything tank top. Something was still wrong. Something was missing.

I rifled through the hangers, then hauled out the pile of stuff that had fallen off the hangers and lay pooled on the wardrobe floor. Then I wandered over to Birdie's room to look at her collection of men's watches. Her wardrobe was open – it's so full it doesn't close – and net skirts and minidresses spilled out between the doors like they were trying to escape. Suddenly I knew what was missing from my outfit.

If Birdie were home, she'd have taken one look at my Rupert trousers and put on her red miniskirt and yellow knee socks, and we'd have walked to school together feeling like we were strutting around Camden Market in London. I forced her wardrobe doors closed and frowned at myself in the mirrors on the front, then I went back to my room and dug a pair of jeans and the plainest T-shirt I own out of the back of a drawer. Turns out Birdie is my main fashion accessory and everything I own looks odd without her.

At school the reactions were as strong as Hector's. A couple of teachers told me I looked "very smart today" (kiss of death to any outfit), a few people stopped dead in the corridors and said, "Finch?" and my class went silent when I walked in the door, like in those Westerns when the gunslinger walks into the saloon. I just scurried to my desk, blushing like I'd arrived in my underwear. Only Kitty Bond seemed disappointed with my new look. I could almost hear her thinking, *River Island? What am I supposed to do with* that!

I didn't care. They'd get used to it. For the first time in years, I had no interest in my clothes. I wanted to sit at the back of the room and do nothing more than exist until the bell rang at the end of the day and I could get to the hospital. The less obvious I was, the less I'd have to deal with in the meantime.

Hector kept doing double takes and frowning at me. "Too weird," he said for the millionth time. "Promise you'll wear a hat tomorrow at least."

I sighed. "Whatever."

Of pyramids, twins and other disasters

Posted by Birdie

Our dad may not have the Franconi dare-devil genes but he makes up for it by being a bit of a circus-history ~~nerd~~ expert. While Mum taught us how to fall into the net without getting hurt, how to dust our hands for grip and position our thumbs on the bar, Dad did his bit to ensure our safety by telling us horror stories on the way to practice.

One of these was the story of the Flying Wallendas, an old circus family, and their Seven-Person Pyramid (which is exactly as dangerous as it sounds). The act involved three tiers of people (and a chair) on one high wire with no safety net, but it all went wrong in 1962 when the lead man faltered and three people fell. Two were killed and one was paralysed from the waist down.

Finch and I were always more interested in how this

trick was done than in how it went wrong (much to Dad's annoyance), but I've always wondered what it was like for the other four people up there on the wire. It's hard enough to stay upright on a high wire, but it must be nearly impossible to watch your partner fall and stay focused enough not to go after them. Not to even lean over or stretch out a hand.

Finch and I have a tendency to follow each other around. It's a twin thing; we're the original buy-one-get-one-free offer. And sometimes I have a nervous feeling that if one of us fell from the trapeze, the other would go sailing after, just out of pure habit.

< < Previous Post

"Hiya, Birdie." I pause, raising my eyebrows exaggeratedly at her, then hiss, *"That was your cue!"*

Nothing.

"Nothing. You're so predictable." I sit cross-legged on the bed, raise her hand into a limp high-five, then set it down and hold her fingers.

"I read your blog today. Another weird one. You're getting all deep and meaningful since being in a coma. I think we should go back to unicycle tips. Hector, for one, could use them. Do you think he'll ever get better at it or has he peaked?"

Nothing.

"Janie made you a new bracelet." I slip the plaited band of red silk around her wrist, next to the blue hospital bracelet with *Bridget Sullivan* and our date of birth scrawled on it. "She said something about tactile objects helping people in comas. I don't know what that means, but it feels nice, see?" I twist the bracelet around so she can feel the silk slide over her skin. "Like it?"

Nothing.

"Py said to tell you 'Keep 'er lit'. He also suggested coming in and doing some tricks for you, but I think he just wanted to get near the compressed oxygen tanks. Can you imagine the size of the flame-thrower he could make? He said the fire alarms would wake you up for sure. Hector said burning down the hospital *might* not be the best thing we can do for you and Py gave in, since he now does *everything* Hector says. It's bizarre – just because Hector helps him with his homework, Py's decided he's Einstein or something and no one's allowed to contradict him. Not that Hector didn't have a point about not burning down the hospital, I suppose. I'll thank him for you, yeah?"

Nothing.

I settle myself more comfortably beside her and dig a packet of crisps out of my bag. Pickled onion, her favourite. I open them and wave the bag under her nose.

Nothing.

"*Everyone* from school's been to see you. I bet you were super humiliated to be seen in that hospital get-up. Teachers came too. That must have been weird, though

I suppose they're used to you not listening to a word they say, yeah? Yeah? Oh, come on, that was funny!"

Nothing.

"You won't believe who I saw coming out of your room on my way in today. James Keane and Sinead Adeyemi, with their *arms round each other*! The Dream Machine is cheating on Kitty with one of her own Bond Girls! Poor Sinead, I almost feel sorry for her. Kitty will *end* her when she finds out. James went scarlet when he saw me. I'm not surprised; this is the gossip of the *century*. Not that I have anyone to gossip to, do I?"

Nothing.

"Dad's coming after dinner; he'll take over until bedtime. Our bedtime, not yours, since you're in bed all day, you lazy lump. I'll probably head over to the warehouse. We're not open, but people keep showing up. Jay's there tonight with the Juggulars, and I'm sure Py and Janie will call in. And Hector, *of course*. I'll just make the pizza, since there's not much I can do on my own on the trapeze. Mum's not really in the mood. You know, you're really setting us back here, Bird. What kind of a flying trapeze act only has one flyer? And if I can't be a flyer in the show, what am I going to be, hey, tell me that?"

Nada. Nil. Niente. Zip. Zilch. Nothing.

25

"Hey, Finch, you have to come see this, it's hilarious!" Janie calls as I walk through the warehouse door. Everyone's crowded around a messy pile of clothing on the floor, which suddenly groans and reassembles itself into Hector. As he gets up, everyone applauds.

"You shouldn't encourage him, he'll wreck himself," I say.

"Yeah, but it's brilliant, watch!" Py says.

Hector rights his unicycle, climbs on with a bit of help from Wren, and starts pedalling across the warehouse, torturously slowly, the wheel jerking in every direction but forward. "Whoa! Whoa! WHOA!" he shouts. I feel like covering my eyes but everyone else is killing themselves laughing. As he passes Janie's silks dangling from the ceiling, one of them gets twisted around his flailing arm. The unicycle keeps going, taking his legs with it, while his upper body is trapped in the silk, till he's almost horizontal. Everyone's waiting for him to let go and plummet to the floor but he starts pedalling backwards, and the unicycle gradually rights itself. We all start breathing again.

Soon he's back to vertical, looking relieved, but he can't stop pedalling and the bike goes from under him again, in the other direction this time. We wince. He pedals forwards and gets back upright, but the bike starts going sideways. We hold out our hands involuntarily as if to catch him, but he rescues it again.

And he keeps doing this, each time managing to turn in a circle and wrap the silk tighter around himself, until he's spiralled in it like a caterpillar in a cocoon. Then he gives up, lifts his feet with the unicycle still dangling between his clenched legs, and the whole Hector/bike/silk parcel starts to spin back the other way, faster and faster, while Hector yells helplessly from within. Py and Janie are leaning on each other laughing, which I think is a bit mean, to be honest. When the last twist of silk unravels, Hector and his bike fall to the floor in a pathetic heap and everyone cheers.

"Hey, you lot made mistakes when you were learning, you know. There's no need to be cruel." But no one's listening to me. I walk towards Hector, looking for a hand or arm I can tug to help him up.

"That was great, Hector! Even better than last time," Janie says.

"I think he added an extra turn," Py says.

"What do you mean?" I bend down to Hector, who untangles himself and stands up without my help, grinning manically.

"He's done that six times now," Janie says. "He has it perfect! I think you should add it to the show. Hey, we could incorporate it into my act, like a comedy silks routine? He could spin me around above him!"

"That would be so funny, Janie!" Hector walks off with her, already discussing ways they can merge their acts, and everyone follows.

"Hey! Wait a minute!"

Hector turns back. "What?"

"You did that on *purpose*?"

"Yeah. I've been working on it since ... well, for a few weeks now. You weren't around to teach me so I've been practising alone.

"But that was—"

"Yeah?"

"I mean, it wasn't—"

"Yeah?"

He's going to make me say it. "That was good, Hector. It was really good."

He gives me the most triumphant smile I've ever seen.

"All right, don't get cocky, your landing needs work."

He rolls his eyes.

★ ★ ★

Before long, the CLOSED UNTIL FURTHER NOTICE sign is a rain-tattered scrap blowing around the car park. We're not teaching classes, but Janie, Py, the Juggulars and the Tuesday Acrobats turn up whenever they feel like it, and Hector and Janie's act is getting better every day.

"They look pretty good together," Py says as we sit on the sofa watching Janie spin gracefully above Hector, who's spinning helplessly, arms and legs flailing in every direction.

"Of course they do. It's all about contrast: she's super talented, he's a disaster — that's the basic recipe for comedy."

"Do you think there's more to it than that?" Py says, examining his ragged fingernails and looking slightly too casual.

I almost spray my Diet Coke over him. "Hector and *Janie*? You've got to be kidding."

"No?"

"Definitely not."

He looks relieved, and I almost laugh. It's ridiculous. Even if he's crazed with jealousy, he can't possibly believe that Hector and *Janie*…

"I guess they *have* been spending a lot of time together," I say, more to myself than to him.

He frowns, then gets up quickly and shouts, "Hey, how about teaming up with me, Hector? Have you ever worked with fire?"

★ ★ ★

Soon, Hector has been added to nearly every act in the circus. They're even designing new ones around him. He gets trapped in the middle of a water-balloon-missile war the Juggulars are having, riding his unicycle up and down No Man's Land while balloons whizz past his nose to a belting soundtrack of the Saw Doctors' "Will It Ever Stop Raining?" He dresses as a tenpin skittle on stilts and the Tots Acrobats turn themselves into human bowling balls and tumble along a giant bowling alley while he teeters around them, trying not to get knocked down. He even does a series of unicycle ride-pasts behind an "unsuspecting" Py, blowing his torches out before Py can swallow them (Dad has *serious* reservations about Hector and fire).

And he's hilarious. He never gets it *exactly* as planned, but he's always funny, and when things go a little wrong, the rest of the performers are quick and agile enough to get out of the way so no one ever gets hurt.

I think it's the expression on his face more than anything. A nervous clown is instantly funny because you *know* something awful is about to happen to him. Hector's not faking the nerves but he does ham it up for maximum effect. He looks no more confident than he did the first time I handed him a juggling ball, but he's concentrating so hard you can't help but root for him, and the more you don't want him to fall, the bigger the laugh when he finally does. And he doesn't care how ridiculous he looks, he just wants to entertain everyone. I start to worry he'll kill himself just to get a bigger laugh.

The whole of the Easter holidays I sit on the sofa, watching them all creating new routines, practising old ones, writing notes, making mistakes, falling, laughing, applauding each other. The whole warehouse is ringing with voices, music and energy, just like it's meant to.

Janie flops onto the sofa beside me on the Thursday before we go back to school, shiny-eyed and breathless, and says, "I think it's really coming along, don't you?"

I look at her. "What's coming along?" I gesture at the various routines going on all over the warehouse. "What's the *point*?"

Her face falls, and I get up and go back to the hospital.

26

"You know, I'm getting sick of these one-way conversations," I tell Birdie peevishly.

"Really? I'd have thought they'd be right up your street."

I almost leap out of my skin for a second before I realize the voice is coming from behind me.

"No one to interrupt or contradict or tell you to shut it? Just an unfiltered stream of Finch. If I were Birdie, I'd wake up just to ask for earplugs."

"Helpful, Hector. Anyway I don't think she can even hear me."

He comes in and sits on the chair next to the bed. "Hiya, SB."

"What's SB?"

"Sleeping Birdie. Like Sleeping Beauty but—"

"Yeah, I get it."

"She *can* hear you. People in comas can hear

everything going on around them."

That's what Tony says too. But it's getting harder and harder to believe, because if Birdie could hear Mum and Dad sitting by her bed crying, she'd have woken up by now.

"I thought I could read to her, if you like?" Hector says.

"What, books on the First World War? She's already *in* a coma, Hec."

"How about a new biography of Buster Keaton?" He produces the book from his bag.

"Oh. Well, that might be OK. And can I borrow it after you?"

"No, you're behind in history – it's First World War for you."

"Great, two comas in the family. Franconis' is in trouble."

He laughs, but stops when he sees I'm not laughing too.

"No, really. Mum says the rent's going up and the income's going down. We're going to have to close. Permanently."

"What about the show, won't that help?"

"What show? There's no show without Birdie – the trapeze was our big act. Anyway, we'd need more routines, rehearsals, equipment. It's a lot of work, and Mum and Dad just don't have the energy at the moment.

No one does." I gesture at Birdie and say, a little louder, "You hear *that*, Bird? You're ruining everything."

"She can't help it," Hector says reasonably.

But I don't feel like being reasonable.

"I knew this would happen someday," I say. "That we might have to close, I mean. I just thought Birdie would be here to help me do something about it. It's like she's given up on us. Whatever, I don't even *care* about Franconis'. I just want her to…"

I gulp and blink furiously because I am *not* going to cry in front of Hector, and he says quickly, "Hey, the trapeze isn't everything. You've still got Py and Janie and the Juggulars. And Wren and Jay and the Acrobats. And me." He looks away and shrugs. "I mean, I can make the pizza and stuff."

"Your Four Cheese and Peanut Butter Surprise *is* pretty special," I admit, getting my face under control again, and he smiles.

"It's not hopeless," he says. "Birdie would want us to try." Then he hands me the Buster Keaton book. "Here, why don't *you* read this to her. She'd like that."

27

"Life is on the wire, the rest is just waiting."
– Karl Wallenda

Posted by Birdie

I've been reading about the Wallendas and discovering there's much more to them than a tragic accident.

What makes a person decide to devote their life to walking on a wire 1.5 centimetres thick, six metres (minimum) in the air? For the teenage Karl Wallenda, it started with a job advert asking for "A hand balancer with courage". How often do you get to apply for a job that specifies "courage" in the ad? IT skills, yes. Courage? Not so much.

The job turned out to be doing handstands on the shoulders of his new boss while the boss walked a high wire, which was all very well but not dangerous enough for Karl, and he soon created his own act. By 1928 his high-wire human pyramid involved four people, three tiers and two bicycles. The two men on bikes would ride across the high wire with two planks of wood between them on their shoulders. Karl would sit on a chair balanced on the planks and his future wife, Helen, would stand on his shoulders. They got the name the "Flying Wallendas" when they fell one night. All four of them managed to catch themselves on the wire, no one was hurt, and people in the audience said they fell so gracefully, they looked like they were flying.

That act became the seven-person pyramid that kept going until the fatal accident in 1962.

The accident was shocking. But not as shocking as the fact that the surviving Wallendas performed again the very next night.

Today, five generations on, there are still performing Wallendas, but now they are skywalkers, which means high-wire walking outdoors, between skyscrapers and over rivers and canyons, using highly sophisticated equipment to monitor weather conditions and construct their rigging. Nik Wallenda trains six hours a day, six days a week, and in 2011 he successfully made the walk between the two ten-storey buildings in Puerto Rico that, in 1978, killed his great-grandfather, Karl.

That's the nature of circus acts – they have to get bigger and better all the time because otherwise the audience will get bored.

But the story about the Flying Wallendas that impresses me most is a very simple one. When the Wallendas first performed in Madison Square Garden, New York, in 1928, they did it without a net. They weren't trying to impress anyone, they weren't being brave and they weren't being cocky. They'd just managed to lose the net in transit.

They could have cancelled the act or postponed until they got a new net, but there was a show to do, a crowd with tickets, and Madison Square Garden was their big break.

You can plan a trick for months. For years. But you can't control everything. *That's* where courage comes in; sometimes you have to just go for it.

The crowd in Madison Square Garden had no idea that the Wallendas hadn't planned to do their act net-less. They just gave them a standing ovation.

<< Previous Post

We've only ever tried one trick without a safety net.

It was last winter and Dad had decided the net was looking tired, so he ordered a new one and we took the old one down the night before it was due to arrive. Birdie and I were in the warehouse alone, tidying up after the Tuesday Acrobats, when I noticed her standing under the trapeze and looking up, chewing her lip.

"The Franconi Twins did everything without a net," she said as I came to stand beside her.

"Yeah, and look what happened to them."

"We don't know what happened. It might not have been an accident at all, it might have been deliberate."

"And that's better?"

She shrugged. "It would mean they didn't make a

mistake." Then she turned and raised an eyebrow at me. "Dare you," she said.

I raised my eyes to the top of the rigging. Without the net hanging halfway between it and the ground, it seemed higher than ever. "Mum would murder us."

"She won't know. Just a simple catch. When was the last time we missed a basic catch?"

"Exactly. We're probably due."

"Rubbish. And we'd be able to say we'd performed without a net, just like the Franconi Twins."

"Not *too* like them, preferably."

"Go on, Finch, it'll be me in the air anyway – all you have to do is catch."

"Yeah, so it'll be my fault if you pancake!"

She was already heading for the ladder. "It'll be fine," she called, and I followed her, because that's what I do.

Before I reached the top, she'd already swung out and landed on the far platform. She sent the bar back to me, I caught it and we stood facing each other. She seemed very far away but I could make out her grin.

"Wait!" I called as she lifted the bar on her side. I applied a hefty amount of chalk dust to my hands, which were beginning to sweat like a beginner's. She did the same. "One catch," I yelled. "Basic knee-hang grab, no funny business, no somersaults. I'm serious, Birdie!"

"OK, *Dad!*"

I swung out on the bar.

I don't look down when I'm up on the trapeze, there's no need. But I couldn't help noticing that something was missing from my peripheral vision as I flipped over to hook my knees around the bar: that blurred expanse of white hovering below us was gone, and the concrete floor looked grey and hard and very, very far away. All at once I realized how big a psychological effect the net has. It keeps you calm. It doesn't just stop you from hitting the ground, it stops you from falling in the first place, because you're not worried, you're not sweating, you're not thinking about the distance beneath you. So you perform flawlessly, and you think you don't need a net. You don't need it because it's there.

Birdie was swinging faster and faster, hanging by her knees, and we were starting to synchronize. If I had a penny for every time we'd done this catch, I'd be loaded, but suddenly it felt like the very first time. My arms felt weak, my hands like boneless dough. I started to second-guess the position of my knees, which way my palms should face. I wanted to call it all off but Birdie was hurtling towards me, stretching out her hands, and this was the one. I reached out automatically, saw her legs unfold, her body start to drop. As she left the bar, there was a huge bang as every light in the warehouse went out and we were plunged into darkness.

I had a split second to find her.

★ ★ ★

It happened so fast, but I remember thinking, or just *knowing*, that there was no point in trying to see her. There was no point in waving my arms around hoping to hit her. The fact was, if she wasn't where she was supposed to be, then it was all over.

Instead I closed my eyes, stopped questioning myself, held my arms out exactly as I'd done a million times before, and when the small dusty hands landed on my wrists, I grabbed hold, tight enough to crush them.

We just swung for a bit, until our eyes adjusted to the smudge of moonlight at the dirty windows and I could see enough to deposit Birdie back on the platform and then swing onto it myself. We sat on the edge, trembling and cursing the fact that *everything* in the warehouse is ancient and dilapidated, including the electrical wiring.

For a second I'd lost her. I had no sister. No twin. No Birdie. I put my arm around her. "Love you, sis," I whispered.

She put her head on my shoulder. "Big softie," she said, her voice still shaking.

After my shift at the hospital, I go back to the warehouse but it's deserted. All the lights are out except one, a big spotlight pointed at the empty trapeze platform. There's something lonely about an empty spotlight, like a big white hole in the world.

"Hi, sweetheart." Mum is sitting on one of the sofas in the dark. No, *huddled* on one of the sofas. It's even sadder than the spotlight. I huddle beside her and she wraps her arms around me.

"I should never have started this," she says.

I look at her and realize she's been crying.

"The circus. I should never have put you up there. Who puts their child ten metres in the air and says, 'Have fun, honey!'?"

It hadn't even occurred to me that Mum might be blaming herself for the accident. "That's silly, Mum." I try to imagine life without Franconis', try to imagine being plain Finchley Sullivan, but I can't even picture him.

"I'm a terrible parent," she says.

"No, you're not. I've always thought you're a pretty cool parent."

"Well, that just proves it. You're not supposed to like your parents, you're supposed to hate them because they stop you doing dangerous things."

"It's not like we didn't know the risks, Mum."

"You're children; there shouldn't *be* any risks."

But that's rubbish, there's risk everywhere. Sometimes you risk everything just stepping through the school gates. At least Birdie and I are used to having our hearts in our mouths. This isn't Mum's fault. *I'm* Birdie's partner and I wasn't there. If anyone's to blame, it's me.

"It'll be OK, Mum, we just have to wait. And …
and in the meantime, we have to focus on the show."

"Show? We can't have the show now, Finch."

"I know, but, Mum, we *have* to! You said yourself,
it's our last shot at keeping Franconis'."

"I don't care about Franconis'. I don't care about
anything except…" She can't finish because she's crying
again.

"But *Birdie* cares. Mum, we can't let her wake up
and find Franconis' is gone, can we? What would she
say? She'd be furious."

Mum cries for a while, then she takes a few shaky
breaths and dries her face with her sleeve. "She would.
OK, Finch. But you have to know, even if we do the
show, it might not make any difference. We might lose
the place anyway."

"I know. But at least we can tell Birdie we tried."

We've got until the end of term to make this happen. I
try to imagine Birdie standing up there in that spotlight
at the show, but all I can see is her tiny body falling in
the dark.

Sign up for Franconis' ~~Dating Service~~ Circus!

Posted by Birdie

If you google "famous circus double acts", you'll be surprised to discover how many of them were husband-and-wife partnerships.

Clyde and Harriett Beatty were both lion tamers, Karl and Helen Wallenda were high-wire walkers, Nik Wallenda proposed to Erendera Vasquez *on* the high wire (who could say no?), Elizabeth and Martin Collins performed the Wheel of Death together, and Texas Slim and his wife, Montana Nell, were a knife-throwing Western act.

I could go on; the list is long.

But when you join a double act and discover just how many hours you have to spend with your partner, how many fights you have to have and times you have to make up, you'll be less surprised. Basically, if you don't like your partner enough to *at least* marry them, your act won't survive. A circus partnership is based on trust, loyalty, devotion, commitment, long hours and not minding the smell of each other's sweaty tights. Marriage sounds pretty casual in comparison.

Which is all very romantic, but the other reason for all these husband-and-wife teams is that if you're spending seven hours a day, seven days a week training together, you might as well get married too, because you will have exactly zero free time to meet/date/kiss/marry anyone else.

Sibling acts are also common, for all the same reasons. In fact, they're even more guaranteed to succeed long-term because you can't divorce your brother or sister (believe me, I've looked into it). You're stuck with them, so you might as well make an act out of it.

The upside to sibling teams is there are no romantic hassles. The downside is there are no romantic hassles.

So if you want to join Franconis' and you've got a sibling handy, bring them with you. And if you're a Single Pringle, come along anyway. Maybe your double act awaits!

< < Previous Post

"You and me, Finch, how about it?" Hector says as we sit together on the yard wall the first day back after Easter, eating lunch and reading Birdie's blog. I almost choke on my sandwich.

"Wawmph!"

He frowns at me while I brush crumbs off myself, then he says, "Why don't we put an act together?"

"Oh," I say. Then, "*Oh!* You've got to be kidding."

"Why not?"

"Because falling off stilts is one thing, falling from a trapeze is another. If you don't believe me, let me introduce you to my sister. Oh, that's right, she's not here, she's in *hospital*. In a *coma*."

He twists his lips at me. "There's more to the circus than the trapeze, Finch. I meant, why don't *you* join *my* act?"

"*Your* act?"

"Yeah, why not? You're good at coming up with stuff. I thought we could design a comedy routine. And it's OK, I'll be the funny one, you can be the straight man."

I bite my lip. It's that or literally growl at him.

"I'm not saying it'll be easy," he says, "but if you work hard, I think we can pull it off. And it would give you something to do in the show. I mean, without Birdie." He shrugs apologetically. I'd quite like to kick him.

"I do *not* need a charity bit part in the Hapless Hector Show, thanks all the same. Birdie will be fine by show time and if she's not, then … then I'll do something on my own! And I won't need to make an idiot of myself either; I can upstage the likes of you any day!"

Infuriatingly, he's trying not to smile. "*The likes*

of me? Snob. What happened to *we're all people on the fringes?*"

"Shut up, Hector."

"Oooooh, did someone dare insult the Famous Flying Finch Franconi?"

I pick up my bag and start to walk away but he's still laughing and calling after me. "Hey, don't worry, I'll teach you everything I know!"

I wave over my shoulder, but not with all five fingers.

29

"What's with all the tragedy on the blog, Bird? It's getting morbid. Why were you reading about all those accidents? Why am I asking you all these questions when you can't answer back?" I grin at her, but she can't grin back either. The monitors beep instead.

Four weeks is the longest we've ever gone without speaking to each other, and that was when I had mumps and Mum made all the others go and live with Lou so they wouldn't catch it. I was only quarantined for two weeks but Birdie wouldn't speak to me for another two weeks after that because it was my fault she'd had to live with Lou, who had given her a haircut with the kitchen scissors and taken her to Karaoke Bingo.

So I think, somewhere in my mind, I had this four-week deadline marked. *Birdie will be back on the trapeze in four weeks.* And then, *Birdie will be recovering in four weeks.* And then, *Birdie will be awake in four weeks.* And now it's been over four weeks and she's exactly the same. Which isn't even "exactly the same", because if she hasn't woken up by now, then "exactly the same" actually means "worse".

Birdie and I both have a tendency to get angry when we're upset. When we hurt ourselves, we don't cry; we shout at each other, or Jay, or whoever's handy. These days it's usually Hector. But it wasn't Hector's fault Birdie fell. And it wasn't Mum's or Dad's or Wren's or Jay's. Py wasn't there, Janie wasn't there. I wasn't there either and maybe I should have been, but Birdie warms up alone all the time; me not being there probably wasn't why she fell. It was no one's fault, and that's almost worse because there's no one to get angry at.

I lie beside her on the hospital bed and remember that night. What a great day I'd been having, bouncing down the road like a bubble, no idea that everything was about to pop, big time, until I ran into James Keane and he ruined my good mood by being a total josser. And for no reason, as usual; probably just lashed out at me because I'd caught him sneaking around with Sinead at Murragh's unofficial make-out spot. Kitty wouldn't be seen dead in that pigeon-infested hole of a biscuit factory, so I reckon it must have been Sinead he was with. I never thought I'd say it, but Kitty could do better. If she'd seen all that grey dust on his clothes that night, she would have known he was up to something shady.

No, I muse, falling asleep, lulled by the regular beeping of Birdie's heart monitor, it wasn't grey, it was white. Would they still have flour in an abandoned biscuit factory? That's what it looked like: flour. Or chalk. Like blackboard chalk. Or chalk dust, for your hands.

Chalk dust.

I sit up so fast I tumble off the bed.

James Keane was there! It wasn't dust on his clothes, it was *chalk*. He wasn't coming from the factory, he was coming from the warehouse! What the hell was he doing down there? And why didn't he say anything after the accident? He must have been the last person to see Birdie before she fell.

Or had she already fallen when he left? A cold blade of an idea slices through my brain. What if he did something; some cruel prank that went wrong? What if he distracted her? Frightened her? He acted so edgy when I saw him.

I pace the room, not knowing what to do, who to tell. Who would believe me?

Birdie just lies there, beeping calmly, the only person who could tell me the truth. I can't prove it, but I *know*. I'm certain. James Keane was there. And whatever happened, it was *his* fault.

30

"That's ridiculous."

"Ugh, I *knew* you'd say that." I fling myself backwards on the bed and Hector perches on my desk, looking down at me.

"James Keane may be a prat but he's not a cold-blooded killer."

I raise my head and growl at him, "Birdie's not dead."

He holds his hands up. "Figure of speech."

"Anyway, I'm not saying he masterminded a whole murder plot. This isn't an episode of *CSI*. But he did *something*; he made her fall, I know it."

"You don't *know* anything."

"I know Birdie! She's always careful, especially when she's working alone. She only does warm-up stuff by herself and she hasn't fallen during a warm-up since we were ten years old. And even when she does fall, she hits the net right; she wouldn't bounce out like that."

"Accidents happen."

"There *are* no accidents. Everything is caused by something. I'm going to confront him at school tomorrow."

Hector looks alarmed by this. "I don't think you should do that. If he's guilty, he'll hardly tell you anything, will he?" he says. "In fact, he'll probably just punch your lights out."

"Well, I can't just do nothing!"

"Look, maybe James *was* with Sinead that night. If he was with her at the biscuit factory, he couldn't have been at the warehouse, could he? So why don't I just ask Sinead for you?"

"That won't look *at all* suspicious. If James heard you'd been asking questions, he'd know we were onto him."

"I'll do it subtly."

I raise my head plus one eyebrow.

"I *am* capable of subtlety, Finch."

"No, you're not; you say everything that comes into your head out loud."

He says "Hah!" so loud it startles me. "You'd be amazed," he mutters. "Leave it with me, and don't go accusing anyone of anything in the meantime, OK?"

"Fine," I agree, reluctantly.

Rules, bones and other things you don't want to break

Posted by Birdie

A good circus always seems anarchic, but like our trapeze bars, if you look closely you'll see that the anarchy is firmly bolted to some heavy-duty rigging. There are rules at the circus. There is etiquette:

1. Do what you're told, when you're told. The rig team (that's me and Finch) are responsible for your safety. If we tell you to check your harness, you check your harness. If we tell you to wait while we examine the rigging, you wait while we examine the rigging. (And if we tell you to make tea, you run for the kettle.)

2. Don't walk, stand, sit or ride unicycles under the net. You'll distract whoever's on the trapeze and when they fall, they'll land on your head.

3. Leave the piercings at home, unless you want to leave them, along with parts of your ear, lip, eyebrow, nipple, etc., embedded in the safety net.

4. Wash your hands! You know where they've been, and if it's anywhere near sun cream, moisturizer or the butter off your toast, we don't want them anywhere near our trapeze bars!

5. Check your partner's safety harness. It's what friends do.

6. Don't wear out your catcher. Remember, while you're having a blast up there, feeling lighter than air, they're knackered and feeling like an overstretched elastic band.

7. Be aware of your own limits. This means more than your skill level: it's your mood that day too. Don't fly mad, sad, sick or while experiencing a major sugar rush. And don't fly to please anybody else; they might have fun for a while, but they won't enjoy scraping you off the concrete.

< < Previous Post

Saturday lunchtime, we're sitting at either end of Hector's bed, cross-legged, lobbing three tennis balls back and forth between us. The bed is good because you don't have to bend down to pick up the ones you drop, or to be more accurate, the ones Hector drops.

"How's Birdie?"

"Horizontal. No change. I thought her eyelids flickered yesterday, but Tony says that's normal and the doctor said it doesn't mean anything."

"You never know, though."

I shrug. "I don't like the doctor; she never says anything good. At least Tony's optimistic."

Hector's doing all right – he must have been practising – so I start to speed up my throws. "Nice date with Sinead last night?"

"Blissful. No one yelled at me *the whole time!*"

"You didn't show her your juggling then."

"If I could think and throw at the same time, I'd come up with a *scorching* response to that."

"If you could throw and *catch* at the same time, we'd be getting somewhere. Did you ask about James?"

"Not yet. I only walked home with her after school; there wasn't time."

"I'm surprised she let you get that far."

"Hey, I can be pretty charming when I have to."

"Hmm, maybe she felt sorry for you."

A tennis ball hits me square in the nuts. "Ow! You little…!"

I make a lunge for him and he laughs, trying to fend me off as I stuff tennis balls down his T-shirt. "I was aiming for your head!" he gasps, writhing and wriggling beneath me. I've almost got him in a headlock when suddenly he freezes. Then he rams himself into my chest so hard I fall backwards and he falls on top of me, his hands pinning my shoulders down. I stare up at him, kind of stunned and heart pounding, not sure what's going on, but he just frowns at the bedroom door and says, "Did you hear something?"

"Yeah. Why?"

He gulps. "You're not supposed to be here." He scrambles up and grabs my arm. "Quick!"

I follow him out to the landing, both of us on tiptoes, through a door and up a narrow staircase to the attic. He shuts the attic door silently behind us and holds a finger to his lips.

"What's going on?" I whisper.

He shakes his head and presses an ear to the door. Floorboards creak on the landing below. Hector's dad coughs, and his mum calls something from the kitchen.

"Just a sandwich, I'll take it with me," his dad calls back. "Where's Hector?"

I make out the word "library" in response.

"I'm supposed to be at the library," Hector hisses. "I thought they'd be out all day."

"Why can't you just say we were at the library and came back here for lunch?"

He looks apologetic. "I'm not supposed to be with *you*."

"Why? What did *I* do?"

He shrugs. "My dad thinks... He thinks I see too

much of you. He thinks all the circus stuff is a waste of time and I should be studying more. Or doing proper sports."

"*Proper* sports?!"

"*Shusssh!*" He goes back to listening at the door and I wander off to look around the attic. It's a huge room floored with random offcuts of wood jigsawed together and it's stuffed with old furniture and packing crates. Different sections of the ceiling slope in different directions, so there are various heights and shadowy corners everywhere. It's lit by one window, which overlooks the side garden, and in front of it sits a wooden desk piled with books, and a chair, the only objects in the room that aren't covered in dust.

"Do you study up here?" I whisper.

"Yeah. It's quiet; no one bothers me."

It's not like Hector's house is noisy. He should try living in mine. I notice a set of juggling rings on the chair, so I pick them up and start throwing them for something to do.

"Stop that!" Hector hisses. "If you drop one, he'll hear – his study's right below us."

I give him a disdainful look. "Drop one? Me? Drop one? I'll show you *proper sports*." I throw the rings higher, faster.

"Seriously, Finch."

I throw one high, spin around, catch it and keep going.

"I mean it!"

I give him a wicked grin and close my eyes for a second. The rings land neatly where I want them, but when I open my eyes again Hector is hyperventilating.

"You really have no faith in me, do you?" I whisper. "Or do you want to join in, is that it? Here." I make as if to toss him a ring. I'm only joking; surely he knows I'm only joking. But he panics and makes a grab for it, knocking my arm in the process. Leaping sideways, I manage to save two of the rings, but one hits the floor behind Hector with a clatter and we freeze, clutching two rings between us and staring at the attic door.

"Sorry!" I breathe.

"Hello?" Hector's dad calls up the stairs.

Then his mum shouts from the ground floor. "Who are you talking to, Brian?"

"Is Hector in the attic? I thought I heard something up there."

"He said he was going to the library. Maybe something fell over. You should check in case it's that bookcase. I *told* you the shelves were rotten. It's probably collapsed."

They're coming up the attic staircase but I've already grabbed Hector and wedged us both in the little triangular gap behind a tall bookcase, which is jammed against the sloping eaves of the roof. We're curled up with our chins on our knees and his elbow in my ribs, but I can't tell him to move because the attic door is opening and his parents are coming in.

"I don't think it's rotten, it just needs to be sanded," Mr Hazzard is saying. "It seems fine."

"Must have been something else then. We really need to sort through all this junk, Brian. It's dangerous the way it's all piled up. We could make a proper study for Hector. With a sofa so he can bring his friends round."

"He can't study and have friends round at the same time, Nuala. He spends too much time at this sort of nonsense as it is." There's the sound of something being set on the desk and I realize it's the ring we dropped.

"I think it's nice he has a hobby, and some friends at last. He's always had trouble making friends."

Ouch. Poor Hector. I can feel him cringing in the dark beside me.

"I'm sure that's not true," his dad says.

"Oh, it is too! He's never been popular. And he's so sensitive; remember how his little bottom lip used to tremble when the bigger boys were mean to him?"

I wince and Hector puts his head in his hands. His parents seem to be poking around the junk in the room while they discuss their son's social problems.

"And I think it was worse than he let on," his mum mutters. "They used to call him Hector Spectre. I heard them."

"Kids always have nicknames, that's normal."

"Oh? Remember that birthday party we had for him and only two kids came? That's not normal."

Hector grabs fistfuls of my T-shirt and buries his face in my shoulder in agony. I kind of want to die on his behalf but all I can do is pat him silently on the arm.

"He didn't *want* a party, Nuala. He never liked parties."

"Because he knew no one would come! It broke my heart that day, seeing him in his little paper hat eating his cake all alone."

Hector starts silently banging his head against my shoulder. The cringe factor is just *rocketing*. If it wasn't so awful it would be hilarious.

"Well, things will be better here; small-town kids are nicer than city kids."

"Exactly. So we should be pleased he has some friends here. I'm going to take this vase downstairs. It'll do for the dining room, it just needs a wash."

"Yes, but it's only *one* friend, isn't it. That's not normal either."

"You just don't like that boy, do you?"

"It's not that—"

"Brian, if Hector likes him, he likes him, there's nothing we can do about it. And if he knows you disapprove, he'll only want to see him more. He never stops talking about him as it is."

Hector reaches an arm around my neck and claps both hands tight over my ears.

It's not funny, but something about tension always makes me want to laugh, and this is about as tense as a steel high wire. I clamp my hands over my mouth and hold my nose, but my shoulders are shaking and I know I'm going to give us away. Surely Hector would prefer us to get caught. Surely he'd prefer *anything* to this. He takes his hands off my ears and covers my mouth instead, but his parents' voices are moving away now and I realize they're going out the door.

"We should invite him round for dinner sometime, and his parents too! I'm sure if you got to know him…" his mum is saying as they leave.

The door closes at last. Hector's body crumples and the two of us spill out of the little space behind the bookcase, me weak with laughter and Hector trying to clamber over me and hold his hand over my mouth at the same time.

"Will you be quiet!" he hisses. "They're still in the house." But a few minutes later we hear the front door shut and the car start, and Hector lies down on the floor, spread-eagled and panting like he's run a marathon.

I stand over him, hands on my knees, out of breath. "I'm so sorry!" But I probably don't sound very sorry, what with all the laughing.

"Kill me," he says.

"Oh, come on, it wasn't that bad."

"I'm serious, just batter me round the head with something. There's probably a heavy bit of wood somewhere – apparently the bookcase is rotten."

"At least your dad stuck up for you. That was pretty cool of him, even if he is a circus-hating freak."

"Dad? He has *no idea*... Ugh!"

"OK, it was awful. But everyone's got embarrassing stories."

"Yeah? Tell me one of yours then," he says.

"Are you kidding?"

"I hate you."

"So why do you never stop talking about me?"

He throws both arms over his face. "Seriously. Kill me now."

"Hey, I'm hardly Mr Popularity myself, you know. At least two kids came to your birthday."

"They were my cousins."

I burst out laughing again.

"It's not funny." But he starts to laugh too as he sits up. "I'd forgotten that party. I was eight. When we played blind man's buff, they blindfolded me, stole my presents and ran off."

It's really not funny; it's the most tragic story I've ever heard. But we're both on our knees now, clutching our sides and shaking. My eyes are streaming, my jaw hurts, and Hector's laughing so hard no sound comes out.

Tension is a strange thing. That's how you get the biggest reaction out of an audience; you put them on the edge of their seats with nerves, and then when you make the leap, or catch the flaming torch, or fall off your unicycle, they need to release it. The more you ramp up the tension, the bigger the gasp, the scream, the laugh. Three minutes of agony behind a bookcase and the two of us can't stop.

And it's not just the bookcase. I realize, as I collapse on my back, that I haven't raised a *smile*, never mind a laugh, since Birdie's accident. In fact there's been nothing but tension, inflating painfully like a balloon in my chest, for weeks. It was going to come out somehow or other, and as I wipe my tear-streaked face and feel my body relax, I'm so grateful to Hector I could hug him.

Instead, when I've calmed down enough to speak, I say, "When *is* your birthday?"

"June."

"I'll come to your next party."

He grins. "OK then."

"Invite the cousins too."

"Yeah?"

"Yeah. We'll kick the crap out of the present-stealing little jossers."

32

Thanks to Hector, I am now *always* early for school; it's really annoying. This morning we're sitting on the yard wall waiting for the bell to ring and he's making us a study timetable. Well, he's making *me* a study time-table. I doubt he needs one.

"What's with the felt tips?" I ask.

"I'm colour-coding your subjects."

"Why?"

"I thought making them brightly coloured would hold your attention better. You know, like they do with toys for three year olds."

"Ha ha. And frankly, it would have to be made of chocolate to hold my attention."

"You know, I don't think drinking Coke for break-fast can be good for you. Your attention span is bad enough without adding sugar."

I take a large swill from my can. I didn't even want

Coke for breakfast but since Birdie's accident Wren and Jay have taken over the grocery shopping so Mum and Dad can spend more time at the hospital, which means our fridge is full of tofu, kale smoothies, pizza and Coke, but not much else. "What are you, the breakfast police?"

"You have a lot to get through. Have you done the geography homework about the earth's core yet?"

"I don't give a flying diabolo about the earth's core. Don't you think teenagers have enough delving to do without taking it to planetary levels?"

"Yup, but that's not going to get you any marks from Mr Geography." Hector has adopted my mum's system of naming teachers.

I'm about to complain that he's not putting in enough blue (circus school) squares when I hear "Aww, such a cute couple" from behind us. I can't see her face but I can tell from her voice that one pencilled eyebrow is right up in her hairline. "*One* of them could probably do better," she adds as she passes. "I just don't know if it's him or her."

She's gone before I can think of a good comeback. Because it's one of those ones where there *is* no good comeback. What am I supposed to say? *Eugh, gross, we are NOT a couple*? Or, *Sod off, Kitty, Hector would be a great boyfriend*? Or, *Yeah, right, he'd be lucky to have me*? I wonder which one Hector would be the most offended by.

Hector just sits there staring at his notebook, like he's pretending he hasn't heard. I wonder if he's regretting ever hanging out with me. Train-track braces and Star Trek toys don't make you popular but at least you grow out of them. By Year Twelve he might have actually achieved complete inconspicuousness. If he keeps hanging out with me though...

When it's quiet again, Hector says, "I have some stuff on the First World War. Do you want to look at that tonight?"

"What?"

"For the history assignment. It's not in the textbook so you'd get brownie points."

"Oh. No, I think I've got enough for that, thanks anyway."

Usually when Kitty says mean things, Birdie and I laugh, not because she's funny, just in disbelief that such a nightmare of a human being actually exists. It's sort of interesting to hang around and see what she'll come up with next, like watching nature documentaries about predators. I try not to take it personally, because I really can't believe she means it personally. It's more like she was assigned a job at the start of term, like Class Representative or Prefect, except her job is "Official Torturer of the Vulnerable". She probably has a badge and everything. I imagine her getting up every morning, putting on her most intimidating outfit, practising her eyebrow-raise in the mirror, jotting down a few scathing remarks to use later, and then complaining to her mum because actually she's bored with the whole thing and wishes she'd gone for the debating team instead.

Birdie does a hilarious impression of the eyebrow that always sets me off. But Birdie's not here; there's just Hector, who won't look me in the eye, and I don't feel like laughing.

I remember Hector's parents talking in the attic and say, "Does your dad really think small-town kids are nicer? Did you move here because you were being bullied?"

"Not exactly. My dad grew up around here. He never wanted me to grow up in the city; he thinks kids in small towns are more … I don't know…"

"Boring? Narrow-minded? Decades behind everyone else?"

"Innocent."

I choke on my drink. "You should introduce him to Kitty."

"I know. I think you're much safer in the city; you can get away with being different. In a big crowd, it's like you're invisible. This place gives me the feeling I'm being looked at all the time. Maybe that's what my dad wants. To be honest, I don't think he wants me to grow up at all."

We still have ten minutes before the bell rings, so

I tell him about being friends with James, and *Oklahoma* Monday and the Ginghams.

"And ever since I've been *she* and *her*, and the guys all avoid me, like I might try to snog them or something, and the Bond Girls act like I'm public enemy number one because I embarrassed Kitty's boyfriend, or because I'm weird or an easy target, or because I don't even *know* why. It's so stupid; it was years ago! And it was nothing! But it's like it's just simpler for them to give you a label on day one, and then everyone knows exactly how to treat you for the rest of your life."

Hector's just frowning at me; maybe I'm not explaining it well.

"It's like what happened with Chunk Magee," I say.

"Who's Chunk Magee?"

"Chris Magee? The guy who runs the newsagent's?"

"Oh yeah. Why do they call him Chunk?"

"Because he's fat."

"But he's not—"

"Exactly. He was fat when he was a kid so everyone called him Chunk. He was practically *anorexic* before anyone noticed he'd lost weight. He ended up in hospital. And they *still* call him Chunk. So what chance have I got?"

He doesn't say anything for a while and I'm starting to wonder if I should have told him any of this. Then he says, "So you were just *friends* with James?

I mean, you don't … *like* him?"

"You're as bad as Birdie! No! Of course not."

"OK. But you do talk about him a lot."

"Because I think he had something to do with Birdie's accident!"

"But the chances are he didn't, so you should stop obsessing about him."

"I am *not* obsessing; I couldn't care less about him."

"OK." Hector shrugs like it doesn't matter but he looks relieved, and I can't help feeling disappointed that he's no better than the rest of the guys. I half want to point out that *he* wouldn't be in any danger anyway, but the bell rings and we both drop the subject.

33

For someone who told *me* to stop obsessing about James Keane, Hector's taking this undercover investigation stuff pretty seriously. He spent breaktime yesterday in the library with Sinead, passed her notes during history, and today I saw them walking home together.

I text him a few times to see what he's found out, but he doesn't reply, and by bedtime I can't stand it any more. I walk to his house and run straight into Sinead coming down his front path.

"Oh, hi, Finch."

She seems embarrassed, which is understandable. If Kitty Bond knew she'd been hanging out at Hector's, there'd be a public excommunication at the very least. Possibly a beheading for treason.

"We were just doing homework," she says.

So that's it; she's sponging off Hector's planetoid

brain. Well, fine, so long as he got some information out of her.

"Right... Well... See ya."

Sinead Adeyemi and I have never spoken a word to each other before, and apparently we haven't been missing much. We nod awkwardly and I carry on up the path.

"Finch?" She's stopped by the gate. "How's Birdie? It's so weird seeing you around school without her."

"Smaller target?" I say. She opens her mouth to reply and I brace myself, already planning the retaliation, but then she turns and walks away. I guess she's not as tough without half a dozen Bond Girls flanking her.

I knock on Hector's front door.

"Hello, Finchley." Hector's dad is one of those parents who call you by your full name, even though no one calls you by your full name, not even your *own* parents. "My goodness, Hector's popular tonight. Late, isn't it?" he says, glancing at his watch. I wonder if Hector's ever had two friends over in one night. The Rev must have fallen through the floor when Sinead Adeyemi showed up in her designer skinny jeans, swishing her hair at Hector. Even his parents know he's at the Special end of the Geek Spectrum.

"Yeah, but I'll be quick, it's just a school thing; I'm stuck on one question of my maths homework and I totally won't sleep unless I figure it out."

"Mmm-hmm." He's not buying it for a second. "Is that a bowler hat?"

"Uh, yeah."

Hector's dad gives a tiny shake of his head and stands aside to let me in. He's obviously decided there's no point in talking to me because we will never understand each other; the bowler hat is just the final proof of this.

I run upstairs and burst into Hector's room. He's juggling plastic rings and wearing Star Wars pyjamas. I think he'd rather I'd caught him naked.

"Nice PJs, Hec."

He goes crimson. "They're old, and... Can't you *knock*?"

"Can't you answer a text message?"

"I was going to but Sinead was here. She just left. I was about to go to bed."

"I know, I saw her. Why is it taking so long to get some answers out of her? You must be bored to death. I appreciate it, Hector, really. Sorry I laughed at your terrible PJs."

"Thanks," he says drily.

"So what did she say? What have you found out? Was James with her that night?"

"Well, I wanted to lead up to that – I thought it would look weird if I just came out and asked, so I started by talking about some other stuff first."

"Like what?" What could they possibly have to talk about?

He shrugs. "School, movies, books..."

"She reads?"

"She actually likes some really cool sci-fi, but you're not allowed to tell anyone; Kitty doesn't approve of sci-fi."

"That's because all the slime-spewing monsters look tame compared with her."

"She likes poetry, too, and her taste in music isn't bad. She's making me a playlist."

Poor deluded boy. "Hector, I hate to tell you this, but she's just saying all that."

"What?"

"She knows you're smart and she's just saying what you want to hear so you'll do her homework for her. It's a classic and you fell for it. At least I'm trading you circus skills. What's she teaching you, how to accessorize? I bet you spent all night doing her chemistry or something, didn't you?"

"Well, no." He looks embarrassed. "She was helping me with my English."

"*She* was helping *you*?"

"She's good at English. And I'm not good with all that symbolism and 'there's no wrong answer' stuff. I *like* there to be wrong answers; that's how you know you've got the right one. Anyway, we're going to work on our essays together."

"You're seeing her again?"

"Yeah, we thought she could come over in the evenings."

"Oh, I see. And what about circus skills? Five minutes' practice in your most embarrassing PJs every night is not going to get you into Cirque du Soleil, you know."

"I'll still have time to practise."

"You have to be dedicated. Like Py. You don't see *him* wasting time on homework."

"I guess not; maybe I should stop doing yours then."

"Fine with me." I slouch against the wall and start picking up random things from his dresser and setting them down again. A lot of them are made of Lego.

"We'll still have time to hang out, Finch," he says. "And do your homework."

"I don't care whether we hang out or not; I just think it's pathetic you believing Sinead Adeyemi is your new bezzie. She's not a nice person."

"Have you ever talked to her?"

"I don't need to. She's a Bond Girl. A Gingham. At worst she'll crush you like a bug and at best she'll turn you into one of them. I *told* Birdie this would happen."

"Told her what would happen?"

"*And* she's going out with her best friend's boyfriend,

who, might I remind you, is potentially a cold-blooded killer who she's covering for. Yeah, you're right, she should be up for a Humanitarian of the Year award."

"You can't prove any of that. She seems OK to me."

Suddenly I realize what's happening. "Oh my God, you fancy her!"

"What!"

"Jeez, one pair of skinny jeans and you're anybody's! She probably knows you suspect James and she's flirting with you to buy your silence."

"What? You've been watching too many movies, Finch. *Bad* movies."

"I bet you didn't even ask her about that night, did you?"

Hector looks uncomfortable. "Well ... we just never got round to it."

"Un-fricking-believable."

"I was going to ask her next time. But honestly, Finch, I don't think she knows anything. She doesn't seem the type—" He stops when he sees me glaring at him.

"You're an idiot, Hector. You're the smartest idiot I've ever met."

"Why, because I think a nice girl might want to spend time with me?"

"A nice girl *did*. Birdie! And I wasn't keen on you two... But I thought at least you cared about her. And now she needs your help and you've gone all puppy-eyed over the first girl to look at you."

Hector folds his arms over Darth Vader's face grill and says, "I am not puppy-eyed over Sinead Adeyemi. You know I'm not."

"Could have fooled me," I mutter.

"Yeah, but then you're not that bright."

"Ha ha."

He unfolds his arms again. "I'll ask Sinead about James, I promise. We're going to the cinema at the weekend – I can ask her then."

"You're going to the *cinema* with her?"

He rolls his eyes. "Good *night*, Finch."

"Whose idea was that?"

"As in *goodbye*?"

"Do you have to wear a paper bag over your head so Kitty doesn't see you?"

"As in *sod off home, will you*?"

"Gladly. But when James Keane finds out you're taking his secret girlfriend to the cinema, I'm not sticking around to put your face back together."

I try to storm out but run into Hector's dad on the landing. I swerve past him and start down the stairs, but he follows and stops me in the hall.

"Finchley, I'm glad Hector has made some new friends here," he says. I wait for the "but". "But I don't want him to neglect his school work."

It doesn't matter how annoying your mates are, when it comes to parents, you lie through your bowler for them. "Oh, he's not, Mr H, he's doing great at school. He's even getting better at the circus skills, believe it or not; we'll have him juggling chainsaws in no time."

He doesn't look reassured. "After-school activities are all very well, but I'm not sure clowning around with beanbags is going to be beneficial for him in the long run."

I'm not sure if he means actual clowning or if "clowning around" is just a general term for spending time with me. Either way he's probably right, but I reckon that's up to Hector, not his dad.

"Actually, I've read articles online that say circus skills are good for personal development. Like problem-solving and fitness and social skills and stuff." This is true; Mum's always going on about it. She basically thinks that if all kids were allowed to drop maths and take acrobatics, the world would be a better place.

"Be that as it may," he says (which is adult for "whatever"), "I'd prefer it if Hector wasn't distracted from his work. This is an important year for him. For both of you."

"Is it?" No one told me. "I suppose so."

"Good, good," he says, like that's all settled. He opens the front door and I have the distinct impression

I'm being ushered towards it. "Oh, and, Finchley? I wanted to ask how Bridget is doing? It must be very hard on your parents."

To be fair, he does look genuine about this, but I can't help myself. "*Birdie*'s doing great. *Hec* has been in most days reading to her." He winces at the "Hec". "When he's not helping me with my homework, that is. Or tutoring Py at the warehouse. Or *clowning around*." On the doorstep I turn back for a second. "Night, Mr H." And I tip my inexplicable bowler hat at him before I go.

The daring young man on the flying trapeze

Posted by Birdie

The man who invented the flying trapeze was in fact a solo act; Jules Léotard (he of the unflattering stretchy aerobics outfit) was a French acrobat who, in 1859, had the bright idea of hanging trapeze bars over a swimming pool. When he introduced his new act at the circus, he drew sell-out crowds; they even wrote a song about him – "The Daring Young Man on the Flying Trapeze". It's quite catchy. (CATCH-y, geddit? Sorry. Trapeze joke.)

Trapeze acts happen so fast, sometimes it's hard to see what's going on up there. There are hundreds of tricks, most of them with bizarre names like Shooting Star, Hocks Off, Straddle Whip, Bird's Nest, Reverse Suicide and Angel. But actually, what we're mainly doing is somersaults.

Single and double somersaults are your basic bread-and-butter tricks, but the triple? That's scary biccies. Italian flyers used to call it *salto mortale* – the deadly leap.

Trapeze artists have great spatial orientation, but the triple has to be done so fast that your brain loses track of where you are and it's hard to know when you're in the right position to reach for the catcher.

Even having a net doesn't make this trick safe, because there's falling and there's *falling*. If you're aware of where you are when you fall, you can get yourself into a good position for hitting the net; but if you've lost all sense of direction, you'll land awkwardly, which can easily result in a broken neck.

The first successful triple was performed by my hero, Lena Jordan, in 1897, when she was only eighteen. After that it became a lot more common, and of course the new goal became the quadruple.

Which took nearly a hundred years. That's how tough it is. In 1982 Miguel Vazquez, spinning at over one hundred and twenty kilometres per hour, performed the first quad in front of an audience.

Only a few flyers have ever managed the quad. Finch aims to be the next, and I guess I'll be hanging around, waiting to catch him.

All these somersaults involve two people, of course – a flyer and a catcher – but only the flyer's name is remembered, which is fair enough because all the catcher does is wait with their arms out.

But I've spent a lot of time doing exactly that over the years, and catching can be hard too. In fact it can be agony, seeing your partner do something so difficult, so dangerous, and being completely unable to do anything but watch.

< < Previous Post

I dream about flying all the time. I do doubles, triples, quads and quints in my sleep every night. Stratospheric somersaults at hundreds of kilometres an hour or endless rolls in slow motion. Falling asleep is just that for me – falling.

"Are you dreaming, Birdie?" I ask, perched on her bed as usual. She beeps at me as usual. If she *is* dreaming, then I'm there with her, like she's always with me, because a flying dream with no catcher isn't a dream, it's a nightmare.

I listen to the beeps, watch the drips, study the charts, and try to connect all that with Birdie's heartbeat, her pulse, her veins, her temperature, her brain, all that activity going on inside her motionless body. She's fighting hard, I know that. And she's right; it's really difficult to sit here, completely helpless, and watch.

Mum doesn't do things by halves. Already there's a folder full of plans and a sign-up sheet for the show hanging in the warehouse kitchen area. So far it says:

ON WITH THE SHOW...

Dad – ticket sales/props/lighting/general dogsbody

Mum – ringmaster

Janie – aerial silks and aerial hoop

Janie and Hector – silks and unicycle

Py – fire poi and fire eating

Py and Jay – fire juggling

Py and Hector – comedy fire routine < over my maggot-ridden corpse! – Dad

Juggulars – team juggling

Juggulars and Hector – comedy juggling

Wren and Mum – high wire

Tuesday Night Acrobats – tumbles 'n' stuff

Tots Acrobats and Hector – acrobatics and stilts

Finch – ?

We still don't have enough people, but everyone's desperate to do all they can, especially now we're doing it for Birdie, so they're expanding their usual routines, combining acts and creating new ones. The performance schedule looks exhausting, never mind all the rehearsals we'll need, but we're determined to make it work. Even Lou offered to revive her high-wire act, but Mum took one look at the pint of Guinness in her hand and suggested she support us some other way. She took a book of tickets and went around threatening the neighbours instead.

I wish more than anything I could write "Finch and Birdie – flying trapeze" up there, but I can't, and I don't know what to write instead. I could join in with the Juggulars, but they're such a tight team, I'd feel like a spare part. I can walk a high wire but I'm not as good as Wren and Mum, and I've never worked with fire so Py's act is out. Anyway, I don't want to do some lame unicycle bit part in someone else's routine.

Unfortunately there's only one other option.

"I suppose," I whisper during physics next morning, "since I'm teaching you stuff anyway, and since you did get me through my geography coursework, and since I'm at a loose end, and since you'll probably injure yourself on your own, I could *maybe* work on an act with you. A short one."

Hector does a deadpan blink. "That's big of you," he whispers back. Miss Deshpande lowers her glasses and looks pointedly at us.

I rest my hand in front of my mouth and talk from behind it. "But just for the show. And you have to work really hard. And do what I tell you. And refrain from telling me facts about the circus or suggesting in any way that you know more about this than I do."

"Is that it?"

"And I'm not wearing giant shoes."

"Shh," Miss Deshpande hisses.

I lower my voice even more and pretend to be staring at my textbook. "So what sort of act did you have in mind?" I ask.

Hector grits his teeth. "How about a knockabout act? I could go for some mock violence."

"I think you've given me enough bruises. What about mime?"

"If that's your way of shutting me up, forget it."

"Worth a shot."

"Do I have to separate you two?" Miss Deshpande says.

We read a few more paragraphs in silence and

then Hector whispers, "How about something classic – a Whiteface clown and an Auguste? You'd be the Whiteface."

"I don't want to do make-up, it's old-fashioned."

"You don't *have* to have the white face, it's just what you call the straight man," Hector says. "And I'll be the Auguste, the silly one. We don't have to wear big shoes and red noses. Although I kind of like the red noses."

"And what will we do?"

He shrugs. "What those characters always do: you set stuff up and I wreck it."

"Sounds like an average day for us."

"That's it." Miss Deshpande sets her pen down. "You two, in the corridor for the rest of the period. Leave the door open and if I hear one word..."

We spend the next few days experimenting with classic clown routines – Busy Bee, The Whip Skit, Funnel in your Pants. Hector has clearly been doing his circus homework (as well as my homework, Py's home-work and presumably his own homework). He marks the "ring" out with chalk, makes me watch YouTube videos, and then propels me around the floor, but the whole thing is excruciating. I thought, since Hector's still not great with juggling or stilts and he's already using a unicycle in his other acts, a simple classic comedy routine would be best. But if anything it's even harder.

And for once, it's not Hector who's the problem.

"You need to work on exaggerating your move-ments," he says. "Don't just walk across the ring, do a big comedy march! Don't just stand up, *jump* up. And when you look surprised, you have to make your eye-brows hit the ceiling. Everything has to be bigger and sillier than real life."

"Believe me, *nothing* is sillier than my real life right now," I mutter. "I feel ridiculous."

"You *look* ridiculous. But you'd look less ridiculous if you were trying to *be* ridiculous. You only look silly because you're trying *not* to look silly. I've watched mil-lions of YouTube videos, I know what I'm talking about. I think we need costumes to make it more real. Would this help?" He pulls two big red sponge noses out of his pocket, looking pleased with himself. "I got them online."

"I'd rather die."

"Put it on," he says sternly. I do it, reluctantly, but continue to glare at him. Unfortunately, glaring with a big red nose on your face just makes you look funny. Doing *anything* with a big red nose on your face just makes you look funny. He smirks. "See, better already! Now let's see your comedy walk."

I stride up and down, knees almost meeting my ears, arms swinging wildly. "How do I look?"

"Like the Hitler Youth."

I sag.

"You need to loosen up," he suggests. "It's the facial expression; you don't look like you're enjoying it."

"I wonder why. We've been here for *hours*, let's take a break."

"No breaks! Work! We can juggle while we think." He tosses some clubs at me and we start passing them between us.

"I need the loo," I moan.

"Rubbish. You have a bladder of iron. If you were in a horror movie, you'd be Blad the Impaler. If you were a Russian city, you'd be Bladivostok. If you were an animal, you'd be a duck-billed bladypus. Or a piss-filled bladypus."

"Making me laugh is not helping the situation."

He sets the clubs down. "Let's try a different skit. How about Dead and Alive? You get to pretend to be unconscious for half of it – even you can't mess that up."

So we start with the mistimed handshake and then he has to pretend to get so annoyed he punches me and knocks me out (I think he enjoys this bit a little too much) and we go into the unconscious clown routine. It's better than the other stuff because at least I don't have to do a lot of facial expressions; I just lie there while he lifts my arms (my legs go up) and then my legs (my arms go up), but it's still not fun.

At the end he has to get me on his back and run out of the ring while I "wake up" and wave at the crowd, but we can't seem to get me from the floor to his back without toppling over.

On our millionth try, we land in a tangled heap.

"That was pathetic!" Hector yells, his voice muffled by my upper arm. "You need to have more energy; you're not jumping high enough!"

"Energy? It's eleven at night, I'm *wrecked*! You're a slave driver! And you know what else? I *quit*!"

"Fine! Good! At fricking last!"

I heave him off me and we get up, panting. "This was your idea in the first place, you know," I yell. "If you didn't want to work with me, why did you even suggest it!"

"Well, I didn't think you'd take me up on it!"

I stand there making disbelieving noises. "What? So why did you ask me?"

"I thought you'd be so horrified by the idea, it might make you get off your big cowardly arse and get back on the trapeze!"

I'm too stunned to be angry. We just stare at each other for a moment.

"What are you talking about?" I say. But quietly, and his shoulders drop their defensive hunch.

"You haven't been up there since Birdie fell," he says.

"Why would I go up there? We're a double act; there's no point in going up there alone. I'm waiting for her to get better."

"You can practise with Wren, or your mum. You'll lose muscle tone if you don't practise, and … you'll lose your nerve. If you don't go back up soon, I'm worried you never will."

I fold my arms across my chest and stare petulantly at the floor. "I don't have nerves. I've never been scared in my life, not up there. Anyway, no one's in the mood to practise; in case you haven't noticed, Birdie's in hospital."

Hector puts a hand on my shoulder, but I pull away and he stuffs both hands in his pockets instead. "She'd want you to keep going. You can rehearse some tricks alone; Birdie was working alone when—"

"Yeah, and look what happened!" The words burst out of me and he takes a step backwards. He looks like he's going to apologize, but the only thing worse than his interfering is his sympathy, so I brush him off. "Look, forget it, Hector, I have to go. It's late anyway."

"But, Finch—"

"Whatever, see you later." And I run out the door.

36

"Remember, it's not the thrower that counts – it's the target."

– Gabor from *Girl on the Bridge* (directed by Patrice Leconte)

Posted by Birdie

The impalement arts include knife-throwing, archery, sharpshooting and bullwhips, and they're all about firing dangerous things (daggers, arrows, bullets, axes) into a wooden target. But with a human standing in the way.

It's an interesting fact that it's always the *thrower*'s name that's famous. There's The Great Throwdini (who was an ordained minister before taking up knife-throwing), Paul Desmuke (an armless knife-thrower who used his feet) and countless others. But in fact, the thrower isn't really important. You can throw daggers with both hands while blindfolded and unicycling, but it won't mean a thing if you're throwing them at a plank of wood. It's the human target that sells tickets.

Target girl Sandra Thompson proved this when she was struck in the ear during an act and so badly injured that six women in the audience fainted. But the performance the next night sold out. People are like that.

Knife-throwing is as popular with magicians as it is with the circus, but I believe it truly belongs to the circus, and for one reason – it's *real*. There's a myth that knife-throwers use tricks or fake knives. Not true. Knife-throwing is not a trick, it's a skill.

Getting someone to be your target is an even bigger skill. No target, no act!

< < Previous Post

A few days later we're in Hector's kitchen, steadily munching our way through a huge tin of chocolate biscuits and discussing new acts for the show. Mainly to avoid discussing our own failed double act and my complete lack of a trapeze routine.

"Do people still do knife-throwing? Seems a bit old school," Hector says, in response to my latest suggestion.

"Exactly! It's kitsch. We could have the whole 'glamorous assistant in a bikini, tied to a wheel' routine."

He grins. "Can we make Py be the glamorous assistant?"

"Do they make black denim bikinis?" We both shudder at the image.

"It'd take years to get good enough, though," he says.

"I bet I could take a fair stab at it."

"Yeah, *stab* being the appropriate word."

"Come on, stand over here." I take him by the shoulders and move him, amid biscuit-crumbed protests, to the kitchen door, arranging him with his back against it, limbs spread. "Like a star shape," I instruct him. Then I open the cutlery drawer.

"You are NOT throwing knives at me, Finch."

"Lack of faith, that's your problem, Hector. You read Birdie's blog: *No target, no act.*"

"How about *No Hector, no homework.*"

"Don't worry! Have you ever seen me throw a dodgy club? Have I ever misplaced a ring or a ball? These hands are infallible." I blow on my fingers as if they're smoking hot.

"I don't care, I am not ending up in A&E!"

I grin evilly at him as I rummage in the drawer, but then I lift out a clutch of teaspoons. "Relax, oh fearless one, we'll practise with these."

"Hang on, I'm not ready, I'm— *Jeez!* That was close!" He flinches as a teaspoon hits the door just by his left ear.

"That's the point; they have to get close enough to make it exciting but not actually hit you. And stop *moving.*" I throw a couple more spoons and they hit the door, one just above his shoulder, one right between the legs.

"Bullseye!"

He goes pale, or pal*er* anyway. "You are NOT throwing knives at my vitals, Finch!"

"Like you have any use for them. Fine, I'll stick to the head then."

I go on throwing and my aim isn't bad, though I have to admit a couple do graze his shirt and one lands in his hair, but that's only because he keeps twitching. When I run out of spoons, I lift a steak knife out of the drawer and stand there, poised to throw. "Right, enough practice!"

He laughs and holds his hands out to protect himself, but I can tell he doesn't believe I'll throw it. "Don't you dare!"

"Stand still!"

"Finch!"

"Ears or armpits? I'll let you choose."

"Finch!"

We're both laughing so loud, we don't hear anything from the hallway until the kitchen door suddenly opens. Hector is flung out of the way and I'm left standing there, aiming a steak knife at Mr Hazzard's stunned face.

He raises a hand slowly, calmly, the way the police do when they say, "Put the gun down, son."

"Do you want to set that down, Finchley?"

"Oh! Yeah, sorry." I put the knife back in the drawer. "I wasn't going to throw it, honestly, Mr H. We were just mucking about."

"With knives?"

"Well, no, spoons mostly."

Behind his dad, Hector is trying not to explode with laughter, but he swallows it when Mr Hazzard turns to look at him and then at the spoons scattered across the floor. Hector and I quickly start gathering them up.

"We were just practising some circus stuff, Dad. It's for the show."

"Show?"

"I told you about it. The show at Franconis'. I'm going to be in it!"

"Are you." Somehow, this isn't a question.

"As a clown," Hector says. "Finch and I—"

"Hector, I'm not sure about that."

"But they *need* me. With Birdie in hospital, they're down an act."

"It's interfering with your school work; your maths exams aren't far away, you know."

"I have to practise."

"And that involves spending every waking minute with…" He glances at me. "At the circus?"

Hector's face hardens a little. "There's nothing wrong with the circus."

"I'm not saying that. It's just … you've already got

into trouble with Mr Cooper over hitting people with juggling balls, and now you're playing with knives and being sent out of classes for talking? That's not like you."

How did he know about that! "That was my fault, Mr H," I say, but neither of them are listening.

"And there's more to Little Murragh than the circus," Mr Hazzard goes on. "I have no problem with social activities, but if you want to make friends at school, you should make time for more varied interests."

"So you think I shouldn't be a clown because I won't fit in at school?" Hector folds his arms and stares huffily at the ceiling.

"I didn't say that."

I think he pretty much *did* say that but I'm keeping my mouth shut. I have the weird feeling I've walked in on an argument that's been going on for years, like a long war, with worn-out sentences being lobbed unenthusiastically between trenches.

"But why make life difficult for yourself?" Hector's dad says. "You're new here, your priority should be keeping up with your school work and *not* getting into trouble with the head teacher, and if you have time, you can get involved with some after-school groups. Isn't there a chess club?"

Mr H has just fired a dud and everyone knows it. Hector looks him in the eye. "I'm a clown, Dad.

Turning me into a chess-playing clown isn't going to make me inconspicuous."

His dad sighs and glances at me. "We'll talk about this later."

Hector shrugs. "If you like." But what he means is "It's not going to change anything." His dad trudges off upstairs, looking tired, and Hector mooches against the wall, looking sulky.

I put on my coat. "I should go, Hector, it's getting late anyway."

"OK. I'll see you tomorrow."

"Are you sure? If your dad doesn't want—"

"I *said* I'll see you tomorrow."

Unlike Mr H, I know when to give in. "See you tomorrow, Hector." I leave him there with his teeth gritted and his hands full of teaspoons.

Sometimes I add up all the hours I've spent playing
football since I started high school (about 150 so far)
and think about all the things I could have been doing
instead. I could have flown to Australia and back three
times, watched six complete series of *The Vampire
Diaries*, mastered the art of sword swallowing. Or had
300 root fillings, which would still have been more fun
than running around in the mud on a freezing cold
morning being kicked in the shins.

It's a little-known fact that I was once asked to be
in the junior school football team. You wouldn't expect
a guy who owns eight bow ties to be good at football, but I was. I was fast, had good reflexes, good aim
and I never let a goal in. One day Mr Duggan pulled
me aside and informed me, with a big grin like he was
making my day, that I could be in the team.

"Er … no, thanks, Sir."

He put a finger in his ear and waggled it, as if he must have misheard. "What's that now?"

"I said no, thanks all the same, I'd rather not."

"Don't be ridiculous. You're not too bad, you know – your ball control is good. You just need to remember which half of the pitch your goal is in."

"It's not that. I know I can kick a ball, I just don't see the point." And I had better things to do than participate in organized violence four times a week.

He let me go but he clearly didn't believe a word I'd said, which is ironic because I was being honest for once. He just couldn't imagine that any boy wouldn't be desperate to be in the football team. I never told anyone I'd been offered a place. You get enough grief around here for being rubbish at sport; it would be a million times worse to be good enough for the team and *turn it down*.

I still have to play during PE though. I deliberately fluff my passes, and Duggan lets me and Hector play on the wings, because he's not interested in anyone who isn't the next Wayne Rooney. We usually ignore what's going on and muck around with the spare footballs. I can balance one on my neck, flip it up in the air and catch it on my head, but you get zero credit for that, except from Hector, who applauds every time.

PE is last period on a Tuesday and we take the long way round from history to the changing rooms. Today we're being slower than usual because Hector can't walk and talk at the same time without tripping.

"I spent all last night researching," he says excitedly.

"Researching? Do we have homework?"

"Not homework. Way more important. The secret of success in any battle is preparation: I am totally set to convince my dad that clowning is a legitimate career and I should be allowed to do the show. I'm going to talk to him tonight."

"I don't know that he was against clowning itself; it was more the idea of *you* as a clown. Probably dreading the injuries. And you did tell him you wanted to join an organization that has one member in a coma already."

He waves away my concerns. "Did you know that the first proper clown was a guy called Joseph Grimaldi? Way back in the early nineteenth century!"

"Hector, have you been to my house? Have you met my parents? Do you know what we do at weekends? *Yes*, I know that."

"And did you know that coulrophobia is the fear of clowns? Loads of people have it."

I look him over critically. "I can see how that could happen."

He ignores me. "But they reckon there were clowns right back in ancient Egypt too!"

"Who are 'they'?"

"Wikipedia."

"If you wanted to know about clowns, you could have just asked me. For example, did *you* know that clowns are the least dateable people in the whole circus?"

"Ouch! Anyway that's rubbish; everyone likes a good sense of humour. Did you know that some people think the reason clowning has been around so long is because humans have a deep psychological need to deal with difficult issues through comedy?"

"Well, duh." (I did not know that.)

"And that in ancient times, clowns also traditionally worked as *priests*!"

"What!"

"So if you think about it, I'm following in my dad's footsteps!" He pops his red nose on and waves his hands about like *ta-dah!*

I laugh. "I don't think he'll see it that way."

His face falls. "No? That was sort of the whole basis of my argument. You don't think he'll go for it?"

"I think calling him a clown, and his religion a circus act, might not be a strategically clever move. Why don't you show him your beanbag tricks instead?"

"I tried that."

"And?"

"I smashed a bottle of communion wine."

"Oh."

Someone behind us says, "Hey, Bert and Ernie! Move it!" and we're almost knocked over by Kitty and the Bond Girls as they barge past in their PE kits, hockey sticks slung over their shoulders like rifles. Hector's still wearing his red nose and one of the girls shudders and says, "God, I am, like, *terrified* of clowns. I think it's the make-up; I mean, they could be *anyone* under there."

Kitty swings round and stops, blocking our path. "Don't be stupid, Jas, they're not scary, they're just sad. And if you want to see who's under there, you just…" She reaches out and plucks the nose off Hector's face. "Oh, look, it's Hector the Holy Ghost. I had no idea, what with your clever disguise and all."

"Give it back, Kitty," I say.

"Why don't you let him speak for himself, princess?"

"That's OK, Finch, she can have it," Hector says. "I just hope she doesn't mind that I sneezed into it five minutes ago."

Kitty's expression turns to deep disgust and she drops the nose. "*Beyond* gross," she says, narrowing her eyes at us before spinning on her heel and walking away.

"Bye, Kitty!" we chorus after her, grinning and high-fiving each other.

Thanks to Kitty, we're even later for PE than usual, not that we mind. In fact, we take so long getting changed that we're last out, and when we reach the pitch, everyone else is already doing sit-ups. Duggan, who's never forgiven me for turning down the opportunity to be damp, cold and muddy four times a week, looks us up and down and says, "Took you lads long enough. I'd ask what you were doing in there but I don't want to know." The rest of the class bleat their collective sheep-laugh at him.

"Good one, Sir," Davy says, and Duggan says, "Shut it, you lot!" but you can tell he's delighted at his own joke. They lower it to a titter and Hector lies down on the ground and starts forcing his elbows to his knees with everyone else.

"Problem, Sullivan?"

I'm still standing there. And there is a problem, but I don't know how to say that. I just know I'm so furious my chest is tight. It was just a joke, not even an original one, and the thing about Duggan is he's so sarcastic, if you argue with him he'll reduce you to a crimson, whimpering infant.

He'll never apologize, not to a student, not in front of a class, not in a million years. There's no way I can win this, but the thought of lying down at his feet makes me feel physically ill.

"I'm not playing."

"You're *what* now?" He gives me a nasty grin, like he's enjoying this.

"I won't play."

"Are you sick?" Everyone's sitting up now, watching the entertainment.

"No. I'm just… I'm just not playing."

"Oh, come on, Sullivan," he says pleasantly. "You can play on the wing if it's too rough for you. Even Mr Hazzard here doesn't object to that, do you, Hazzard?"

Hector doesn't answer, but he does make a motion as if to get up and I know he'll walk off the pitch with me if I want him to. But that would only make everything worse and I shake my head subtly at him.

I walk away, legs shaking, and consider my options while Duggan's voice booms out behind me. "Right, you lot, press-ups! Start now, stop when I say so!"

I could go straight to Cooper and complain that Duggan humiliated me and Hector in front of the class. I could talk to Miss Allen; I can't see her having much impact on Duggan but she'd listen at least. I could tell Mum and Dad, who'd march straight down to Cooper's office. I even think about telling Lou, who would follow Duggan down a dark alley and make him wish he was never born.

But I know I won't do any of these things, because they all involve telling people what Duggan said. And then Duggan would say I'm getting my knickers in a twist over nothing, it was just a joke and he says it to the last two boys out of the changing room every week so they'll hurry up next time, and no one else minds so why should Hector and I be any different?

In the end I stand there in Duggan's office and stare

at the wall over his head while he reads me the riot act. And I take my week's detention meekly and my essay on sportsmanship without a murmur, hating him so much I could kill him, and the only person I tell anything to is Birdie.

38

They give me lunchtime detentions so I can still go to the hospital after school. I'm supposed to be grateful for that, and I would be, except that lunchtime detention is picking up litter; Coop believes in us making ourselves useful. I have to scour the yard and the sports fields with a bin liner and a pair of rubber gloves, picking up all the filthy crisp packets, Coke cans and takeaway wrappers wedged under hedges and in damp, manky corners. Hector tries to walk with me, but the rule is you have to do it on your own. So he sits on the yard wall and drops biscuit wrappers so I have to come over and he can tell me the latest Wikipedia circus fact that I already know.

Of course, when there's a litter picker, people search their bags and rifle through their pockets for extra stuff to drop, which means I spend half my time following Kitty and the Bond Girls around. They chuck bits of sandwiches and everything, and my only consolation is that they must be starving by the end of lunch.

I've almost got the whole yard clear when I spot a last crisp packet, blowing in and out between a few pairs of trainers. Pretty nice trainers. And a lot cleaner than mine, which are now muddy from tramping about the football pitch after Coke cans. I walk as slowly as possible towards James, Adi and Davy, wishing the bell would ring.

It doesn't, and I have to spend several humiliating seconds chasing the fricking crisp packet around their feet while they laugh and kick it out of my way. James puts a foot out and steps on it just as I grab it. I look up murderously at him and he steps back.

The bell finally rings and Adi and Davy move off, but James is still standing there as I tie up my bin bag and take my gloves off.

"You doing this all week then?" he says.

"Yep, feel free to raid your bins at home, folks!" I pat the bin liner, which is starting to leak fluid. "Plenty more where this came from."

He just looks blankly at me. "Well, if you wouldn't rile people up… Duggan's a bully; you shouldn't get in his way."

"You think? Thanks for the heads-up! Do tell me *more* about what you think, please, because I really care."

His face hardens. "I'm just saying. Why do you

always have to turn yourself into a target?"

I blink at him. Does he think I'm standing here with my sad bin liner for fun? By choice? I'm about to open my mouth and say God knows what when I suddenly think, You know what, I can't be arsed. I shake my head and walk away instead.

"I'm only saying," he mutters again, but this time I'm not turning round. Birdie was right. Even James is right. No target, no act.

But on the way out of school, Kitty and her whole crowd walk past me (or *through* me, to be more accurate), dropping rubbish every few steps between the school doors and the yard wall. Kitty turns to blow me a kiss as they walk out the gates and I stand there with tomorrow's litter swirling around my feet.

Right, that's it. I tried fighting back, I tried walking away. Nothing works. I'm sick of Kitty, I'm sick of Duggan, I'm sick of school. I'm sick of being everyone's punchbag. I can't do a thing about any of them, but there's one thing I *can* do. I turn and march back into school, down the deserted corridors, and knock loudly on Cooper's office door.

One good thing about Coop is he's never too busy to talk. You might have to watch him eat his lunch or help him tidy his office, but he never sends you away. I sit in my usual chair and wonder if this is the first time I've ever been invited, rather than ordered, to sit in it.

He says, "What's up, Finch?" and I take a deep breath and tell him about the night of Birdie's accident. I tell him about seeing James, I tell him about chalk dust and how it gets everywhere if you're anywhere near the trapeze, I tell him that Birdie would never do anything risky alone. I tell him about James and Sinead coming to the hospital, I tell him that Kitty and James have had it in for me and Birdie for like *ever* (which he knows, *everyone* knows), and I tell him that I am one hundred per cent certain that James had something to do with Birdie's fall.

Throughout it all he never moves. Then, when I'm done, he folds his hands and props his chin on them. I wonder if he'll phone the police right away or talk to James's parents first.

"Finch," he says eventually, "you can't go around making unfounded accusations."

For a second I'm speechless. But only for a second. "*Unfounded!* It's not unfounded. It's totally founded! I've just told you all about it; it's *obvious* he had something to do with it!"

"I know you boys don't get on—"

I roll my eyes. "That's the understatement of the year. But it has nothing to do with this. Or maybe it does! Maybe he went down there to do something to *me*, and Birdie just got in the way! That's even more evidence! But whatever happened, it was still his fault, and you have to do something about it."

"Listen, I'm sure there's a logical explanation for all of this. And without any real evidence, Finch..." He all but shrugs at me. "As I say, it's just an unfounded accusation."

I snort at him. "Typical. All they *do* is make unfounded accusations about me, but when *I* do it... What about all the stuff they've said about me over the years? No one bothered to stop all that, did they?"

"I know what they're like, Finch, but they say that sort of thing to all the boys. They say it to each other; it's just a joke."

"It shouldn't be a joke. I mean..." I swallow. "I mean, what if it was true?"

"Oh." He sits back in his chair. "I see."

"No, I'm not saying it is, that's not the point. But it's true for some people, isn't it? So it shouldn't be a joke."

"Do you want me to speak to them?"

"No! Look, this isn't about me, I just wanted to tell you about James!"

"Do you want me to talk to your parents about this?"

"No, they've got enough to deal with." My head is starting to ache. I take fistfuls of my hair in my hands and say slowly, through my teeth, "I *want* you to ask *James* about *Birdie*!"

"OK, Finch, calm down, I'll have a chat with James." But I can tell he's just saying it. "I know you've got a lot going on at the moment and—"

"Forget it." I stand up. If he's not going to take this seriously, I'm not sitting here listening to him feel sorry for me.

Hector is sitting on the wall outside. "There you are, I thought I'd missed you. Why are you late?"

"I had to talk to Cooper."

"Why, what did you do?"

"Oh, right, just assume the worst about me, like everyone else in this dump."

"Well, when was the last time you talked to Cooper when you *weren't* in trouble?"

"Very funny."

"Very true."

I slump on the wall beside him. "I told him about James."

"You didn't!"

"Yep. I told him he was there that night, that he knows something, and that he probably *did* something."

"I thought we were going to wait until we had proof."

"I couldn't wait any more."

"What did he say?"

"He ignored me."

"Oh. Well, we knew he probably wouldn't listen," Hector says. "Not without proof. But you did your best, that's all you can do."

"I'm not upset about that. Birdie will tell me what happened when she wakes up anyway."

"Then what's the problem?"

I fold my arms. "I'm just sick of it. Of everyone."

"Yeah, but what can you do? Don't waste your energy on them, they're not worth it."

"Easy for you to say, you've only just got here. I've been putting up with this crap for years."

Hector snorts. "You think I didn't get this kind of thing in the city? There were a hundred and eighty kids in my year alone. And *two* of them came to my birthday party. Do you know what that is as a percentage?"

"No, I'm crap at maths." He's trying to cheer me up and I'm not having it. "It's still better to be ignored in a big crowd than be treated like a freak every day," I say.

"That's just a small-town thing; they've nothing more interesting to do. I think in the city you'd be pretty cool."

"That's great but I'm not *in* the city, I'm stuck here." I hunch over my folded arms and kick at the wall with my heels. "I suppose you'll move back to Belfast as soon as you get the chance."

"I don't know, I'm starting to like it here."

"Seriously? I thought you said you hated being

looked at all the time. You said in the city you can be invisible."

"I know, but the city has downsides too."

"Name one."

He shrugs. "You can be invisible." He nudges my shoulder with his shoulder. "Look, there are jerks everywhere. You might as well be somewhere you have a few friends too."

I suppose now he's besties with Sinead he thinks Little Murragh is wonderful. "There has to be somewhere in the world you can just be yourself and not get crapped on for it," I mutter. "It's just too depressing otherwise."

"There's Franconis'. Everyone *there* likes you."

"That's not much of an achievement when the place is run by your mum. Your parents *have* to like you."

He snorts again. "Not necessarily."

"I wish this year was over. I wish *school* was over."

"Well, it's not," he says briskly. "There are fifty-seven days until summer and about a thousand until university, and there's nothing we can do about it."

"That helps, thanks."

"All the more reason to ignore them. Don't let them ruin the rest of the day – cheer up."

I fold my arms even tighter. "No."

"If you don't cheer up, I'll *make* you cheer up."

I give him a sceptical look. He puts a hand in his

blazer pocket. I know what he's got in there.

"Don't do it, Hector."

"Don't make me do it."

"I mean it, I'm not in the mood."

"Then you leave me no choice." He takes his clenched fist out of his pocket and holds it between us.

"Don't you dare."

"I'm doing it."

"Hector."

"It's happening."

"Hector."

He turns away for a moment.

"Hector, stop it right now."

He turns back, big red nose taking up half his face, rests his chin between his palms and gazes challengingly at me. I stare back, face rigid.

His smile slowly widens.

I clench my teeth.

His cheeks balloon.

I purse my lips.

His eyes cross.

I try *so* hard, but once the corner of your mouth goes, you're doomed, and you can either give in and laugh, or sit there looking constipated.

"I hate you," I mutter through a very reluctant grin.

He waggles his eyebrows. "Don't care."

I shake my head at him. I'm still grumpy, but, if you

have to be grumpy, being grumpy at Hector is a million times better than being grumpy at everyone else.

"Come on." He hops off the wall and clown-marches down the road, nose in place. "We can go to yours after we see Birdie. I'll let you throw teaspoons at me if you like."

I grin and follow him.

A post on ... er ... throwing stuff

Posted by Birdie

The Juggulars are our Friday-night juggling club (except they're here pretty much every night). I tried to get them to lay down their weapons for a couple of minutes to talk to me, but they refused, so we conducted this interview while they stood on each other's shoulders juggling clubs over my head.

So, ladies and gentlemen, boys and girls, here are the Juggulars!

BF: OK, guys and guyettes, what's the secret of great Juggling then?

TJ*: Practice.

BF: That simple, huh?

TJ: It takes a while, but once you get the basic skills, you can build on them quite quickly.

BF: And why would you recommend learning to juggle?

TJ: Because you meet cool people. And team juggling is fun.

BF: What tips would you give to beginners?

TJ: You can concentrate too much. Stress won't improve your juggling! Unless you thrive under pressure, in which case you should put all your most breakable possessions on the floor around you.

The Juggulars' chillaxation tips for anxious jugglers:

1. Try singing while you juggle; it takes your mind off what your hands are doing and they start to behave more naturally.

2. Don't watch the balls. Focus on a point about thirty centimetres from the end of your nose.

3. Drop your shoulders and you'll stop dropping the balls!

4. If you're becoming a "wandering juggler", try facing a wall so the balls hit it instead of moving away from you.

BF: What would you say to people considering joining the Juggulars?

TJ: If you've got two hands, get down here – we can use you. Actually, if you've only got one hand, we can still use you. And if you have no hands, we can use your feet.

*I would never suggest that the Juggulars aren't a diverse

group of individuals. But they do tend to all talk at once. And finish each other's sentences. And dress alike. And Dad calls them "the Clones".

<< Previous Post

When I get down to the warehouse, Hector is already there. (Mum gave him a key. Everyone has a key. The only person who doesn't have a key is Py.) He must have been reading Birdie's blog because he's got his headphones in and he's singing "Half a Person" by The Smiths at the top of his voice while juggling three rings. He's facing away from the door, so I sneak in behind him and settle on the sofa to watch. He's not doing too badly – maybe Birdie was right and I do make him nervous. Or it could be the singing. He's even dancing a bit.

A ring goes over his head and he tuts and turns to pick it up.

"Holy…! *Finch!* You could have said you were there!"

"Are you kidding, that was priceless."

He looks so embarrassed; apparently singing is more humiliating than doing pratfalls in baggy trousers. Or maybe he's just embarrassed to be caught listening to The Smiths. Actually, The Smiths is one of my favourite bands (I inherited them from my dad) and I'm impressed that he likes them.

"You were doing really well!" I say.

"Yeah?"

"Maybe work on the high notes."

He chucks a ring at me.

"Come on, let's try some tandem stuff." I plug his phone into the sound system and then we stand there with our arms round each other. I launch into the song myself and he gives me a look of complete mistrust, but then shrugs and joins in.

Three Smiths albums and a "Best of" later, we're hoarse, knackered and I officially award Hector his *Franconis' Level One Juggling* certificate.

You'd think it was a Nobel Prize. He tears up, makes a speech and then we go out for pizza to celebrate.

40

I've hardly seen Birdie all week because she's been having millions of tests; every time I showed up at the hospital, they were wheeling her off to another department. So we've all had a nasty, nervous feeling hanging over us, like when exam results are due at school. Except this matters.

Hector and I are still with her on Friday when Mum arrives to take the evening shift. But Dad has come with her this time, and the doctor follows them into the room, holding Birdie's chart like a shield between her and us. We stand, as if the head teacher's just walked in, then the adults make small talk about the weather and the traffic and the canteen food and how the doctor's been on duty since midnight – "you poor thing" – but I realize no one's listening, because everyone in the room is staring at the chart.

Mum and Dad are craning their necks a little, as

if they might be able to see over the top of it, looking scared and hopeful. The doctor grips it with both hands like it weighs a ton, and frowns at the scrawled writing, even though I get the feeling she knows what it says already. The adults never make eye contact, and Hector and I glance between them, wondering who's going to cave first and actually say something about what's scribbled on those green pages.

Eventually the doctor raises her head, and her smile is a lovely one; kind, reassuring, as if it's been lifted from a box labelled "kind, reassuring smiles". Mum and Dad smile back determinedly, like being nice to the doctor will make her say Birdie is going to be fine. Dad is squeezing Mum's shoulder so hard it looks painful.

"Thanks for coming in, Mr and Mrs Sullivan. I thought we should have a chat about Bridget's progress."

I almost laugh. It sounds like something Mr Cooper would say at school; *has* said, on several occasions. "We're concerned about Finch's progress, Mrs Sullivan. Perhaps we could have a chat?" *You're in trouble now, Birdie,* I can't help thinking. A month's detention for sleeping through class. And lunch. And dinner. And all your favourite TV shows and many, many conversations with me.

"Of course," Dad says.

The doctor looks at me and Hector.

"I'll wait outside," Hector says.

"Perhaps you could wait with your friend?" the doctor says to me.

"I want to stay."

"Finch is Birdie's brother. Her twin," Dad says. "Can't he stay?"

The doctor puts her head on one side and the smile says *Best not.*

I follow Hector out of the room but stand close to the door, trying to listen. I hear muffled voices, but the corridor's too noisy to make anything out.

"Do you want to know what they're saying?" Hector asks.

"Of course."

He bites his lip, considering, then he says, "If you're sure. Follow me," before dashing off down the corridor.

"Hector, wait! Where are you going?" I don't want to leave the door, but the muffled sounds are only getting quieter, so I give up and run after him. At the end of the corridor I find him standing round the corner, at a fire exit.

"This goes outside," he says.

"It's a fire door — there'll be an alarm."

"There isn't, I've been watching. There's a little garden where the nurses go to smoke — they go in and out all the time. Birdie's room looks out onto it and her window's open."

"Are you *actually* Sherlock Holmes?"

"Come on, do you want to hear or not?"

I follow him through the door, which *doesn't* summon the fire brigade as we open it, then I almost trip over him because he's crawling along the ground by the hospital wall. The top half of this wall is lined with windows and one of them must be Birdie's.

Of course, Hector knows exactly which one, but I'd have found it anyway, because about six windows down I hear Mum saying, "What do you mean by brain damage?"

Hector looks back at me, his eyes wide, regretting bringing me out here. We hunker down, side by side, backs against the wall. The window is only open a crack, but the garden is quiet and we can hear every word.

"We can't know for sure until she wakes up; it's just one possibility we have to consider. After a head trauma, people sometimes have memory loss or difficulties with speech, vision, hearing, or there could be learning difficulties or motor impairments."

"That's difficulty with moving your body," Hector informs me in a whisper, but I shush him.

"So she might not remember us? Or be able to talk to us? Could she be paralysed?" Mum's voice.

"There doesn't appear to be any damage to the spine, so she shouldn't be paralysed. But movement, like everything else, is controlled by the brain, and we don't yet know how her brain has been affected."

"But she might be all right?" Dad says. "There might be no damage?"

"I had hoped she would be awake by now," the doctor says. I notice she didn't answer the question. "With a head injury it's normal for the brain to sort of switch off for a while, to recover," she goes on. "But the longer the coma continues, the more likely it is that the person has suffered some permanent damage, or that…"

"What?"

"Or that they may not wake up."

The voices float on over our heads, mingled with the beeps from Birdie's machines. The doctor is talking about "care options"; Mum and Dad aren't saying anything. On the concrete between us, Hector's hand moves over and takes mine. I turn to look at him, but everything feels sort of unreal and I can't quite focus on his face. I pull my hand away, place it on top of my knees and examine it instead.

My hands look like the feet of a hiking enthusiast. Trapeze artists wear leather hand guards called "grips" for a more secure hold and to protect their skin, but you end up covered in calluses anyway. Sometimes I cut the tops off the calluses with a knife or a razor, because if they stick out too much, they can rip and bleed, and then you get blood all over the trapeze bars.

My knuckles are huge, my fingers are skeletal, my skin is dry and rashy from the constant contact with chalk dust, and my palms are like sandpaper. I've always been a little ashamed of the state of my hands, and I don't want Hector to touch them.

"I'm sorry, Finch. I shouldn't have brought you out here," he says.

"I have to go."

"OK. They'll be finished soon. We can wait in the canteen if you like?"

"No, I mean I have to get out of the hospital."

"Don't you want to see your mum and dad?"

"No. I have to go." I'm crawling back to the door. I don't know why I'm crawling; I could just walk, since it doesn't matter now, but I keep crawling and Hector crawls after me. The concrete under my knees feels good for some reason.

At the door I stand up, and then run unsteadily down the corridor. I pass Birdie's room without looking in, jostle through groups of nurses and people in dressing gowns at the hospital entrance, and run on down the street, faster and faster, leaving Hector panting miles behind.

Birdie's hands are as bad as mine. Later that night, after Mum and Dad have gone and there's no danger of running into them, I sit on her bed, take one hand in mine and turn it over. Raw, red, still rough, but definitely softer than it used to be. She complains about her hands as much as I do, but she never uses hand cream. The thing about the calluses is you earn them. You have to work hard to get them, and even though they're ugly, they protect you, like armour. As soon as you take a break, they start to soften. If the break is too long, they go altogether.

Sometimes Birdie and I compare hands to see whose are worse.

"God, they look terrible," she always says, holding her big-knuckled, rough-palmed hand up next to my bigger but identical one.

I lift her hand now and hold it palm to palm with mine. It's like trying to slide two pieces of sandpaper over each other. Our hands are designed to lock together and hold on tight.

Tony comes in then and tells me I'll miss the last bus if I don't go soon. When I let go of her wrist, Birdie's hand flops, lifeless, onto the bed, leaving mine empty.

41

For a few days Hector does little more than trail after me everywhere I go (including litter detention and even the bathroom on one occasion), bring food to my house (Mum's stopped cooking again) and send me text messages every five minutes from the time he leaves my house in the evening until I fall asleep. He's even started talking about "our act" again, which I know is just to keep my mind off Birdie.

"I'm fine, Hector, you don't have to keep fussing," I tell him repeatedly.

"OK," he says, and then keeps fussing anyway.

What are you doing? he texts one evening, even though I told him ten minutes ago I was going to bed.

Going to bed. You?

Watching TV. Did you see Vampire Diaries tonight?

You watch that?

Vampires, werewolves – what's not to like?

Whiny girls, convoluted plot – what's not to hate?

So you do watch it.

I may have accidentally seen it once or twice.

Liar.

Geek. Go to bed. Do you even get free texts?

No.

Your dad is going to freak out when he sees your phone bill.

I'll blame you. Night then. ☺

Night. ☺

Actually I don't mind the texting. Or the company on the way home from school. And the food comes in handy.

I turn my lamp off and leave my phone next to my alarm clock, which I don't even use any more because Hector texts me at 7.35 every morning without fail.

42

I can only sit with Birdie for so long before the silence makes me want to scream. Besides, other people want to sit with her too and we're not supposed to crowd the room. So I take to sitting in the garden Hector showed me, doing my homework below her window. The first few times the nurses catch me out there, they usher me back inside, but soon they get used to me and we start chatting about how terrible their day has been or doing my homework together. The nurse I see most is Tony, because he smokes so much – he goes through more lighters than Py.

"All right, Finch, how's it going?" he says one day, squatting beside me and lighting up. He blows the smoke out like it's the breath he's been holding all afternoon.

"She's about the same."

He fans the smoke away from me and says, "I asked how *you* were, not how Birdie is."

"Oh." I have to think about that for a minute. "I suppose I'm OK. Apart from Hector driving me nuts talking about clowns."

"Is he the one who trips over Birdie's heart monitor or the one who smells like a petrol station?"

I laugh. "He's the blond one. The other one is Py; he's a fire eater."

"Each to their own. The doctors all seem to know him."

"He gets treated for burns a lot. I expect they'll be getting to know Hector soon too."

"Do your friends have any *safe* hobbies?"

"Says the guy who smokes like a chimney."

"Good point. But at least I'm trying to quit."

"This is you quitting?" I wave a cloud of smoke away from my face and cough pointedly.

Dad's been sitting with Birdie, but a few minutes after he leaves I hear the door open again and someone else come in. There's no fake-cheerful "Hiya, Birdie!" to tell me who it is, though. Footsteps. Chair legs scraping. But no one speaks. It could be a doctor, but doctors never sit down, and Tony's out here with me. It could be Wren, but she tends to sing to Birdie. Actually, I think Wren knows I'm here and she sings to both of us. But today there's just silence. I listen for a few minutes and then my attention drifts back to my homework and Tony telling me about his weekend, so I'm startled to suddenly hear a voice say, "I'd better go. I shouldn't be here, I'm sorry," and then the chair legs scraping again. It's a familiar voice but for a second I can't place it.

As I jump to my feet and press my face to the window, I catch sight of the unmistakable back of James Keane's head disappearing through Birdie's door.

"What's *he* doing here?"

Tony stands and looks through the window. "Who?"

"That guy. The one who just went out."

"Didn't see him. But there are a couple of boys who come to see her besides you. Do you mean the good-looking one?"

I roll my eyes. "I guess so. If you like that sort of thing. Tall, dark, etc."

"Yeah, he comes on his own, after your dad leaves and before your mum gets here for her shift."

"That sneaky..." I can't think of anything bad enough to call him. I don't care what Cooper says, this confirms everything. And if James thinks sitting in Birdie's hospital room feeling guilty makes up for whatever he did to put her there, he can forget it.

"I think you're jumping to conclusions," Hector says the next day when I tell him about seeing James. It's Saturday afternoon and we're on our way out of the hospital. "Loads of people from school have been to visit Birdie," he adds. "Maybe it doesn't mean anything."

I throw my arms up in exasperation. "Tony says he comes *all the time*. That's got to mean something. Why are you being so negative?"

"Because it doesn't count as evidence. And because I don't want you to look like an idiot, going around accusing innocent people of terrible things again."

"Oh, so I look like an idiot now?"

"Not *yet*," Hector mutters.

He starts talking about costumes for our act, but I know he's only trying to change the subject. I remind him that I haven't even said I'll definitely do the act and that in fact it's probaby a terrible idea, given how our first and only rehearsal went.

"Oh, come on, we weren't *that* bad." I give him a look. "Well. We still have time to work on it. How about trying some improvisation? I've been reading about it; you don't have to have an act planned at all, you just go with whatever you feel like doing."

"That sounds like my worst nightmare."

"You don't know till you try. Napoleon said the mark of a great general is the courage to improvise."

"Well, luckily I have no ambitions to lead the French army. Look, it just isn't me." This is true; you don't improvise on a trapeze. If you so much as grin in the wrong place, you can throw your partner off. It might look exciting from the ground, but in fact we aim for total predictability, mind–numbing repetitiveness. Asking a trapeze artist to improvise is like asking a cat to bark.

"I know you look down on clowning," Hector says, "but it takes guts."

I scoff. "You think it doesn't take guts to let go of a trapeze bar in mid–air?"

"It's not the same. You and Birdie are only taking a chance on each other. A clown has to trust a crowd of complete strangers to laugh in the right places. And not throw fruit. Being that vulnerable is terrifying, and if you haven't the guts for it that's fine, but just admit it."

"You're right, the trapeze and clowning *aren't* the

same. Because the worst that can happen to you is you get humiliated. The worst that can happen to *me* is a long list of stuff, starting with broken bones and ending with killing your partner. But, yeah, your job is harder."

"Exactly!"

"What?"

"You're not scared to go up there and risk your neck, but you're terrified of looking silly in front of a few kids from school? It's not about danger; it's about being too chicken to do the stuff you're not good at."

"I'm just not the clown *type*. Even you can see that."

"Oh, you're too cool for clowning, is that it? Clowns always have the lowest status in the circus and you're not used to that, I get it. But that's kind of the *point* of clowning. If they minded being laughed at, they wouldn't be funny, they'd just be sad."

"I don't know where you've got this idea that I don't like being laughed at. Have you seen my clothes? I'm a clown 24/7." I gesture at my bowler hat, which, admittedly, is the only odd thing I'm wearing, but I like to think putting it with jeans and a hoodie kind of makes an anti-statement.

"Yeah," Hector says, "but maybe that's like a costume – you give them something to laugh at so they never get a chance to laugh at the real you."

I look around helplessly, like someone might tell me what he's talking about. And then I realize we're lost.

"Where are we?" We've been arguing so much, we've taken a wrong turn. In either direction there's just more corridor; I can't see an exit. We stop at the open door of a large ward and Hector peeks inside.

"Children's ward," he says. I look over his shoulder. There are two long rows of beds down either side of the room, and the walls are painted with rainbows, suns, trees and animals. The kids are lying or sitting on the beds, some of them trussed up in plaster casts, some with less obvious problems. They're reading, playing on iPads or with board games, and at the end of the room there are toys in a big heap and a TV playing cartoons at low volume. Apart from the plaster casts and pyjamas, it looks like a standard roomful of kids, but quieter; you'd expect a roomful of kids to be making more noise. There's something unnatural about it that reminds me of talking to Birdie and getting no answer.

I start to move away but Hector says, "Hang on."

"What are you doing?"

He shrugs, puts a hand in his pocket and pulls out his red nose. "Going for a walk."

I watch him stroll casually into the ward, hands in his pockets, whistling. The kids all turn to look at him. This could be because he's wearing a red sponge nose, but I get the feeling these kids are so bored, they'd turn to look at anyone who walked through that door.

I can't watch. I put a hand over my face and peek

through my fingers. Hector strolls on, ignoring the eyes following him down the ward. About halfway, when there's complete silence apart from his whistling, he "trips" over something on the floor and lands in a heap. The kids titter. Some of them move to the ends of their beds to see what he's fallen over. There's nothing there, but Hector gets up and starts making *What idiot left that lying there!* gestures. He shakes his head, picks up an empty Lego bucket and makes a big show of collecting the obstacle and putting it in it. Then he stops. He looks at the bucket cradled in his arms, then around at the ward, and narrows his eyes in a sneaky *I have an idea* look.

He goes on a fake-casual walk around the room, looking left and right as if to check no one's watching, like a cartoon burglar, and starts nicking random objects from the kids' bedside tables and putting them in the bucket. He takes a little girl's toy lipstick, pretending to apply it to his pouted lips and then fluttering his eyelashes before tossing it in. Then he steals another kid's toy car, a single slipper, a plastic tiara (which he tries on in front of a mirror and then discards), a few building blocks (which he juggles into the bucket), a bag of sweets, a can of Coke, a book, a doll – oblivious to the kids watching him. They're looking at each other, bemused, half disbelieving the nerve of this guy who's nicking their stuff, and half waiting to see what the punchline will be.

A few of them start to follow Hector around, reaching for the bucket to take their possessions back. Each time they get close, Hector does a sharp turn or switches the bucket to his other hand at the last minute, all the while pretending he doesn't see them at all. He never says a word, but the expression on his face is priceless as he "finds" things to steal, looking under pillows and behind curtains, and then sneaking each item gleefully into the bucket, while the kids laugh at each other's attempts to steal them back.

As he passes me, still standing in the doorway, he neatly grabs the bowler hat off my head, puts it on his own and keeps going.

The kids all stop to see what I'll do.

In the circus, if someone gives you a cue, you really don't have a choice. It's the equivalent of someone trying to high-five you in public; it's just plain rude to leave them hanging. So I react exactly as Hector knows I will – instinctively.

I have no idea why that stupid red nose is still in my pocket but, heart pounding, I jam it on, put my hands on my hips and make an exaggerated *Hey!* face. Then I do my best comedy march down the ward after Hector, who pretends to notice me coming and quickens his pace.

The kids all stand back to watch my attempts to get my hat back. Every time I get near Hector, I do a massive dive at him and he swerves or ducks or dodges and I do a somersault, ending up on my back or my arse, splayed on the floor and looking confused. I may not be a natural at improvisation, but somersaults I can do.

And it's weird, but this feels different from rehearsing in an empty room. It's *fun*. The kids squeal with laughter every time I make a leap at Hector, and it's easy to be silly because I know they *want* me to be.

I start wordlessly directing them to help me. They cut him off for me, drag him towards me, they even make jumps at the hat themselves. There are too many of them to avoid and soon it gets knocked off Hector's head onto the floor and they all cheer.

I leap about triumphantly, then make *Stand back, I'll get it* motions. I walk purposefully towards the hat and bend down to pick it up, but as I do, it skids a few centimetres along the floor away from me. The kids gasp and I shake my head as if I must be imagining things, then walk towards it again. It skids away. I try coming at it from different directions, I sneak up on it, I run at it, but every time the hat magically dashes away from me. The kids are killing themselves laughing at my ineptitude and shouting, "Get it!", "It's stopped!", "Jump on it!"

This is the oldest trick in the book. It was old when *Lou* was a kid. But people are always impressed because it looks so effective. And it's dead simple: as you step towards the hat and bend down to pick it up, you kick the brim so it scoots out of reach. If you do it quick enough, it totally looks like the hat is moving by itself and running away from you.

By now a few nurses have come in, wondering what all the yelling is about. One of them, thinking we're mucking about and bothering the sick kids, strides towards me. Hector immediately gets in her way. He grabs the clipboard out of her hands and runs, and she whirls round to follow him as he pelts down the ward, in and out between the other nurses, looking terrified and throwing toys out of his bucket to slow her down. She couldn't have done better if she'd rehearsed with us. The kids bounce on the beds, hysterical with laughter. Even the other nurses start to laugh, and soon the nurse chasing Hector gives up and just stands there watching as he runs back to me and the hat.

This is it; I reckon we've got about thirty seconds before they chuck us out.

I motion to the kids, the ones who can get off their beds anyway, and direct them until we're all standing in a big circle around the hat. Then Hector and I take silly, tiptoe steps towards it, fingers to our lips, and the kids follow suit, all trying to stifle their laughter, eyes shining as we creep up on the surrounded hat.

I hold a hand up and count on my fingers. *One. Two. THREE!* I don't need to tell them what to do. With a roar we all dive at the hat and land in a big heap on top of it. I emerge, waving it in the air, then push it onto my head, battering it down like it might try to escape again, while the kids do victory dances.

Finally Hector and I stand to take a bow. I bend at the waist and the hat falls off. Hector grabs it and runs down the ward with me in pursuit, and the kids clap and cheer behind us.

We don't stop till we get to the hospital exit, and we're halfway down the road, panting and laughing, when I realize we're still wearing our red noses.

"That was incredible!" Hector says. Or *yells*. I know the hyper look in his eyes, the way he's bouncing around like he's being electrocuted. There's nothing like the rush you get when you've just finished a performance and the applause is still ringing in your ears. Your heart pounds, your blood fizzes, you feel like you could run a marathon, and you're certain, absolutely certain, that you don't want to do anything but *this* for the rest of your life. Hector's just done his first ever show and he's been bitten by the bug, big time. He throws an arm round me and bounces me up and down with him. "Wasn't that fantastic! And you were so good! You're a natural! You're a natural clown, Finch."

"Take that back, how dare you!" I laugh, but I can't help being pleased that he thinks I was good. "Calm down, Hector, you can't fail to be entertaining in a place where the alternative is injections and bed-rest."

"Admit it, we were brilliant! Oh my God, Finch, that was terrifying. I had no idea what I was going to do!"

"Yeah? You didn't *look* scared."

"My legs were like jelly!"

"I can't believe you did all that just to make a point."

"I didn't." He looks surprised at me. Or at himself. "I did it because those kids looked miserable; I couldn't stop myself. That was so not like me at all!" He looks suddenly frightened. "God, what's wrong with me?"

I put a hand on his arm and say gently, apologetically, "I hate to be the one to break this to you, Hector, but you're a clown. I'm afraid you will be physically incapable of acting like a normal human being for the rest of your life. You will go on to frighten and irritate many, many people."

"I'm a clown," he breathes, looking awestruck, like I've revealed his cosmic destiny.

I slap him on the back. "Come on, Bozo, we'll miss our bus."

44

MONDAY 18 MAY

"When great actors die, people are sad. When the great clowns die, people grieve."
– The late film critic Andrew Sarris

Posted by Birdie

Clowns are the backbone of a circus (and the funny bone). They fill the gaps between acts while the props are changed, they caper around doing silly versions of all the serious acts so there's always something to laugh at, and they have running gags that go all the way through the show and tie all those different acts together.

When people join the circus, they always want the glamorous jobs, with drum rolls and sequinned costumes, because those acts look the most impressive. But clowning is harder than you'd think.

Buster Keaton was one of the big stars of silent cinema, but he was basically a clown who did all his own stunts. He was once asked how he did all those falls. He said,

"I'll show you," then opened his jacket to reveal a chest covered in bruises.

Clowning can teach you a lot, and not just pratfalls and somersaults. You learn that it takes a lot of guts to be the butt of everyone's jokes, and that some things are worth taking a few bruises for. Most of all, you learn to really value the people who make you laugh.

< < Previous Post

I'm sitting in the nurses' garden when Tony comes out for a smoke.

"Hiya, Finch, what have we got today?"

"Maths."

"Eugh."

"Exactly."

He sits beside me. "I heard about your little stunt in the children's ward."

I wince. "Really?"

"*Everyone's* heard about it."

"Crap, sorry. Are they raging?"

He laughs. "They want you to come back and do it again."

"Seriously?"

"The kids loved it; they've been talking about it all weekend. The nurses thought you could make it a regular thing if you want. Would Hector be up for that?"

"He'd be so up for that, it would frighten you."

"Gotta love an enthusiast."

"*Obsessive* is more like it."

"Could be worse," he says. "*My* boyfriend is obsessed with antique musical instruments."

I drop my gaze back to my maths book. "Hector's not my— You have a—" I cough, swallow, take a breath and look coolly up at him. "What kind of instruments?"

He grins at me, clearly amused. "All kinds. I have an old cinema organ in my kitchen at the moment. It's not even a big kitchen."

"Does he at least play for you while you cook?"

"Yeah, that's why we eat out a lot."

There's a silence, and then he says, "Hector seems like a nice guy. He was pretty popular with the kids."

"Yeah. If he could be as popular with people at school as he is with seven year olds, that'd be great."

"Seven year olds are smart. Teenagers, less so. Give him a hard time, do they?"

"They're idiots, he knows that."

"I doubt knowing they're idiots makes it any easier to live with."

"Yeah. Why are people such assholes? Just because you're a bit different. Don't you think it's depressing, the way people are here? If you try to be even a tiny bit interesting, they just descend on you like 'Who do you think you are?' As if it's a *sin* to actually *like* yourself.

Especially if you happen to be fat or skinny or short or talented or geeky; or have acne or glasses or crooked teeth or a weird family or a bizarre hobby or, God forbid, a *personality*. You're supposed to keep your head down and spend your life apologizing for your existence or something."

Tony frowns. "Are we talking about Hector now, or you?"

I shrug.

He stubs out his cigarette and puts the pack back in his pocket. "Kids at school will always have stupid things to say. Why don't you say something intelligent back?"

"Hmm. *Sarcastic*, I can do. Intelligent, not so much."

"So say something true. That's even better."

"I think you and Birdie would get on well."

Tony grins. "I'm sure we will. Right, I'd better get back to work; there's a bedpan on the second floor with my name on it."

Speaking of death-defying...

Posted by Birdie

As part of my investigations into the Franconi family history, I've (rather bravely, if you've ever met her) interviewed veteran high-wire performer, the Amazing Alouette Franconi! (Aka, our granny, Lou!)

BF: Hiya, Lou, thanks for agreeing to speak to me today about the original Franconis.

LF: It's about time one of you took a bleedin'* interest!

BF: In your opinion then, the old days were the best?

LF: Course they were. There was none of this flipping health-and-safety malarkey for a start. My granny on my dad's side could do a handstand on horseback at full gallop, did you know that? There was no namby-pamby prancing about on soft mats in leotards; back then, the circus was about danger, and "audience participation" meant you let the tiger off its chain.

BF: But surely, given your own family history...

LF: You mean Aunt Avis?

BF: Yeah.

LF: (Shrugs) They knew the risks. We all did.

BF: What do you think about the rumours surrounding the accident? I know a lot of people accused your father, Carlo, of having something to do with it.

LF: That's why I don't go around listening to "people" and neither should you, Miss Know It All.

BF: So he was innocent?

LF: Oh, I wouldn't say that, now. Guilt's a funny business. My ma never got over Avis; she felt bad because they'd been arguing before their act that night. About Carlo. Let me tell you, you don't want to go up there with anything on your mind. Distraction's a killer.

BF: So you think the argument was enough to put Avis off her game?

LF: Ma thought so, but of course she'd blame herself; she was Avis's partner. If your partner's not happy, you do whatever you need to do to make them happy, or you suffer the consequences when they bugger things up.

BF: I guess. Do you think if they'd both given up Carlo, Avis might have survived?

LF: Who knows? Relationships with people outside your

act are just a botheration. And they're not worth risking a partner over. Partners aren't ten-a-penny like boyfriends.

BF: I guess your first loyalty has to be to your partner, huh.

LF: If you've got one. That's why I preferred to work alone.

BF: Did you ever have a circus romance?

LF: You mind your own bleedin' beeswax, miss.

BF: Well, thanks for talking to us, Lou. Just before we wrap this up, what would you say to kids who are thinking of joining the circus school? Would you recommend it?

LF: Yes, kids these days need the stuffing knocked out of them. When I was young, if you weren't bruised before bedtime, you'd wasted your day. Bunch of mollycoddled china dolls, the lot of them! Learn to play your flipping Zboxes on a high wire, then you can snigger at my shopping trolley in the street. Bleedin' brats, what they need is a good kick up the... (Stomps out of earshot in direction of pub).

*Swear words have been modified to meet the standards of our censor (i.e. Dad).

<< Previous post

For someone in a coma, Birdie has a lot to say. Like "your first loyalty has to be to your partner". And you don't ditch them when they're in hospital so you can team up with some guy in a red nose.

But Hector is so thrilled about being asked to entertain the hospital kids again, it's hard to tell him that.

"Calm down, Hector, it's not exactly Ringling Brothers; it's a hospital ward."

"Exactly! It's practically charity work – even my dad can't argue with that."

We're sitting on the yard wall during lunch break. It's cold, it's starting to rain, and we're puffed up inside our coats. I couldn't face the canteen clamour, but I don't have any lunch with me. Hector offers me half his sandwich.

"I'm fine."

"Eat it or I'll stuff it under your hat. And no one likes the boy whose hair smells of tuna."

"OK. But only because this is Jay's hat. You don't have to sit out here with me, you know."

"Do you want me to go away?"

I shrug and he looks down, hurt, but actually I don't want him to go away. "No, I don't want you to go away," I say and he grins.

Since we're being friendly, I add, "Do you want to come over tonight?"

"Sure! Oh no, wait, I told Sinead I'd be at home. We got paired up in English for an oral presentation."

"You got 'paired up'? Kitty Bond won't believe that any more than I do."

"Well, Sinead had to pick *someone* at my table. It

was me or Marc Norris, and I'm not convinced he can actually read."

"Whatever. Have a great night."

"I could come to the hospital with you after school first. I'd like to see Birdie. I can't *wait* to tell her about the hospital kids."

"No! Don't tell her."

"Why not?"

I shrug again and I'm about to tell him to do what he likes, she probably can't hear him anyway, when he says, "Here she is now."

"Birdie?" What's he talking about? But when I turn to look, a lone figure is walking towards us, buttoning her coat and pulling her hood up as she approaches.

"Hiya, Sinead!" Hector waves.

She waves back, runs the last few metres to the wall and then plonks herself down beside him.

"Hi! Hiya, Finch." She leans around Hector and nods at me. I take a large bite of Hector's sandwich and nod back. "Just wondering if we're still on for tonight?" she says. Hasn't she heard of text messaging?

"Definitely! I was telling Finch about our presentation." He turns to me. "It's a debate on the literary merit of sci-fi novels. We're 'pro'."

"No kidding."

He turns back to Sinead. "I want to go with Finch to see Birdie first, though."

"Of course, sure."

"Hey, you could come with us!"

"Wawmph!" Too much sandwich.

"Then we could go straight to my house after," Hector adds.

"Yeah, that'd be great. I'd like to visit her," Sinead says. "That is … if it's OK with Finch?"

Hector looks pleadingly at me. Well, I can hardly say, "No, you can't come and sit by my very ill sister's bedside", can I?

"Sure, why not." Because you're an evil cow, that's why not.

By the end of school I've decided that if Hector can't bring himself to offend Sinead by calling her a psycho-shielding scumbag, I'll have to do it myself. I find her waiting for us outside the school gate.

"Hiya, Sinead!" I say, *super* nice.

"Hiya, Finch!" She looks relieved. I suddenly realize that every time she talks to me, it's like she's nervous, which is weird because the Bond Girls are right at the top of the food chain around here. She is *definitely* hiding something.

"It's nice of you to visit Birdie."

"No problem. I hope she's better soon; school's sort of boring without her – you two always made me laugh."

"Yeah, we noticed that."

"I didn't mean…"

Hector's running across the yard towards us, school bag bouncing on his back, and I wince, waiting for the moment he trips over his shoelaces, or a rock, or thin air, and takes a chunk out of the tarmac with his teeth. He makes it, but not without misjudging his braking distance and slamming into me. Sinead looks relieved to see him.

We set off, but I'm not dropping it. "A lot of people have been to see Birdie actually," I say. "Didn't I see you visiting with James once? Or was that Kitty? No, no, I'm pretty sure it wasn't James and Kitty, it was James and *you*."

She looks uncomfortable.

"I've seen you and James together a couple of times, now I come to think about it."

Hector gives me a warning look, which I ignore.

"I had no idea you were such good friends," I go on.

"Finch," Hector says.

"In fact, the only time I've seen him on his own recently was that night. The night Birdie fell. I was on my way to the warehouse and I saw him down there, but he was alone; I guess you weren't with him *that* night?"

She looks alarmed, glancing at Hector as if he might tell her how she's supposed to answer.

"I… That was so long ago…"

"Ten weeks," I supply helpfully. "Ten weeks exactly, I've been counting."

"I don't remember. I think—"

"I am *starving*. Can we hit the hospital canteen on the way in?" Hector says.

I give him my most convincing *I am going to throttle you* look. I'm certain she was about to crack.

"Ooh, I could murder a doughnut," Sinead says. "Kitty and the girls are all on this protein diet. I don't understand it, because you can eat loads of cheese but you can't put it on toast. Basically anything that makes life worth living isn't allowed."

"Sounds rough," Hector sympathises.

"Sounds self-inflicted," I mutter.

"Doughnuts all round then," Hector says loudly, determined to drown me out.

I am actually going to throttle him. That is, if I ever get to see him alone again. But he can't hide behind a Bond Girl for ever. Not one that skinny.

Another week passes and nothing happens. It's like Birdie and I have become statues while the rest of the world whirls around us. The show is taking shape, no thanks to me; I'm too miserable to even go down there any more. I just stay at home, where at least everyone else seems as slo-mo as I am.

Saturday afternoon and I've been lying on my bed for hours, scrolling through stupid selfies of us on Birdie's Instagram account and listening to the playlist on her phone. There's some awful stuff on there – not *one* Smiths song – but it was nice arguing with her in my head about it.

I'm watching her YouTube videos of us on the trapeze when I'm interrupted by footsteps racing, tripping, up the stairs outside my room.

"It's me!" Hector calls.

"You're kidding. Come in."

He hops through the doorway, rubbing one ankle. "I had an idea," he pants.

"Oh God."

"We need to sort out costumes for our act. I thought we should do it here."

"Why here?"

He grins, flings open the doors of my overstuffed wardrobe and gestures at my clothes like *ta-dah!*

I fold my arms and jut out my chin. "How rude. I'll have you know my clothes are extremely stylish. Or were. When they were made."

"Hey, I'm not knocking your sartorial brilliance," he says, flipping through hangers already.

"What's 'sartorial brilliance'?"

"Fashion sense."

"Oh. Thanks."

"But I reckon if we mix and match a few things, we could come up with something hilarious." My Rupert trousers tumble off a crammed shelf and land on his trainers. "See, we didn't even have to look."

"Ha ha."

He starts dragging clothes off hangers and shelves and chucking them at me. "How about this?"

"That was expensive; you're not throwing cream pies at it."

"This?"

"I was going through a Gatsby phase. I'm over it."

"What *is* this?"

"It's vintage Versace! Versace is not even remotely funny."

He sighs, drags a chair over to stand on and digs around on the top shelf. Then he pauses, head and shoulders deep in the wardrobe, and I start to worry, trying to remember if I've left any posters of Damon up there.

But it's not that. It's worse.

He glances at me, embarrassed, and tries to put the photo back, as if I haven't just seen him look at it.

"That's old," I say quickly, which it is, but the fact that I obviously know exactly what it is kind of proves that it wasn't just accidentally left up there three years ago.

"Hey, what about this!" He drags a red bowler hat from the back of the shelf, determined to pretend he didn't see the photo. He jumps down and jams the hat on my head. "Perfect." Then he wraps a red skinny tie around my black bowler, puts it on himself and we stand there facing each other. "There! We match!"

He sticks his right hand out to shake, and I roll my eyes, but you can't ignore a cue so I stick my hand up in the air to wave hello. He sticks his hand up to wave as I bring mine down to shake. And then we do it again. And again, faster and faster. It's the start of the Dead and Alive skit, and if you get the timing right, it's pretty funny. We end up laughing and whacking each other's hands as it gets too fast and falls apart.

"See, costume makes all the difference," he says.

When it comes to clowning, he's *unstoppable*, so while he goes back to rifling through my wardrobe, I just lie on the bed listening to him go "Ooh!" and "Yeah!" and "Eugh!" as he throws clothes at me until I'm buried under a huge pile. The Eau de Charity Shop is pretty pungent.

He's right though, a costume does make you braver. Wish I'd been wearing one when he saw that photo of me and James, our arms round each other's shoulders, posing at Adi's birthday party. I swear I haven't looked at it in ages, but I'm ashamed that it's still there. I'm ashamed that it's so dog-eared. Mostly I'm ashamed of how happy I look in it.

When it goes quiet, I lift my head out from under a paisley shirt to find Hector stripped to the waist and unbuckling his belt. He waves me away, frowning, and I pull the shirt back over my face, blushing. I wonder if he's thinking about the photo and freaking out in case I'm eyeing him up, like the idiots at school. *As if.*

I've thought about telling him the truth. I always thought he wouldn't be a josser about it, not like James and Adi and Kitty and that lot, but now I don't know. Even if he's only *thinking* all the things they say out loud, then that's just as bad.

"What do you think of this?" he says eventually.

He's wearing my baseball shoes, which are enormous on him, my brown suit trousers – far too long – a baggy Hawaiian shirt, and a tartan bow tie that he's tied too tight.

"I guess if you're going for comedy."

"Exactly!"

I sit on the bed, reading the Buster Keaton book while he experiments with more bow ties in front of the mirror.

"So what will your clown autobiography be called then, Hector?"

"Hmm. How about *'Sixteen, Clumsy and Shy' and Other Smiths Lyrics That Basically Sum Up My Life.*"

"You're not sixteen."

"I will be by the time I write the book. And I'm pretty sure the Clumsy and Shy parts will be eternally applicable."

I don't disagree with him.

"OK, now what about your costume?" He looks me over critically. "I think we should work with what we've got. I mean, we already look kind of funny together; we can exaggerate that with clothes."

"What do you mean, *funny*?"

"Well, you know, I'm sort of skinny and pale and geeky, and you're … you know…" He gestures at me vaguely. "Taller, and broader … and … you know … kind of … goodlookingandstuff."

Goodlookingandstuff? What's that supposed to mean? But he's already rambling about trousers.

"You have to find a person's comical features and exaggerate them. You should wear trousers that are too short, to make you look even taller, and I can wear baggy ones, to make me look skinnier. Here, put these on." He pulls his own school trousers out of his rucksack, then plants himself on top of the pile of clothes on the bed, folds his arms and looks expectantly at me.

"Do you want popcorn?" I say. Apparently it's OK for *him* to watch *me*.

He rolls his eyes and lifts the Buster Keaton book. "Like you have anything to worry about," he mutters.

"Didn't say I did," I mutter back, suddenly wishing he'd just leave but not knowing how to say that without saying why.

The trousers almost fit around the waist but are a good ten centimetres too short. We add orange socks, white trainers, a custard-yellow shirt, a wide green tie and a tank top of Birdie's that just about reaches my belly button, so you can see the red braces poking out underneath.

He hands me the red bowler and my red nose, drags me to the wardrobe and closes the door so we can see ourselves side by side in the mirror.

I can't help laughing.

"We look totally professional!" Hector says.

"If by 'professional', you mean 'deranged'."

"Yep. Imagine making a whole career out of being certifiable."

"If that's what you're aiming for, then we're done here. I'm starving," I say. "Do you think it's physically possible to eat dinner in this lot and not throw cream pies around?"

"Lose the nose."

So we go down to the kitchen, minus the noses, where Mum looks straight at me and says, "Finch, if you're out this afternoon, can you buy loo roll?" And then Hector walks in behind me and she goes, "Oh, are these costumes? They're fab, guys!"

Way to knock my sartorial brilliance, Mum.

She leaves us to make pizza and throw cream pies.

"We'll need a name for our act," Hector says. "And a logo. And a theme tune!" He's sitting on the kitchen table juggling Jay's abandoned beanbags while I make pizza. It feels weird and familiar all at once: planning, juggling, dreaming. If I close my eyes, it could be Birdie sitting there.

"And when we learn to drive, we could get a van and call it the clown-mobile and have a travelling show!"

I picture Hector behind the wheel of a car. "Yeah, maybe I'll do the driving."

★ ★ ★

That was *our* big dream, mine and Birdie's, to go on the road. A travelling circus, doing street shows and festivals – we talked about it all the time. We'd been talking about it not long before her accident, in fact. I remember because she was in a mood. I was in a mood too; the guys at school were going through a phase of wolf-whistling every time I walked by.

"It'll be great, Birdie, it'll be just us. Just our own little circus family," I'd said.

"Yeah."

"I mean, we'll go to lots of towns, but if you're always travelling, you never really have to get to know anyone except your family."

"Yeah."

"What's wrong?"

"I don't know if I want to travel," she said.

"What!" We'd been planning this since we were like *in the womb*. You'd think I'd just brought it up that minute. "Why not?"

She shrugged. "If you're always travelling, you never get to know anyone except your family."

"And we'll have a Facebook page!" Hector is saying. "And a YouTube channel!"

"What?"

"For the act."

"Oh."

He frowns. "Are you rehearsing 'sad clown' or is something wrong?"

"No, just thinking. About costumes." I have a wicked idea. "Hey, do you think you could nick your dad's dog collar?"

He chokes on his pizza. "Oh my God, he'd spontaneously combust!"

"Ladies and gentlemen!" I boom, drum-rolling with my cutlery. "Boys and girls! Today's sermon will be read by Reverend Hector the Hazzardous on his two-metre unicycle!"

He laughs so hard his bowler hat falls off.

"Speaking of which," he says then, glancing at the clock, "they'll be home in half an hour. I'd better go."

"In that?"

"Bugger!" He dashes upstairs while I rinse the dishes, and comes back in his own clothes. "You can keep the school trousers," he says. "I'm not wearing the uniform any more."

He opens the back door and sort of lingers there awkwardly. "This was fun. I had fun. Thanks."

"Um … OK? I mean, yeah. It was fun. I'll see you Monday?"

"OK."

"OK."

Then he disappears. Seriously weird day.

About five seconds later the door opens again and

I think he's forgotten something, but it's Jay. He looks straight at me, fully clowned up, and says, "Finch, Mum told me to get loo roll but I forgot. Can you get it?" Then he runs upstairs.

Whatever. Apparently I am goodlookingandstuff.

47

I see, or rather, hear, Hector before Monday, though. I'm at the hospital on Sunday afternoon, sitting in the garden with my geography homework, when he arrives. Wren is in there already, singing songs from Birdie's terrible playlist (but I don't mind when Wren sings them), and Hector says he'll take over so she can go home.

I haven't told Hector how much time I spend sitting out here now. But what else can I do? Being at Franconis' is depressing, being at my house is depressing, sitting in Birdie's room is depressing, I'm not allowed at Hector's house and there's literally *nowhere* else to go.

Hector starts reading *The Lord of the Rings* aloud, which seems like a pessimistic choice, since I'm hoping for a recovery that's slightly shorter than the journey to Mordor. Still, the geography of Middle Earth is more interesting than the geography of oxbow lakes, so I give up on the homework, lean back against the wall and listen. His Orc voices are pretty cool.

After half an hour, he snaps the book shut and starts talking to Birdie about random stuff – school, the show. He tells her about his English presentation, and that leads on to Sinead, and I know I shouldn't listen but I don't move.

"Finch thinks I fancy her, but it's not like that. We're just friends." He's told me this a million times and I've never believed him, but somehow I believe him now. Why would he lie to a girl in a coma? Then again, why would he lie to me? But then he says, "I wish you were awake so I could talk to you. It sucks not being able to talk about things that actually matter to the one person you really like. It's starting to drive me nuts."

Oh. So I was right all along, he *does* like Birdie.

"And I hate that we're hiding stuff from Finch. He suspects something, you know. I wish you hadn't made me promise not to tell him; it's getting awkward. But you were right, he won't take it well. No one will *ever* be good enough to date a Franconi." He gives a sad little laugh and adds, "Especially not me."

I have a sudden vivid memory of being punched in the gut.

Birdie and Hector have been dating the whole time, and keeping it from me, like I'm some kid who'll throw a tantrum because someone's nicked his favourite toy.

My heart sinks as I imagine Birdie waking up and asking for *him*, not me. And him helping her recuperate, spending every minute round our house, holding her hand and disappearing into her room with the door shut.

Birdie's never kept anything from me before. She obviously felt guilty because she knew she was ditching me, leaving me to survive school on my own, basically breaking up the act. The reason she never said a word is because she knew it was going to ruin everything.

The worst part is, I feel so *stupid*. It was obvious; of *course* they're dating. I am *beyond* stupid. I even thought… But I don't know what I thought.

I pack up my books, slink out of the garden and make my way home so I won't have to see Hector. I don't want to see him ever again.

Lions, boys and other wild animals

Posted by Birdie

OK, so we don't actually have lions.

Franconis' doesn't have any animals because we think it's cruel to force animals to perform. We've put a lot of effort into taming Jay, but we think it's unfair to do it to more intelligent creatures, like dogs and fleas and stuff.

Still, the history of animal taming is fascinating, and every big circus used to do it, so here are the facts:

— Your average lion can open its mouth thirty centimetres wide. That's big enough for your head to fit in comfortably (comfortably for the lion anyway). Isaac A. Van Amburgh was the first lion tamer to put his head in a lion's mouth. He would also bring children from the audience into the cage with him. I don't think health and safety had been invented back then.

— Lion taming is not only dangerous but tough. Try training your pet cat to "sit". Now imagine it has eight-centimetre claws and can crush a bull's spine with its jaws.

— The first person to breed a lion in captivity was George Wombwell, who had his own travelling menagerie in 1810. He had a longstanding rivalry with Thomas Atkins, who had a show called Atkins' Menagerie. On one occasion, when they were exhibiting at the same fair, Wombwell's only elephant died en route. When Atkins heard this, he put up a sign saying that he had "the only live elephant in the fair!" Wombwell retaliated with a sign saying his show had "the only dead elephant in the fair!" Everyone came to see the dead one because they were allowed to poke it. People are like that.

— Animals do attack. In 1860, lion tamer Martini Maccomo was mauled by a lion, and the pistol he used in his act accidentally fired into the audience, injuring a spectator. And in 1861, his hand got wedged in the mouth of a tiger for five minutes.

— Tiger tamer Mabel Stark would face eighteen big cats at once. In 1916, a lion called Louie mangled her arm. Her lion-tamer husband, Louis Roth, saved her by firing blank cartridges at Louie. The bizarre coincidence is that Roth had been mauled himself earlier in the day by a lion named Jeff (presumably he was ticked off about being a lion named Jeff).

- Lion tamers use chairs to hold the lion off, because having four legs thrust at them confuses a lion enough to distract them from clawing your face off. This works with all simple-minded creatures. Seriously, just wave four different items of junk food at a boy; he'll do whatever you want.

- It's surprising what you can get a wild animal to do. Irina Bugrimova could get her big cats to form a pyramid, and sit behind her on a motorbike.

My question is, *why*?

Some people reckon animal attacks are due to boredom and frustration, because wild animals are being forced to learn behaviour that is unnatural for them, in an environment that doesn't suit them. When was the last time you saw a tiger in a nature documentary sit on a giant glitter ball and "beg"? This is a standard trick in animal circuses and I think it's depressing.

So I'm afraid we don't offer classes in lion taming at Franconis'. If you've got a whip and a chair, you can practise on Lou, but we can't guarantee your safety.

To be honest, it's not the mauling I find interesting. The thing that always gets me is that most lions never maul anyone. As you watch them being backed onto tiny platforms and made to do pretend roars, you can't help thinking, *Dude, you're twice the size of this guy. And you have much bigger teeth*. It's like the lion has no idea that it's much more powerful than the puny human in the sequinned lycra jumpsuit.

I sometimes think the same about people. People who put up with a lot of crap because someone's told them, over and over, that they have to; that they're weak. People who have no idea how strong they really are. Sometimes I just wanna yell, "Dude! Check out your teeth!"

<< Previous Post

After overhearing Hector's one-way conversation with Birdie at the hospital, I decided to avoid him, unfriend him, cut him out of my life for ever.

Which would have been much more satisfying if he'd been around. But he spent the whole of Sunday night with Sinead. All I got was a text saying, Plans with Sinead, soz, laters, when I hadn't even tried to make plans with him. Like I'd been pre-emptively ditched!

I guess this is what it's going to be like. As soon as Birdie wakes up, it'll be text messages saying *Plans with Hector (heart emoji), soz, laters*, and I'll be like *(Vomit emoji) Whatevs*.

I spent Sunday night watching Lou shout at quiz-show hosts on TV. Neither of us got a single question right. It seems like whether Birdie wakes up or not, I'm going to be left on my own, so I might as well get used to it. Hanging out with Lou could be my new social life.

At one point she demanded more whiskey, and when I told her Mum said no, she glared at me and said, "Did you know lion tamers only use young lions? After a certain age they're completely untrainable and dangerously aggressive."

"I didn't know you had the internet, Lou. Was that from Birdie's blog?"

"What blog?" she said.

I got her the whiskey.

Monday morning I feel hungover from the fumes of Lou's pipe as I drag myself to school alone. I left home super early so I wouldn't have to walk with Hector.

"Are you all right, Finch?" Miss Allen says before first period. I can see why she might be concerned; I'm early for maths, sitting all alone in the dark classroom, staring out the window.

"Fine, thanks, Miss."

"I can't help but notice you don't look quite … *yourself* these days," she says as she goes around the room setting graph paper and compasses on the desks.

I look down at myself. I'm wearing a plain T-shirt and jeans. Apart from a couple of favourite hats, that's what I wear most days now.

"What would you consider more *me*, Miss?"

"Oh, I don't know, something … *fun!*" By which she means "funny", like I exist to entertain the inmates of Murragh High.

She tries a different tack. "What would Birdie say if

she could see you looking like that?"

Wrong tack. "Humph. I'm not sure I know Birdie well enough to say, Miss," I mutter.

The rest of the class start pouring through the door and trying to stab each other with the compasses. Hector and Sinead dash in last. At least he doesn't sit with me in maths. I go back to staring out the window.

Halfway through class, I realize I still haven't got the hang of Pythagosaurus, or whatever he's called, but I'm determined not to ask Hector for help. I give up on the exercise Miss Allen has set and lean my head on one hand. A little shower of snow rains down on my graph paper.

I frown at it and pick up a few crumbs: tiny chunks of eraser, a couple of minuscule paper balls and some wads of tissue. With a sinking feeling, I run a hand through my hair, dislodging another blizzard and setting off a chorus of tittering from the row behind. If Birdie were here, I'd shake myself like a wet dog and pretend I didn't care. Now I just comb the stuff out with my fingers and go back to my work.

But that's not enough of a reaction for Kitty Bond. I know it's her, because the missiles start getting bigger. I can feel them pinging off the back of my head and shoulders. She chooses her moments; Miss Allen hasn't noticed anything. I'm expecting a compass point to pierce my ear any minute when I hear a *thud* and a yelp.

I turn to see Kitty rubbing her forehead and scowling, a multicoloured beanbag ball sitting on her desk.

He might as well have thrown a signed confession at her. The whole class swivels to look at Hector.

"Oops," he says.

"Those things aren't allowed in school, Miss," Kitty says. "Zero tolerance. He should be suspended."

"I don't think it's quite that simple, Kitty," Miss Allen says.

"Yes, it is, that's what *zero tolerance* means."

"Well, yes, but..." Even Miss Allen is faltering.

"It's mine, Miss, I brought it to school," I say. I might as well get suspended; it's not like the week is going to get any better.

"He didn't, *I* did," Hector says.

"It's my beanbag ball, Hector," I hiss at him.

"So romantic!" Kitty crows. "Coming to the rescue like a knight in shining braces!"

This is unfair because Hector got his braces taken off a month ago. But that doesn't matter; he could grow six inches and become a bodybuilder, and she'd still make him feel like that skinny geek with the braces. And no matter what I do, what I wear, what I say, I'll *always* be a circus freak to her.

Suddenly I'm sick of it. I stand up, knocking my chair over, and turn to face her. Kitty is instantly on her feet, like she's been waiting for this her whole life.

"What is your problem, Kitty?"

"Now, folks, let's just sit down and talk about this," Miss Allen says, flapping her hands at us. Everyone ignores her.

"*You're* my problem, Prom Queen. You and your stupid sister think you can do whatever you want around here! You think you're so weird, the rules don't apply to you! Well, you're not special, Sullivan, you're just a freak."

"Oh, well excuse me for not being as *normal* as you, Kitty. No, really, congratulations on being so completely and totally *average*, it's such an achievement. And you've got some nerve, by the way, standing there talking about my sister when it was your stupid boyfriend—"

"Don't you *dare* talk about him!" she screeches.

"Why would I want to? He's a dick; you're welcome to him!"

Miss Allen is rapping the desk with a paperweight now, but Kitty and I are locked in a death-stare. Even *I'm* starting to wonder how this is going to end when, in between the screeching and Miss Allen's attempts at discipline, there's a second of silence, and an odd buzzing sound fills the air.

Miss Allen could have brought in a riot squad of PE teachers and it wouldn't have calmed us down, but suddenly everyone is stock-still, staring at Hector, who's on his feet at the other side of the room, dodging a bee. He's ducking his head, leaping about and waving his arms at it, following it with his eyes as it chases him. So we all follow it too. Except there's nothing there.

"Are you all right, Hector?" Miss Allen says.

The buzzing continues and Hector jolts forwards, stomach first, as if the bee has prodded him in the back. Then he's up on his chair, then on the desk, hopping from foot to foot as the imaginary insect dive-bombs from above. People are looking at each other, wondering who's going to react first, and whether we're going to laugh or *laugh*. Kitty's still too furious to speak, which is lucky for Hector.

He's had enough of the bee now. He rolls up his graph paper and starts stalking it down the length of the classroom, over the tops of the desks. People grab their pencil cases and phones before he steps on them. The "bee" starts to circle Sinead Adeyemi and Hector's watching it so convincingly, she goes cross-eyed as it "lands" on her forehead and the buzzing stops. He brings the rolled graph paper down – *smack* – on her head. Sinead blinks in disbelief and looks nervously from left to right, from Kitty to Hector. *This is your cue,* I want to tell her, despairing at Hector's chances of cooperation from a Bond Girl. But as the buzzing starts again and Hector follows the bee on down the row, she smiles. Then she starts to giggle, and Miss Allen gives up trying to get Hector back on solid ground and starts to giggle too. Hector wallops a few more people on the head, and they start to laugh as well. Some of them instinctively try to dodge the bee, they can't help themselves, and that makes everyone else laugh. He's reached Miss Allen's desk now. He stands on top, gasps like he's had a great idea, and the "bee" flies right into his open mouth.

He feigns choking, gagging, and then pokes his tongue around inside his cheeks, like the bee is going mad in there. He motions desperately at Miss Allen to pat him on the back. She gives him a thump and Hector does a difficult-looking gulp.

We all stare in silence, as if he's actually swallowed a bee and we're waiting to see if it stings him. But he just hops off the desk, burps, says, "Thanks, Miss," and pretends to pick his teeth as he goes back to his chair, casual as you like. Then the bell rings.

People are still laughing as they leave, and a couple of them give Hector a small round of applause. Kitty and I just give each other the evils as we pack up.

"Finch?" Miss Allen calls me over as I head for the door. "You know, if you want to talk to—"

"I'm fine, Miss," I interrupt. I feel bad for being rude to her, but I'm really not in the mood.

She looks doubtful but says, "OK. Well, if you change your mind... But in the meantime, you can't go around shouting at people."

"I know."

"Although I have to say —" she gives me a tiny wink and whispers — "*that* was much more *you*."

Hector's not in my English class (where people spend the whole period poking their tongues around in their mouths like bees and completely weirding out Mr Morgan) but at breaktime he's on the yard wall as usual. I try to walk past him but he sees me.

"Finch! Did you see that throw? Bang, right between the horns! Luckiest shot ever."

I'm not laughing. "I don't need you to fight my battles for me, Hector."

"I was just trying to help!"

"Well, don't, it's embarrassing. Just stay away from me. I said at the beginning I didn't want to be friends, so just leave me alone."

He sags. "Don't be an arse, Finch, you don't mean that, you're just—"

"I do too mean it. And *you're* the one being fake, Hector. You only wanted to hang out with me to get to know Birdie. And now you're just killing time until she's better and you two can disappear, and I'll be left in Loner-ville. Well, I might as well get used to it, so you needn't bother pretending we're friends any more."

"What are you talking about?"

"I know all about it! I heard you talking to Birdie yesterday. I know your big secret."

He goes pale and swallows hard. "You heard that?"

"Yes! I know you and Birdie are going out."

He looks confused, then exasperated. "You thought me and *Birdie*...! Oh, for God's sake, you moron. Birdie's not going out with *me* – she's going out with James!"

"James who?" It's so impossible, the name doesn't even register with me.

"James Keane. They've been seeing each other for months."

I want to punch him in the teeth. "Liar!"

"It's true. She asked me not to tell you, but this is getting ridiculous."

"It can't be true. And don't you go around saying it; Kitty Bond will tear strips off her!"

"Kitty knows. That's why she's been tearing strips off *you*, you idiot. James dumped her, not long before the accident. And she can hardly take it out on Birdie, can she?"

"She knows!"

"Everyone knows. Except you." He rolls his eyes. "There seem to be a lot of things that everyone knows except you!"

"What's that supposed to mean?"

He looks away. "Nothing. Look, don't get upset that Birdie didn't tell you. I bet *you* have secrets from *her.* You can't know everything about a person and anyway—"

"Wait a minute! What did you say?"

"What? I just meant—"

"That's it!" I let out an enormous "HAH!" and slap him on the shoulder. "I have to go!"

"What? Come back!" But I'm already running out of the yard and down the road. I don't care that it's 11 a.m. and Mr Cooper will have a pink fit – I've just worked out Birdie's password.

49

LOGIN: <u>birdiefranconi@gmail.com</u>

Password: JamesKeane

Password accepted

That proves it then, Hector *wasn't* lying. I don't know what Birdie was thinking, going out with James – she's far too good for him. And she didn't tell me because she knows it. *And* she knows what he did to me. And that I hate him, and that it's a massive betrayal, and that Kitty will murder her. What was she *thinking*!

There's only one more automatically scheduled post, but suddenly I decide not to cancel it. The blog posts are the closest I get to talking to Birdie now and it's horrible knowing there's only one left. I don't want them to stop.

There's also a bunch of comments left by "Anonymous" on some of the older posts, which Birdie has deleted.

Most of them include the words "slag", "bitch" and "slapper". No prizes for guessing who "Anonymous" is. What was she *thinking*?

That's the worst part, I realize, lying on her bed looking up at the Buster Keaton collage pasted on her ceiling. Our whole lives, Birdie has been like the other half of my brain. And now, for the very first time, I have no idea what she was thinking.

50

Home sweet home?

Posted by Birdie

A travelling circus is its own little world. It has its own language and traditions, even its own superstitions. For example, did you know that a bird trapped inside the big top means bad luck? I guess it's bad luck for the bird, anyway.

The circus performers have their own caravan village, and they usually keep to themselves. Finch thinks this is the best part of travelling. He loves Franconis' because it's the only place in the world where he completely belongs. Which is great, and it's why I'd do anything to save the place for him, but I sometimes wonder if there's a downside.

When they arrive in a town, the first thing circus people have to do is find a school for all the kids to go to. A circus kid can attend 300 different schools. They probably pick up a lot of Facebook friends, but not many real ones. I don't know how much of an education they get, but most of them will stay in the circus all their lives anyway. They will grow up there, work there, live there, date there, marry there and have more circus kids there.

They don't have much choice. It's the only place in the world they belong.

< < Previous Post

It's ironic really. Franconis' is Mum's career, Janie's home, the only future Py wants, the only friends Hector has, the only place I belong, and it's family for all of us. But that's not the reason we're killing ourselves trying to put this show together: we're doing it for Birdie.

And it turns out, she was only doing it for me.

I've been rereading all her blog posts. They make a lot more sense, now I know about James. All that stuff about taking a day off from the circus, and Avis and Evelyn arguing over a guy, and double acts not having time to date. I'm starting to wonder if Birdie would even care if she woke up and found Franconis' was gone.

I'm late for my shift at the hospital, but when I arrive Mum's car is in the car park, and as I walk down the corridor I see Dad coming the other way carrying coffee cups. He looks pale, tired and unsteady, and he doesn't seem to see me until I'm right under his nose.

I'm still mad at Hector for not telling me the truth,

and for letting me ramble on and on with my James conspiracy theories, and I'm trying to think of a way of getting out of doing the show with him without having to tell anyone why, so I say, "Dad, do you think this whole clown act is a good idea? I'm just not sure. I mean, do you think Birdie would approve?"

He blinks at me in a dazed way, then laughs like a crazy person. "Ask her yourself, son," he says. "She's awake."

I crash through the door to Birdie's room so fast, I almost knock the doctor over. Then Mum has to stop me launching myself at the bed.

"She's awake? She's awake? Dad said she's awake! Why are her eyes closed? Is she awake?"

Mum's laughing and hugging me. "Calm down, sweetheart. She woke up for a few minutes but she's sleeping again. The doctor says that's normal; she'll only be awake for a little while at a time at first, but she's not in the coma any more."

"You're sure? She was definitely awake?" I peer at her. She looks just the same as last time I saw her, and the machines are still beeping away.

"She spoke to us. She was very weak and disoriented but she said, 'Where's Finch?'"

"Really? She asked for me?"

"Of course she did."

"She also asked for lunch money, but we're putting that down to the disorientation," Dad says, coming through the door with the coffee. "I called Wren — she's on her way with Jay."

The doctor starts telling us what to expect, but she doesn't send me out of the room this time, and her smile is a real one.

"She'll wake for longer and longer periods over the next few days, but she'll have something called post-traumatic amnesia for weeks. She'll be confused and have holes in her memory. She probably won't remember the accident and she might forget things you say to her. This should get better with time, but you'll have to be patient. When she's able to talk to us more, we'll be able to assess any lasting damage to her mental functioning, but the fact that she spoke to you and knew who you were is a great sign."

"Thank you so much, Doctor," Mum says. You'd think the doctor had done some sort of magic trick and brought Birdie back herself. In reality, all she did was wait with the rest of us, but I feel like hugging her too. And all the nurses. And the canteen staff, and the cleaners. I'd hug Kitty Bond if she was here.

Even though I hover over her bed almost every minute, it takes a couple of days before I manage to catch Birdie with her eyes open. I sit there through the afternoons, singing "Please, Please, Please, Let Me Get What I Want" by The Smiths and doodling on my homework.

And then one afternoon, a tiny voice that sounds so far away I think at first it's coming from the garden outside, says, "I hate The Smiths."

"Bird!" I shuffle my chair right up to the bed, grinning manically at her. It's stupid, because I've done nothing but long to talk to her for weeks, but now she's awake, I don't want to say anything. I just want to look at her weak, pale, blinking, tired, *open* eyes.

"Hiya," she murmurs. All these weeks this room has felt like an empty room, and now it's like she's finally walked through the door and there are two of us again.

I find myself whispering. "Hiya. I've missed you."

"What happened?"

"You had an accident, you're in hospital. But you're OK now."

"Were you hurt?"

"No, I wasn't there. And I'm really sorry about that."

"I can't remember."

"It doesn't matter."

"I'm tired."

"Go to sleep then, I'll see you later."

And that's it, our big reunion. She closes her eyes and falls asleep, but now I've spoken to her, it doesn't feel like she's gone away again, and I hum quietly as I do my homework, so as not to wake her.

Over the next few days I have several scintillating, if brief, conversations with Birdie, most of which she has forgotten thirty seconds later:

"What have I missed at school?"

"A lot of homework, so nothing important. Hector says he'll help you catch up."

"Are you being nice to Hector?"

"I'm *always* nice!"

"Are people being nice to you?"

"No worse than usual. A bunch of them came to visit you. Did you see the flowers they sent? Birdie? Birdie?"

"Tony told me about you and Hector in the children's ward. Have you met Tony?"

"Yeah, I know Tony."

"He's nice."

"Yeah. Hector's a maniac; you wouldn't believe the stuff he's making me do."

"Are you being nice to him?"

"I'm *always* nice!"

"Did I miss anything at school?"

"How's Franconis'?"

"Going strong. Well, we haven't folded anyway."

"I told Tony about the show. Have you met Tony?"

"Yeah, I know Tony."

"He's nice."

"Yeah."

"I'm sorry I won't be in the show, Finch. I feel like I let you down."

"Don't be silly, Bird."

"They said I have to have physio for months before I can train again."

"I know."

"Tony said he'd come and see the show. Have you met Tony?"

Hector's back to texting me every five minutes, but now it's to see how Birdie's doing. The doctor's insisted on "family only" visiting for the time being.

How is she today?

Breakdancing and having pillow fights with the nurses.

Did she say anything?

She said Trekkies are losers.

You're hilarious.

She ate three bites of toast.

Wow! That's great!

And she said if you come down tomorrow, Tony will sneak you in to see her.

Really?

Yeah, they're like best mates now or something.

See you tomorrow then!

While Hector's with Birdie, I sit on the steps outside the hospital entrance, imagining her asking him, "Is Finch being nice to you?"

And him replying, "Finch is *never* nice."

Not that Hector would even say that because the fact is, Hector's *always* nice.

I don't know what my problem is; I'd like to blame it on having a lot to deal with since Birdie's accident, but I can't. I just seem to be angry or irritated all the time, and I take it out on everyone. Well, now Birdie's better, I'll have to try harder, especially since she's got a boyfriend and if I'm not nice to Hector, I'll be spending a lot of time on my own.

When I think about Birdie's boyfriend, my new resolve to be less grumpy is immediately tested. And as if the universe is trying to prove that I'm incapable of keeping it, I look up to see James Keane walk through the hospital gates.

He stops at the bottom of the steps, hands in his pockets.

"She's not allowed visitors yet, just family," I tell him.

"Oh. It's just Sinead said Hector was going to see her and—"

"Hector's circus family. What are you?"

He shrugs and sits down next to me. He looks miserable. "Nothing really, I just want to talk to her."

Suddenly I feel sorry for him, because I know what it's like to want to talk to her. But I still don't trust him. "I thought you were her boyfriend."

"She dumped me."

"She did?"

"That night. It must have been just before her accident; when I left the circus school, she was getting ready to practise. She told me we couldn't see each other any more. That's why I was so mad at you when I saw you; I blamed you."

"Me? Why was it my fault?"

"Because she knows you hate me. She thought you'd be upset if she went out with me, that's why we kept it secret. She said you'd take it as a big betrayal or something, and she was your only friend and she couldn't abandon you."

"Wow, thanks, Birdie, that's not at all embarrassing."

"I was pretty angry. But the truth is, it's my own fault you hate me. And it's my fault you get a hard time at school. I tried to talk to you about it a couple of times, but I'm not very good at that sort of thing and you're always so … I don't know, you don't make it easy to apologize."

"Am I supposed to apologize for that?"

"See? Look, I'm sorry for all that stuff back when we fell out. I was a jerk, and I regretted it like five seconds later, but I was getting all this crap from the other guys about hanging out with you, and we were all new at school and I didn't want to be *that guy* right from day one. So I ditched you. But it was cowardly and I regret it."

It was a long time ago and an apology shouldn't make any difference now, but it does. In fact, for the very first time it actually seems like it *was* a long time ago. Anyway, I know how hard it is to stand up in front of the popular kids and say what you really think. Why did I think it would be any easier for James?

I just nod at him, because it doesn't fix everything, but it does mean something.

"If you want to know the truth," he says, "I was better friends with you than I've ever been with anyone else. Until I got to know Birdie."

"How did I not notice you two hanging out?"

"She sat with me in French while you were in Spanish. She gave me a hard time at first, but after I apologized for what happened with you, we started talking and then walking home together. And then she'd tell you she was going to the library to do blog posts, but she'd come over to my house to do them instead."

"That sneaky—"

"If it helps, she felt guilty about it. But she couldn't stand the thought of hurting your feelings, and she knew you'd try to talk her out of dating me. You seemed to want her at the warehouse every spare minute. I never got to see her, which made me mad, and then I'd lash out at you at school. It was just a big mess, and Kitty was all over Birdie because I broke up with her, and I couldn't even stand up for you two because then you'd find out the truth. I think it just all got too much for Birdie, so she dumped me. And I've been so scared that her accident was my fault, because she was so upset that night. I need to talk to her. Please."

I know what it's like to blame yourself too. "Come back tomorrow," I tell him. "I'll sneak you in."

That night Birdie's pretty alert and we're able to talk properly for the first time.

"Hector told me about your act in the show. It sounds amazing."

I shake my head. "It's bizarre; can you imagine me as a clown?"

"That's why it's amazing."

"You might have another visitor tomorrow. James wants to see you."

"Oh." She looks nervous. "Are you angry?"

"No. I'm a bit confused though. He apologized for everything."

"Good."

"And he told me you broke up with him. Was it really because of me? And was that why you fell?"

"I fell because I was an idiot to go up there on my own when I wasn't concentrating. I don't remember how it happened but I know I was in a bad mood. It wasn't your fault, or James's. But I guess I did break up with him because of you."

"Birdie, if you wanted to go out with someone, I'd be OK with it. Eventually."

She grins at me. "I know. But you *would* have been upset; I know you used to—"

"That was ages ago."

"Anyway, it wasn't just that. I wanted a break from Franconis' and I was too scared to tell you."

"You wanted out of the act?"

"Not for ever. I wanted to spend time with James, and then I got to know Sinead while I was hanging out with him and I thought it would be nice to be friends with her. But we never do anything but train and teach classes and write circus blogs and make costumes, and there wasn't time for me to have a life." She takes my hand. "I tried to get you to make friends with Hector so you'd have someone besides me, but you didn't want anyone else around. I even started researching how acts split up; I wanted to know how it happens. I suppose I was looking for a way to tell you, but all I could find were terrible accidents. It seems like acts only end when someone bites it. It's like Lou said: you don't just walk out on your partner. That's why I told James it was over."

I put my head next to hers on the pillow. "Birdie, we'll always be partners, it doesn't matter if we perform together or not."

She smiles but I can tell she's getting tired. "Thanks, Finch. I do want to train again, just not all the time."

"OK."

"And, Finch?"

"Yeah?"

"You know, if *you* wanted to go out with someone, it wouldn't matter who it was, I would be fine with it."

What's that supposed to mean?

"James has changed a lot," she murmurs, her eyes closing. "I know it's hard for you to see that; I know he kind of broke your heart. But he's nice really."

"I know," I say quietly, fighting back the lump that's suddenly in my throat. "I remember."

But she's asleep.

52

The show is coming up fast and everyone's rehearsing like crazy. Hector and I are so nervous, we've managed several rehearsals without a single argument.

Thursday night, two days before the show, we have the big dress rehearsal. Tony promises to take special care of Birdie because the rest of us are at Franconis'. Still, I leave the hospital as late as I can, and when I get to the industrial estate I hear The Clash pumping out of the warehouse sound system already, so I know Py is running through his opening act.

When I get inside, his fire staff is spinning around his body, a strobe in the darkness giving flashes of his dreads and henna tattoos, and his Docs pounding the concrete in time to the music, like something primeval. He's also topless. He does this trick where he covers his skin in an invisible fireproof gel so he can run flaming torches over his arms and chest. I admit to freezing in the doorway for a moment, mesmerized by Py's naked torso, which has a much more impressive six-pack than you'd expect from a guy who lives on pizza and cheap cider.

When the routine ends, he pulls on his grotty, baggy T-shirt, spits on the floor and wipes his nose on the inside of his wrist, and he's back to plain old Py again.

I hurriedly put on my costume and then Hector and I sit at the edge of the circus ring Mum's created out of milk crates, waiting for our turn to go on. Hector's in so many acts, he's knackered already, but at the moment it's the Juggulars' routine so he's getting a rest.

"Nervous?" he says.

"Kinda."

"Bet you wish you'd stuck to the trapeze now."

"Kinda."

"It's not the same without Birdie though, is it?"

I shrug. "I think you were right about me being scared to go up there."

"I shouldn't have said that; anyone would be scared, seeing her in hospital and everything."

"No, it's not that. I don't think I'm scared of falling, it's just..."

"What?"

"It was like, if I went up there alone, I was admitting that she might not come back. And we've always done everything together – I mean *everything*. It turns out I can't even get dressed in the morning without her."

He raises an eyebrow at me.

"I don't mean literally, but you've seen my clothes lately. It takes guts to wear the stuff me and Birdie used to wear; I'm not brave enough if she's not around. What if I get up there –" I raise my chin towards the heights of the warehouse – "and discover I'm just no good on my own? The trapeze is the one thing that makes me special. Without it, I'm pretty ordinary."

Hector glances at me, then examines his fingernails as he speaks. "I don't think you're ordinary, trapeze or not. And I think you're braver than you know, and … I know I'm not Birdie, but you're not on your own, Finch. I mean, *we* could be a double act. A proper one."

There's an awkward silence, like he's given me a cue and I've totally left him hanging, and then he gets up to join Py in the ring. I watch him "helpfully" extinguish Py's torches for him, watch everyone laughing, and I know he's right, but it's not that simple. What did Lou say about partners building trust, and how long that takes? Birdie and I have had for ever; I've known Hector about five months. I can't tell him, but I don't *want* another partner. I'm scared. I'm scared he'll let me down. I'm scared it won't work out. I'm even scared it *will* work out. Because I don't even know what *it* is.

When Hector comes back, his curly clown wig only

slightly singed and Dad batting him with a fire blanket, he has another suggestion.

"Why don't you hang out with me and Sinead sometime?"

"I'm sure she'd *love* that."

"She'd like to get to know you, but you're not exactly welcoming. I think you make her nervous."

"*I* make *her* nervous?"

"Sinead's not having an easy time of it either, you know. Kitty's furious that she's defected."

"What's 'defected' mean?"

"She's crossed No Man's Land and joined the enemy. Which is brave, if you ask me. You could try being nice to her. And you owe her; she's the reason I'm in the show."

"What? Why?"

He looks sheepish. "My dad thinks I'm with her tonight. Most nights, actually. I told him I'm going out with her."

"You *lied* about hanging out with me?"

"I had to — he wouldn't stop going on about it."

I huff down my nostrils. "Well, you're one to talk about being brave, Hector. You know, you're not the only person around here who doesn't want to be seen with me, but at least the rest of them are honest about it."

"Don't be so dramatic; it's not that I don't want to be seen with you."

"Yes, it is. Your dad doesn't like me and you haven't the guts to tell him that you do. I mean, that we're friends. Or whatever."

"Or whatever?" He shakes his head. "Yeah, *or whatever* really sounds like a worthwhile reason to pick a fight with my dad."

But it's our turn in the ring and we don't get a chance to say anything else. We run through our act woodenly, our clown grins stiff and forced. Janie looks worried, but neither of us feels like going over it again. Everyone's nervous actually, so although we get through the whole rehearsal without much of a hitch, it all feels a bit flat.

"Don't worry, Finch," Py says. "It'll be different with an audience; that's where the energy comes from."

But that's what I'm worried about. What if our audience is Mr and Mrs Wood and All the Little Woods? What if no one comes?

On Friday I sit on the yard wall as usual with my lunch, but Hector doesn't run out to join me. In fact, he hasn't spoken to me since yesterday's dress rehearsal. I try to enjoy the silence but actually I feel miserable. I've wanted him to go away pretty much since the moment I met him, and now that I'm used to him being around, he's gone. Flipping typical.

Kitty and her crowd walk past on their way to the canteen. James isn't with them, I notice.

"Has he ditched you, Finch?" Adi calls out. "Never mind, want me to set you up on a blind date? Kitty, do you know any blind people?"

It's ironic, really, that I get teased about my love life when I'm about a million miles behind everyone else in the dating department. People in my year talk about relationships so casually, and when they meet someone they like, they know what to do about it. But they were all kissing behind the bike sheds when they were eight and playing spin-the-bottle when they were eleven. They're on to the serious stuff now and I've still never even held anyone's hand.

I'm about to give up on the celery sandwich Wren's made me when Sinead plonks herself down on the wall.

"Hector's not here," I say, as if that's not obvious.

"Yeah, I can see that. He's in the canteen."

"Oh, well, don't let me keep you."

But she doesn't move. "He's pretty mad at you."

"Me? He's the one—"

"He told a tiny fib, that's all."

"It was *not* a tiny fib. A tiny fib is when I go home and tell Wren these sandwiches were edible. Hector told a whopping great *lie*, if you ask me. And I don't see why you're standing up for him; did you know he's telling people you're dating him? Wait till Kitty gets hold of *that*."

Sinead sighs. "I don't care. So what if people think I'm going out with him – is there something wrong with that? You're supposed to be his friend and you're telling me I should be embarrassed or something?"

"Exactly; I'm his friend, and *he's* the one embarrassed to be seen with *me*!"

"No, he's not, he was just trying to avoid a fight with his dad. You know, if you're his friend you should act like it, otherwise he might give up on you."

"It would be about time," I mutter. "Why do you care anyway?"

She's quiet for a moment. "Look," she says eventually, "I know hanging around with Kitty doesn't entitle me to any favours from the people she's tortured over the years, but I want you to know I'm done with all that. I never liked her; I just kind of got stuck in that group years ago and I've been scared to be on the other end of it. You can understand that, can't you?"

I shrug.

"But I don't want to waste the rest of high school on her. Actually, I've always thought you and Birdie were pretty cool. I'd have liked to be friends with you but you're always so ... stand-offish. You won't let anyone be nice to you."

"Me?" I'm genuinely surprised.

She gives me a look. "Oh, come on. You've never said *anything* to me that wasn't completely sarcastic."

"Basic defence mechanism. Maybe if I didn't have to—" I see her stiffen, waiting for the sting, and I realize she's right; it's like a reflex, and I'm about to do it again. I hold my hands up. "Fine. Point taken. Go on."

"You two never seemed to need anyone else, so I didn't bother trying. I didn't want to ditch Kitty and end up all on my own. But when Hector came and you made friends with him, I thought..." She shrugs.

"I used to watch you in the yard, teaching him to juggle, and I'd be listening to Kitty go on and on about *nothing* and wishing I could be with you guys instead."

"Really?" There's still a bit of me that's certain this is part of some elaborate joke designed by Kitty.

"I got to know Birdie before the accident. She's great. I'd like us to be friends, but it won't work if you hate me. She'd never do anything to upset you."

"Hey, I don't *hate* you." I'm starting to feel bad for her; it sounds like life as a Bond Girl isn't much fun. "I don't mind if you and Birdie are friends."

She smiles. "I want to be friends with you, too."

"Yeah?" I try to look casual. "I guess that's OK."

She nudges me with her shoulder. "And I want you and Hector to make up."

"*Jeez*, you want the moon on a stick, don't you?" I roll my eyes and she giggles.

54

But I don't get a chance to talk to Hector. He doesn't walk home with me after school, and when everyone arrives at the warehouse that night, Dad is already standing in the centre of the floor tapping Mum's ringmaster whip against his palm and glaring at us.

"Right, you lot," he says. "Circus history lesson, listen up. Tomorrow night is the show and you can stick stars on your dressing-room doors and swan about like divas if that's your thing. But you may or may not know that traditionally in the circus, everyone has *two* jobs: a shirt-sleeves job and a spangles job. When a travelling circus arrives in town, everyone – even the star performers – has to help set up."

"Sure, Mr S, we can do that," Py says, slouching towards the enormous pile of rigging for the bleacher-style seating we've rented and now have to construct.

Dad prongs him in the chest with the whip. "Not.

So. Fast, Mr Carson," he says. Then he starts pacing in front of us like a drill sergeant. "This is a *public* performance," he barks. "That means members of the *public*. That means *public* liability. That means conditions of insurance that must be met. That means *health* and that means *safety*. That means *regulations*." His eyes gleam; he looks crazed. Mum pops a ringmaster hat on his head. "Thank you, dear," he says, still glaring at us. "That means that for tonight, *I am in charge*. I am the head honcho, the big cheese, gaffer-in-chief. That means I *own* you lot." He points the whip at each of us in turn. "You *will* do as you are told. *Exactly*. Instructions will be followed." He brandishes a complicated set of diagrams at us. "To the *letter*. There will not be one *screw* left over, misplaced or loose when we are done here."

"What about the one in your head!" Lou shouts from the doorway.

He points the whip at her. "*You* will limit yourself to bagging popcorn, old woman, or I will tell Edna O'Brien who jammed her cigarette machine with foreign coins!" Dad is in his element. Mum looks kind of impressed. Everyone else looks stunned. "Right! To work!"

So we all spend the whole of Friday night constructing seating, running through fire drills and safety checks, rigging up ring-door curtains and setting up changing cubicles behind them. And every time I get near Hector, Dad hands one of us a screwdriver or a hammer, or drags us off to lift something heavy.

When the seating is done, we go home, exhausted, five of us stuffed in the back of Dad's car and five more in the back of Mum's. Hector sits between me and Janie in the back seat, but Wren is sitting on his knee and Jay is jammed onto mine so neither of us says anything when he squeezes out past me.

When I get to my room, I sit at my desk for a while holding my phone. But I don't want to say this over the phone. And anyway, I have no idea what it is I want to say. It occurs to me that Hector didn't text me as usual before going to sleep last night and I wait to see if he'll remember tonight.

At midnight I give up and go to bed.

55

On Saturday we come back to do some more setting up, and by lunchtime the place is starting to look like a circus. All the bare warehouse walls have been covered with black curtains and we've made a "ring" from a semicircle of red and yellow painted boxes, and hung a red silk curtain to separate the ring from backstage. While Dad does final spotlight checks, Hector, who's been flat on his back under a malfunctioning fog machine for most of the morning, stands in the centre of the ring and looks around, smiling like it's Christmas morning. It's the first time I've seen him smile since before our argument at the dress rehearsal, and I remember what Birdie said in her blog about belonging here. Maybe it's not just me then.

Dad orders us all home for a rest before the show, but we'll have to walk because he and Mum are sticking around to do last-minute stuff.

I reckon this is my chance. "Hey, hang on, do you want to walk home?" I call to Hector as he passes me on his way to the door. He stops but doesn't look at me. Then he shrugs. "Some other time," he says quietly, walking away.

I should be rehearsing. Or resting. Or pacing nervously or bouncing around, getting overexcited. Today's the day we've been waiting for, planning for, for months. For *ever*. Today's the day we save or lose Franconis'.

And what am I doing? Sitting on my windowsill absentmindedly picking the stitches out of a beanbag ball and staring at my phone.

I sent Hector a text an hour ago.

Hey, did I leave my bowler hat at your house?

It's not at his house, it's at my house. On my head. What the text really says is, *How mad are you? Are you too mad to even answer a text about a bowler hat?*

And apparently, the answer is *Yes*.

I tell myself it'll be OK, I'll talk to him before the show, I'll apologize properly.

I'll also work out what I'm supposed to be apologizing for.

I guess for calling him gutless for lying to his dad when really he was just trying to help us put on a great show. And for taking things out on him when I was stressed about Birdie. For not appreciating everything he did for me when Birdie was ill. For pushing him away every time he tried to be friends with me, and then getting jealous when he made friends with someone else. For being too scared to be his partner. Oh yeah, and for calling him hopeless about twelve billion times when actually he's one of the best performers we've ever had, and if anyone's going to save Franconis', it'll be him.

A whole seam of the beanbag ball comes apart and it spews its beanie guts all over my lap. I put my phone away. Hector's never going to forgive me and I don't blame him; I've really messed things up. Not leaping into random friendships is all very well, but I guess sometimes you can leave it too late.

I go back to staring out the window, flicking polystyrene beans at the glass and watching the empty lane in front of our house. I suppose I've been hoping all afternoon that Hector might come tripping down it any minute, because when I see a figure come round the corner at one end, from the direction of his house, I jump up in a cloud of beans, and I'm halfway down the stairs before I remember Hector doesn't wear a red denim jacket, knee-high boots and a hairband.

"Hi, Sinead." I meet her in the lane and we walk back towards the house together.

"Well, don't look so thrilled to see me."

"Sorry, I am, really. It's just, I was expecting Hector. Sort of."

Actually, seeing Sinead is making me feel better. I'd forgotten we're friends now, and if I'm friends with her and she's friends with Hector, then he and I can't really avoid each other. Maybe she'll come to the show tonight and we can all hang out after, and maybe he'll be in such a good mood after the performance that maybe—

"Yeah, about that," Sinead says. She looks uncomfortable. "Hector sent me with this." She hands me a stuffed rucksack. Hector's rucksack.

"What is it?"

"Props," she says. "Hector's not coming tonight."

My stomach takes a ten-metre, net-less dive.

"*What?* He's *bailing* on me! On *us*! How could he *do* this!"

"No, no!" Sinead flaps her hands at me. "He wants to come, he really does, but he can't."

"Did he break both his legs! And his *neck*!"

"Worse – he told his dad about the show. And about

lying to him. About everything. He's grounded, effective immediately."

I collapse on the garden wall, dazed. This is a disaster. This is The End.

Sinead sits beside me. "What are you going to do?" she says.

I stare blankly at her. What *can* I do? Cancel the whole thing? Refund the tickets? Lose Franconis'?

There's only one option. "I have to save the show," I say helplessly, not even knowing what that means.

"Are you going to do your trapeze act?"

Hmm. I guess I always had this fantasy about me and Birdie swooping in (literally) to save the day, save Franconis', with our trapeze act, but it's not going to happen that way. Even if Birdie were here, it wouldn't be enough. Hector was our only shot. He's in half the acts, he ties the rest of them together with his skits between performances, kids love him – *everyone* loves him. The show just isn't going to work without him.

I shake my head. "No."

"Then what?"

"I'm going to rescue Hector."

57

Hector's still not answering his phone; it's probably been confiscated. So I go over there, clinging to the hedgerows in case his dad sees me out of a window. I scale a neighbour's wall and creep around the edges of the garden, not really knowing what I'm doing. But if I go to the door, his dad will send me away. My only hope is that Hector will see me and come outside.

When I get to the back of the house, I try pinging his bedroom window with grit but there's no response. I go back round the side via the bushes and then I spot him in the attic window. Of course.

He's at his desk and doesn't look up. I don't know if I can throw that high but I lift another handful of grit. Just then his mum appears at a window right in front of me. I dive into a bush. She sits down with a cup of tea and a book. Great.

I creep round to the front, then right around the

house, looking for open windows, open doors, like a burglar, but there's nothing. I end up on the opposite side of the house to the attic window. There are no windows at all on this side, so at least his parents can't see me, but it means Hector can't see me either.

This is hopeless. I slump against the trunk of a tree, let my head sink back against the bark and stare up through the branches arching high over the garden, the neighbour's garden, the roofs of the houses.

The roof.

I'm kicking my shoes and socks off and shrugging out of my hoodie before I'm even aware of what I'm doing. Then I'm shinning the tree trunk, pulling myself up on sawn-off stumps and knots until I reach the proper branches further up. I stand on the lowest branch and peer upwards through the dense leaves, assessing my chances. The tree must be as old as Little Murragh. It towers over the house, and the branches are thick and sturdy, but they're spaced out and it's not going to be an easy climb.

Unless you happen to be able to fly.

I scale my way up as far as I can, and when I come to a gap that's too big, I stand on the branch, balancing carefully, bend my knees and make a leap for the branch above, grabbing it with one hand, then the other, and dangling there like a Christmas ornament. I start swinging so I've got a bit of momentum, flip upside down, bring my legs between my arms, and hook my knees over the branch. Then I pull myself up to a sitting position. I wish Birdie were here to see this; I can almost hear her cheering from below (I can also hear Dad having an apoplectic fit).

I stand on the branch, feeling it sway and bob beneath my weight as though it wants to throw me higher. The air feels different up here; there's something so peaceful about height. I've missed it, and suddenly I'm *itching* to get back on the trapeze.

But not right now. Right now is about Hector.

I make another leap, then shin around the trunk to some denser branches on the other side, then back to the house side, searching out footholds, feeling more confident. I'm almost there. Another gap, another leap.

This time I miss. I touch the bark but it comes away in my hand and I'm falling.

The reason people fall out of trees is because they're only thinking about two things: the branch they're reaching for, and the ground below. But the trapeze is *all* about spatial awareness. I'm surrounded by options, and the ground is the only one I'm *not* thinking about. I know without looking that there's a branch just below me, to my right, for example, and I'm hooking one arm for it even as the other still grapples for the one I missed. I hit hard, with my full body weight, my chest crashing against it as I grab hold. It's not as sturdy as the other branches; it dips and creaks as I swing there, reinflating my flattened lungs, but it holds, and I swing myself up and start again.

Shake it off, Finch. Keep going.

When I get level with the roof of the house, there's another problem. The branches almost overhang the tiles but they're much thinner out there and they'd snap under my weight. I can't just walk along them and step onto the roof; I'll have to go higher and then jump across. If I get high enough, I can swing and launch myself that bit further, but that also means further to fall.

I climb to a branch about three metres above the roof and dangle there from my hands, starting to swing, pumping my legs to give me more momentum. I can see most of Little Murragh from here. I can see the road to my house and the road out of town. I could still back out of this. I could climb down and go home and try to salvage the show as best I can.

Or I could do the crazy thing. Which is what Hector would do for me.

I put all the *forward* I've got into one last push, and let go, hitting the roof tiles with a thump and centimetres to spare.

The next bit is really Wren's department: high wire. Usually, I wouldn't attempt it without a balance pole and a safety net, but the slope of the roof on either side of the ridge is steep and slippery with moss, and I reckon my only chance of reaching Hector is to walk the ridge pole. I stand, shaky from the climb, on the very apex of the roof, arms out on either side, feeling the cold breeze on the back of my sweaty neck. I look out across the eight metres of narrow tile in front of me.

Lou used to do this to freak out the neighbours. Well, she *said* it was to freak out the neighbours. Probably she was just homesick. She was a fearless wire walker in her day, and I wish now I'd asked her more about it. What would she tell me if she were standing here with me? The only thing that comes to mind, the only piece of advice she's ever offered me, is: "You're a Franconi, Finch."

I nod at the invisible Lou, and start putting one foot in front of the other.

About a million miles, a chimney stack and a close encounter with a seagull later, I reach the other end of the house. The attic window is directly below me and it has a deep sill, but I'm going to need the window to be open when I lower myself down to it. Hoping Hector hasn't gone back to his bedroom, I lie on my belly on the roof, dangle my head down over the edge as far as I dare, and knock politely on the glass.

Hector falls off his chair.

"What the…! And *how* the…!" Hector splutters as I pull myself through the window. "You are *insane*!" he hisses.

"Nice to see you too."

I grin at him, but he doesn't grin back. Instead he goes to the far corner of the attic and sits on the floor, his back to the wall, and says, "What are you doing here?"

He thinks he's hiding it, but the bin by his desk is full of tissues and he's sitting at the dark end of the attic to hide his eyes. He's been crying.

I sit down in front of him. "Look, it's OK, I'm going to get you out of here. I mean, I don't know *how*, unless you know a way to sneak through the house, because there's no way you're walking the ridge pole and going down that tree. What if we—"

"Finch, I can't go anywhere."

"I know you're grounded but we can sneak out. Unless ... oh my God, he hasn't locked you in here, has he? In the *attic*!"

Hector rolls his eyes. "God, you're such a drama queen. My dad's not a fricking ogre! I just came up here to be alone for a while."

"So we can sneak out then."

"No! I'm not sneaking around any more. Look, you can't be here, you'll make it worse."

"How can it be worse? You're going to miss the show. I can't believe you'd do that!"

"That's all you're worried about, isn't it? The show. Franconis'. I'm sorry but I have bigger stuff going on. You don't even need me."

"Of course we need you, you're our clown."

"You *have* a clown. *You're* a clown. You can fill in for me with the other performers and you'll just have to cancel our double act. You never wanted to do it anyway." He folds his arms around his knees and rests his head on them. He might be crying again.

I put a hand out. I want to put an arm round him, squeeze his shoulder, *something*. There's a whole bunch of stuff I wanted to apologize for, but now I can't remember the words and I feel awkward. And anyway, this is about his dad, not me, and I don't know what to do, so I just take my hand back and sit there feeling useless.

I guess he's right; we could do the show without him. I've watched his routines a million times, and if I was out there with the other performers, I could probably manage it. I could make that fantasy come true; I could be the hero and save the show, save Franconis'.

But that's not why I'm here. That's not why I climbed that tree and walked that slippery ridge pole. Suddenly I don't care about the show half as much as I care that Hector is mad at me. And that he's crying. And that he's worked bloody hard for this and he'll be gutted if he misses it.

And suddenly I know that Hector's not half as mad at me as I am at his dad.

"I'm going to talk to him."

"What? What are you doing?"

I'm opening the attic door, that's what I'm doing. I'm walking down the stairs and I'm shouting, "Mr Hazzard? Are you there?"

"Finch! Don't!" Hector tries to hold me back, but the noise of us arguing just brings Mr H into the downstairs hall anyway.

He frowns as we come down the stairs. "Finchley?" As if I might be a mirage. "Hector, you're supposed to be grounded – that means no friends round."

"I sneaked in, Mr Hazzard. I mean Reverend Hazzard. *Father* Hazzard?" I haven't been inside a church since ... actually, ever. We're just not that kind of family. "It's not Hector's fault."

"He's just leaving," Hector says.

"Yeah, but I need to talk to your dad first," I hiss at him.

"How did you get in, Finchley? I didn't hear the door. Are your hands bleeding?"

"Oh. Yeah. Well, the bark was rough." My jeans are torn too and there are red scrapes down the lengths of my bare arms. I suck the blood off my fingers and say, "I climbed the tree and came over the roof."

"What!"

"It's OK, I'm a professional."

But he looks like he prefers Hector's word. *Insane.*

"I should call your parents."

Why do parents think parents should be involved in *everything*?

"No, they're busy, they're at the warehouse. That's why I'm here; the show is tonight and we need Hector."

"I'm sorry, but Hector lied to us and now he's grounded."

"But the show is only for one night! Can't you let him out for one night?"

"If punishments were conditional, they wouldn't be very effective, would they?"

"But he's worked so hard!"

"Finch, just leave it," Hector says. His mum is watching from the living-room doorway now too.

"I won't leave it! You *have* worked hard and you're really good and you deserve this; it's not fair!"

"I'm sure Hector appreciates you trying to help, Finchley, but all that has nothing to do with the fact that he wasn't honest with us. I'm sorry but I've made my decision."

My eyes narrow. I can't make Mr Hazzard do anything, but I'm not about to let him punish Hector for lying and then stand there and lie to us himself.

"You're right, it *doesn't* have anything to do with it," I say. "And the fact that he lied has nothing to do with why he's grounded, does it? It's because you don't like *me*. I don't know why, but you don't like Franconis' and you don't approve of me. *That's* why he's not allowed to do the show, isn't it?"

"That's not true."

"Finch, please just leave it!" Hector is pulling me towards the door now. "You'll just make it worse. It's complicated."

"No, it's not, it's pretty simple." Hector opens the front door, but I turn back to the Rev and say, "I mean, I get it. Sometimes you don't like stuff that other people want to do, and you think you know what's best for them and you want to protect them." I guess I'm thinking about Birdie dating James now, and I can't stop myself rambling. "But if you care about someone..." I look at Hector, because this is the best I can do for an apology and I hope he gets that when I say "If you care about someone" I mean "I care about you". "If you care about someone, you just have to let them do what makes them happy."

I'm waiting for Mr H to chuck me out but he just stands there, and for a second I think he's even going to change his mind. But then Hector takes my arm and pulls me to the front door.

"You shouldn't have come, Finch."

"I'm just trying to help!"

"Well, I didn't ask you to!"

"But—"

"*Please*. Just go."

On my way home to get cleaned up, I pass Lou and Jay pushing a rusty wheelbarrow full of bags of popcorn onto the bus.

Maybe everyone's right. Maybe my family are so completely freakish that I have no idea how normal families work. Maybe in normal families you *don't* clamber over people's roofs covered in blood and accuse their dads of being hypocritical dictators.

Maybe I've just made everything worse. Hector's still mad at me and now I've got him into even more trouble.

As I walk to the warehouse later, I try to psych myself up for performing, running through Hector's routines and cues in my head, but my rucksack of props feels like it weighs a ton, my body is stiff and my feet drag. This is not good. Clowns pretending to be sad can be funny. Clowns who are actually sad? *So* not.

The worst thing is, this is a completely familiar feeling. I've done it again, haven't I? Dared to like someone, dared to let them know it. And then had the door slammed in my face. At least I didn't get beaten up this time.

No, it feels worse than that.

Wren and Janie have attached signs to every lamp post between the town centre and the warehouse saying:

FRANCONIS' CIRCUS THIS WAY!

NO, YOU'RE NOT LOST, IT ACTUALLY IS IN AN INDUSTRIAL ESTATE!

Jay has set up a laptop with Skype so Birdie can watch from the hospital, and he's been posting "Circus tonight!" every fifteen minutes on every social media site in existence.

I arrive half an hour before the doors are due to open. Everything is set up and there's a hum of conversation, laughter and panic in the air. I sit alone in a dressing cubicle backstage, pulling on my clown gear, listening to snatches of conversation from the groups of performers as they do last-minute rehearsals, check their props, lose bits of their costumes.

"No, no, it's one, two, *three*, four. And when she does the somersault, *catch* her this time!"

"Has anyone seen a pink feather boa? No, that's peach, it won't go with my baseball boots."

"Is that my beanbag?"

"This is definitely not your beanbag, this is *my* beanbag."

"I'm pretty sure that's my beanbag."

"All beanbags are identical, dude."

"Then how can you be sure it's *your* beanbag!"

"*Py!* Set that down this minute, you are *not* pouring lighter fluid around the ring!"

"But Mr S!"

"And tell the Tots Acrobats to give those matches back *right now!*"

At 7.30 sharp the doors open.

And nothing happens.

"Give it time, give it time," Dad mutters, running back and forth with his lighting diagrams.

I can't take the strain. I climb the trapeze rigging and sit on the platform, watching the black curtain that separates the front doors from the performance space. It's the first time I've been up here since Birdie's accident. From down there the platform looked so far from the ground, but now I'm up here, it doesn't feel far enough.

And then someone walks through the curtain.

A few Juggulars still running around the ring freeze, staring at the poor family who have just arrived. That'll be Mr and Mrs Wood then. The Juggulars gather themselves and dash behind the red curtain as the mum, dad and three little kids take seats a few rows from the front and look around as if they're as nervous as we are that no one else will show up.

But more people do come. Some more families. Parents of the performers, some kids from Jay's class, some from Wren's. I watch in amazement as the black curtain keeps parting to let them through.

Lou barges her way in accompanied by half the clientele of O'Brien's pub, all of them a few pints too far gone. She's ditched the cardigans in favour of a clinging, glittery dress that reveals her full range of tattoos, and she appears to have taught her crew an old circus song with dubious lyrics, because they're all singing loudly:

OHHH,
The circus is coming to call,
The big top is fifty feet tall.
We'll make you laugh,
We'll make you gasp,
And the lion will bite off your OHHH!

The circus is coming to call...

The mothers in the row in front cover their children's ears, but they can't move seats because the place is filling up now as more and more people arrive.

Miss Allen! With Mr Cooper! Sinead and James and

a couple of the Bond Girls, though I suppose I should stop calling them that if they're going to start doing stuff without Kitty. A bunch of kids who got out of the children's ward recently, and a few who are still patients accompanied by a group of nurses and a doctor. Our next-door neighbours and Chris Magee from the newsagent's, some more teachers and a few people from our year at school, plus a lot of people I don't know at all.

I relax a tiny bit.

We have an audience. They came. They paid money to see us.

There's a small scream followed by an unidentified crash from somewhere backstage and suddenly my stomach tightens.

We have an audience. They came. And they paid money to see us.

I climb down the rigging and head backstage, but before I get to the curtain a familiar voice calls, "Finch!"

"Tony!"

"Hey, this looks great!" He's left his seat to reach me but he points back to the audience and says, "I brought people. That's my boyfriend, Mal, that's Shirl – she's a nurse in cardiology – and that there is…" He grins.

"Birdie!" She's in a wheelchair, wedged between Shirl and Mal in the front row and cocooned in blankets, pale and tiny. But she's here. She's home.

"She was feeling good today and she slept all morning, so we got permission to bring her along, providing there are two nurses with her at all times. Speaking of which, I'd better get back to her before Mal starts talking about mandolins or something, poor girl."

"Should've known she wouldn't miss my debut in making an idiot of myself," I say, but I'm thrilled really; at least if I completely wipe out in the ring, Birdie will be here to pick me up. As usual.

Mum's calling me backstage and the lights are going down already. The seating's full (and *hasn't* collapsed) and I guess we're as ready as we'll ever be.

"I have to finish getting dressed. Tell her I'll see her after the show, and thanks again, Tony!"

"Looking forward to it! Tell Hector good luck!"

"Oh. Yeah. Hector. Actually—"

"Never mind. *Good luck!*" he yells to someone over my shoulder, and I turn just in time to see Hector sprint through the backstage curtains.

We've used more curtains to subdivide the back half of the warehouse into cubicle-sized dressing rooms. Between the excited chatter of the performers back here and the music pounding out front, it's pretty noisy. Hector and I have a tiny space with folding chairs, a mirror, clown outfits hanging on a hat-stand, and props littered around the floor.

"You're here!" I dash in to find him tearing off his clothes.

"Wig! Braces! *Now!*" he yells. He's on after Py, which means he has exactly six minutes to put on a costume and make-up that usually takes us twenty. I throw props at him, fasten his braces, button his buttons and jam his wig on while he paints his face. I hope he can calm down enough to remember his cues. When Dad ducks his head in and yells, "You're on!" he runs to the stage curtain, still tying his bow tie, and I follow and peek nervously from the wings.

I needn't have worried. Hector's air of panic and dishevelment only adds to the comedy as he ducks water balloons from the Juggulars. I don't know how he managed to get here, or if this means I'm forgiven, but I guess we can talk about that when he comes backstage again.

But actually, Hector's in so many acts and there's so much to do backstage that the show's half over before he and I find ourselves back in our dressing room together.

Our act is coming up soon. I'm putting the finishing touches to my white face, clown eyebrows and red lips (I finally agreed to the make-up) when Hector comes in and flops onto a chair, exhausted. Outside I can hear Dad running about with his clipboard, directing everyone, and Mum being ringmaster out front. Her voice booms over the speakers, "AND NOW, LADIES AND GENTLEMEN, BOYS AND GIRLS, GIVE A BIG WELCOME TO THE JUGGULARS AND THEIR WEAPONS OF MASS DISRUPTION!!!!"

Everything seems to be under control and there's nothing for us to do but wait for our cue, which shouldn't be long; we're on after the Juggulars.

But I'm worried. I still don't know how angry Hector is; we haven't talked properly since the dress rehearsal, and I don't want our act to go as badly as that did, so I'm trying to work out the best way to fix things between us when he says, "I can't do this."

I stare at him. "You're bailing on me six minutes before our act? Are you serious? I can't go out there on my own!"

He rolls his eyes. "Not that. You know, you always assume I'm going to let you down or ditch you for someone else or disappear on you. I know today was a close call but, in case you hadn't noticed, I'm *here*. I'm here and I'm still your friend, even though you've never really given me a reason to be."

I don't know what to say to that. It's true, but I still don't know what to say. He doesn't give me time to respond anyway.

"I'm not worried about the act," he says. "But I want us to sort things out before we go on."

"Oh." I let out a relieved breath. "Good idea, I was thinking that too. OK, I'll go first." I turn my chair so I'm facing him, and say, "I'm sorry I yelled at you and I'm *sort of* sorry I broke into your house and yelled at your dad."

He can't help smiling. "Thanks, Finch, that's big of you. But actually, you were right."

"Really?" I try not to look astonished. I'm almost never right.

"About being brave and being honest about everything. That's why I told my dad the truth. About Sinead.

And about you. Actually, I thought it was kind of cool of you to break into my house to rescue me."

"Your dad didn't think it was very cool."

"I think he's torn between being impressed and having you reported as a danger to yourself and others. But he also said you must be a pretty good friend to go to all that trouble and he could see why I liked you."

"Really? So he let you come tonight?"

"They're in the audience."

"That's great!"

"And now I want to tell *you* the truth," he says.

"Me?"

He frowns at the noise around us, shuffles his chair closer to mine and we both lean forward. He stares at the floor between his knees and rubs nervously at the back of his neck as he speaks.

"I've been trying to work out the best way to say this, but it's pretty simple. You know I'm gay, don't you, Finch? I hoped you'd already guessed that."

I sit back. "Oh. Right. I mean, yeah." I had *not* guessed that. I think. I don't know. Mostly I just feel a sort of lurch in my stomach, like the floor's dropped from beneath me.

"It's not a secret or anything; people at my old school knew."

"Yeah? That couldn't have been easy."

He shrugs. "There's always some group of dicks

who think it's *any* of their business. But it was a big school and there were a few gay kids, so most people were OK with it. They just picked on me for being a Star Trek fan instead."

"Understandable. Do your parents know?"

"Yeah, I told them a couple of years ago. They were better about it than I thought they'd be. Mum was great. I think Dad will come round eventually, but he kept saying, 'You're too young to make any big decisions', like I was choosing something expensive out of a catalogue. I think that's why we moved here. He thinks gay kids only happen in big cities and TV programmes, and if I'm surrounded by *normal* kids, I'll forget about it." He rolls his eyes. "He was thrilled when he thought I was dating Sinead."

"So why didn't you tell anyone at school here?"

"I did tell Birdie, but that's all. I've never lived anywhere this small before; I wanted to get to know the place before I stood up and painted a target on myself. And Dad said I should wait. He seems to think the whole thing is OK in theory, but I should keep it low-key and not make life difficult for myself. Like being singled out at school is the worst thing in the world. He even said to me one day, 'You know, it's fine to be gay, but you don't have to be obvious about it. You don't have to be *camp*.' I know he's just trying to protect me, and I thought he might be right for a while, but now I think that's rubbish. It's always harder pretending to be something you're not. You know?"

Yeah. I know. But somehow I can't get the words out.

"I guess that's what all this fuss over you has been about," he says. "I didn't want to pretend or sneak around any more and he wasn't happy about it. But it's my decision. So this is me not pretending." He looks at me properly for the first time since he started speaking. "Do you understand what I'm saying?"

I open my mouth but nothing comes out.

"My dad didn't like me spending so much time with you because he thinks I'm too young to be in a relationship. With a boy anyway. I don't know why he thinks that's different."

I still can't speak.

"I'm saying I like you, Finch."

I *have* to force some words out. Any words. "You do?"

He gives me a nervous smile. "Yeah. I mean, you're annoying and you're tactless and you have zero patience and you're prickly as hell." He shrugs. "But you're also funny and kind and loyal, and you throw yourself in the way every time someone takes a shot at me, which no one's *ever* done for me before, and you're brave and different and talented and … well, honestly? Kind of hot. And you're right about telling the truth, so… I like you and I'm not going to hide it just because you want to ignore all this."

Dad pops his head round our curtain, yells "Thirty seconds!" and disappears again.

Hector's still looking at me. It occurs to me that it's just typical that the first time someone tells me they fancy me, they're wearing a huge painted grin, a curly orange wig and funny trousers. It's ridiculous. A snort of laughter escapes me and Hector jerks upright like he's been slapped.

Crap. "No, Hector, I didn't mean to laugh."

"It's fine, it doesn't matter, forget it. I mean, I know I'm not James Keane or anything," he mutters. He's adjusting his wig, putting his red nose on and heading for the curtain door, and he doesn't look a bit surprised, like he never expected much better from me. But we can't go into the ring like this. I pull him back by the braces.

"Wait! Please listen! I listened to you."

He turns but still doesn't look at me. "OK, but be quick, we're on in a second." He's right; I can hear the audience applauding the Juggulars.

"I didn't mean to laugh, you just made me nervous."

"All right, I can understand that." He waits expectantly. "Is that all you want to say?"

I don't know; he isn't giving me time to think. And anyway, my mouth's dry and my stomach's starting to heave. I can hear Mum's voice booming around the warehouse: "AND NOW, LADIES AND GENTLEMEN..."

"I..."

"BOYS AND GIRLS…"

"I…"

Hector shakes his head, disappointed, and walks off towards the gap in the ring-door curtain. I follow, and he disappears through it, into the ring, as Mum yells, "FRANCONIS' MOST HILARIOUS DUO, HAZZARDOUS HECTOR AND OUR VERY OWN FINCH FRANCONIIIIII!"

About two metres short of the curtain, I stop. I stop like I've hit a brick wall. The sheet of red silk in front of me floods my vision like a tidal wave. A cheer from the audience twists my stomach, the bassline of the music hammers in my head, and I can't hear, can't think, can't move, can't breathe.

"Finch?" Janie is beside me. "Are you OK?"

I shake my head and put my hands on my knees, trying to control the dizziness, trying not to vomit. The colours of my costume swim before my eyes and I tug at my collar like it's strangling me.

"You feel nauseous?"

I nod.

"Dry mouth? Palpitations?"

More nods.

She squeezes my shoulders. "It's just stage fright; you must have had it before?"

I shake my head. Never. I've performed on the trapeze a million times and I've never felt like this.

I don't understand it; I just know I'd rather suffer anything – death, failure, the wrath of every performer at Franconis' – than walk into that ring.

Mum dashes backstage. "Finch! What are you doing? Hector's out there on his own!"

I just shake my purple wig at her, wordless, blank. She could be speaking Dutch, for all it means to me. My whole skull throbs and I can't tell if it's the music or the blood pounding in my ears.

"He's a little nervous," Janie says. The crowd laughs and I know Hector must be out there improvising to fill the time, terrified, waiting for me to rescue him. And I would if I could. I would climb *skyscrapers* to rescue him. But I can't do this.

He's all wrong about me; I'm not brave enough.

Janie leans down and speaks calmly and quietly in my ear. "You don't have to do anything you don't want to, Finch," she says. "No one is going to make you go out there and it's not the end of the world if you don't. But you should know that it's never as scary as you think it will be. It might be great or it might be awful, but I guarantee it won't be as bad as how you'll feel if you let Hector down."

I don't feel any better, but I know she's right. I look up at her and nod.

She leads me towards the curtain.

★ ★ ★

The next six minutes are a blur. It's no wonder Mr Hazzard thought we were spending a lot of time together; we've rehearsed so much, I don't even need to think about what I'm doing. Instead I watch Hector. My nerves vanish the second he flashes his big, relieved clown grin at me. My body loosens and my smile lights up to match my make-up, as if the Finch cowering behind the curtain was someone else altogether. I can feel the laughter of the crowd coming at me like waves, bearing me up, making me buoyant. The spotlights lift me and Hector out of the darkness, like we're the only people in the world, but when I peer through them, I can see the audience. It's the closest I've ever been to an audience. There's Birdie clapping and cheering, Sinead laughing, Mr and Mrs Hazzard smiling in amazement at their son, who seems to be carrying the whole audience along with him on a tide of clown weirdness. Carrying me too. Our movements are like a domino chain, one triggering the next as we react to each other, setting each other up and filling in each other's punchlines; and I know neither of us would be half as good, half as funny, half as brave, alone.

But he has been alone. All this time. I think about him growing up in the city; no brothers or sisters, no friends at school, no one to talk to. Moving to a new town, working out who to trust. I think about how brave he must have had to be. Prancing about in a clown suit must seem like nothing. And suddenly I'm flattered that, even though he could do this on his own if he wanted to, he wants to be partners with me.

If I haven't already ruined it, that is. He's such a good performer, I have no idea if the clown grin he's giving me is real or fake, but like everyone else here, I choose to believe in it wholeheartedly for the next six minutes.

We'll worry about later, later.

In no time, it seems, Hector's galloping out of the ring with me on his back, waving my hat at the kids, and Mum's running on to introduce the Tuesday Acrobats. Behind the curtain I jump off him and the two of us jog back to our dressing cubicle, panting and laughing so hard we have to pull the red noses off to breathe. It feels like the first time we performed for the kids at the hospital, except this time it's me having the adrenaline rush.

"You were brilliant, Hector!"

"I *knew* we could do it!"

"That was freaking incredible!"

I can still feel the energy surging through me. Six minutes isn't enough. I want to go back, I want more. I could do it, I could do *anything*. I've never felt this exhilarated after a trapeze act. Trapeze is nowhere near as scary and nowhere near as exciting.

We're laughing and giggling, and I'm starting to think I might have to run back out there just to vent some of this energy. I can't just sit down, take my make-up off and go home. Not yet.

"Hector?" I pant. "I have to tell you something."

"Yeah?" He looks nervous but holds my gaze.

"If you can be brave, I can too. I haven't wanted to admit this, even to myself, because I didn't want to be any more different than I already am. But I think it's time to face it."

"Yes?"

"Yes. I'm ready now." I take a breath and stare at the ground, as if I can't look him in the eye, but when I raise my head again, I'm wearing my red nose and a deeply serious expression. "Hector, I think … I'm a clown."

There's a second's pause as he shakes his head at me. "You arse!" Then he whacks me on the shoulder as I convulse with laughter.

"I just can't deny it any more!" I yell over his head, in between yelps as he continues to wallop me. "I can't live a lie! This is the real me!"

"It's official, you are a complete and total tool, Franconi!" But we're both laughing. He stops beating me up and starts to turn away.

"Hey, Hector?"

He turns back. "What?"

I pull my red nose off again. Then I take one of his hands in mine, pull him towards me, and kiss him on his ridiculous clown lips.

61

Everyone's buzzing after the show. The whole thing went perfectly, dozens of people have asked to join – even kids from our school – and they liked Hector so much, we've had requests for clown classes. When the audience have gone, we have a big party in the warehouse. We crank the music up loud, tuck into all the food Mum's made, and she and Dad are still dancing like teenagers in the centre of the ring at midnight.

We did it. We saved Franconis'. But for the first time, it feels like it wouldn't matter if we hadn't. We didn't do it for the building or the equipment or the classes. I didn't walk into that ring so we could keep a roof over our heads – I did it for Hector. And Py did it for Janie, and Janie did it for Birdie, and Hector did it for me.

I dance and laugh like a lunatic along with everyone else at the party, but for once I'm not thinking about Franconis' at all.

Monday morning I wait until 8.37. But no Hector.

I've been up since 7 a.m. I dreamed about the show all night, but when I opened my eyes this morning, the first thing I thought about wasn't the circus. And it wasn't Birdie. It wasn't even Hector. It was my wardrobe.

I leapt out of bed and spent a full hour getting dressed. Then I sat on the front doorstep for half an hour, wondering if I'd got confused. If I'd missed something in one of his texts. If I'd dreamed the whole flipping circus/show/kissing event.

At 8.38 I can't wait any longer or I'll be late, so I run down the road and arrive at school out of breath, expecting to find Hector on the yard wall waiting for me, but he's not there. Still five minutes to the bell, so I sit down and start to panic.

A couple of people walk by and say, "Hi, Finch, liked the show!" and others wave from across the yard, which should make me feel great, but all I can think about is the empty space on the wall beside me. Adi and Davy walk past, look me up and down and snigger.

I'm wearing a blue tartan kilt, black-and-white stripey leggings, bovver boots, a black T-shirt and eye-liner. I know turning up to school in a skirt is asking for trouble, but it seemed like a good idea when I got up this morning. Now, it seems less so.

The problem is, the higher you are, the further you have to fall.

That post-show rush is like helium, and since I ran out of the ring I've felt so light, I floated through the whole weekend. On Friday night I was a closeted trapeze artist and by Sunday I was a gay clown. It felt like everything could change.

Even coming out at home was easy because, of course, my family reacted like the super-cool family they are.

Dad said, "Oh my God, you're not dating Py, are you? I don't think my nerves could stand it."

"No, Dad."

"OK, then we're good."

And Mum said, "Hadn't you already told us that? I could have sworn you did."

"Uh … no."

"No? Maybe it was when Wren went vegan."

"I guess so."

Then they went back to their Sunday newspapers and I stood there awkwardly for a minute. Even I was expecting more of a reaction than that. Was I supposed to just go now, or what?

"Um, is that it? I mean, you understand what I'm saying, don't you? You know 'gay' doesn't mean 'happy' these days?"

Mum laughed and then said gently, "Of course we understand. And we knew, sweetheart. Of course we knew."

"Oh. I think Birdie knew too actually. I guess I should stop wearing that *I am gay* T-shirt everywhere."

Dad flapped the pages of his newspaper and said absently, "I think it's very nice. Maybe try a jacket."

When I told Lou, she looked me over, shook her head and said, "I don't know. I've seen gays on the telly and they're very fashionable. I don't think they'll take you."

"You don't have to *apply*, Lou! And there's nothing wrong with my clothes!"

"Can you get me into one of them gay bars? They look like a laugh."

I rolled my eyes. "Still underage, *Gran*. But maybe. Someday." She started practising her club moves and the two of us laughed until my face ached.

But I guess the high is temporary. It tricks you into thinking anything is possible, and then you find yourself sitting on the yard wall on a chilly Monday morning, surrounded by games of football and other minor skirmishes, and the sense of anticlimax is kind of crushing.

I try to remember the costumes, the spotlights, the music, the applause. But then I look around at the whitewashed school and the tarmac yard and all the grey people and think, *What does any of that have to do with this?*

I was an idiot to think anything would be different. The euphoria of the weekend now seems ludicrous. All that talk about being brave suddenly seems like just that – talk. And what it boils down to is a lot of complicated, scary things that I now have to think about.

Do I want to do this? Do I want to be Murragh High's gay poster boy? Do I want to sign up for years of looking over my shoulder and being on my guard and picking my battles? Do I want to have a boyfriend? Do I want to have a boyfriend who's a million times smarter than me and has no dress sense?

If he ever even gets here.

I'm taking my phone out to text him when I hear a scream and some laughter from near the gates, and I look up to see people scattering out of the path of the unicycle lurching dangerously across the yard.

He looks as terrified as ever, but I know he's putting it on; he's not half as bad at the unicycle as he's pretending to be. But he's certainly getting people's attention as he narrowly avoids running them down.

He's wearing plain brown trousers that actually fit him; a white shirt tucked in at the waist, open at the neck, with the sleeves rolled up; his red clown braces; and the black bowler hat, spikes of blond hair jutting out beneath it. He looks pretty cool. And kind of cute; why did I never notice that before?

Everyone's watching, laughing and squealing at the near-misses, wincing and waiting for the crash as he comes towards me. But when he gets closer, he straightens up, winks at me and then sails the last five metres, smooth as Janie on her silks or Py with his poi. I stand up to meet him, slightly confused and with a fluttery feeling in my stomach.

But then, a metre away, he seems to hit a bump and lose his balance, because suddenly he's falling face first towards me. I put my hands out to catch him but he tucks his head in, puts his arms out and does the neatest little tumble. He lands right at my feet and springs up in front of me, grinning and pulling something out of the folds of his rolled-up sleeve like a magician with a bunch of fake flowers.

There's scattered applause from the yard and I laugh, waiting for him to say "Ta-dah!" because it's the perfect ta-dah moment.

But it's not fake flowers, it's two slips of paper. "Movie tickets," he says. "You won our bet. There's a film festival in the city; they're showing old Buster Keaton and Charlie Chaplin films. Come with me? As my date?"

Everyone is staring at us. A whole yardful of Ginghams, frozen, slack-jawed, like they've never seen a boy on a unicycle ask out a boy in a skirt before. We glance around at them.

"This isn't going to be easy, is it?" I say.

Hector shakes his head. "It might be totally shit. Think yourself lucky; I've done it once already and now I have to do it again!" He holds the tickets out. "So, how about it?"

There's no orange wig, no sticky lipstick, no red nose. Just a couple of hundred teenagers gawping at us. I don't care. It's like Mum said; you can't please everyone. One person will do.

"Yeah." I grin at him. "That sounds great."

There's a moment during every trick

Posted by Birdie

It might look like letting go, leaping into thin air, but what it really is, is trusting something or someone to catch you. It could be a ridiculously small part of your own body – your knees, one foot, even your teeth. It could be a bar, a length of silk, a parent, a sister, a friend. A hand reaching out of its spotlight and into yours. The trust part comes in because you have no idea if it's going to work out until you make that leap.

When choosing a partner for your act, remember that you'll spend very little of your time in the spotlight. Six minutes or so, a few times a week. And most of the time you spend holding that outstretched hand *won't* be when your life depends on it, it'll be when you're watching telly, or walking home from school, or sitting in the cinema.

The trick is to choose a hand you like holding, wherever you are.

< < Previous Post

ENJOYED THIS BOOK?
WE'D LOVE TO HEAR
YOUR THOUGHTS!

🐦 #FlyingTips @KMcCaughrain
@WalkerBooksUK @WalkerBooksYA

📷 @WalkerBooksYA

ACKNOWLEDGEMENTS

Drum roll, please...

This book would still be cowering backstage were it not for Helen Nicholl and Liz Carrasco who very gently yelled at me until I sent it to my agent. Everyone needs friends like these.

Massive thanks to – my agent, Kirsty McLachlan, for believing in me in the first place; the truly lovely folks at Walker Books, especially my editors, Lucy Earley and Emily McDonnell, both of whom instantly got these characters and made the editing a breeze (I'm so grateful Finch leaped into such safe hands); Anna Morrison for the beautiful cover; and Michael Bell for school-related fact checking (all errors are his fault).

The spelling of Palari words varies, but I *shushed* most of mine from Micheál Ó hAodha's *Parley with Me: A Compendium of Fairground Speech*.

Most of all, thanks to my husband, Michael, for support and encouragement beyond measure; to my family, who very rarely suggest I get a proper job; and to my sister, Lynsey, who demanded I put her name in the book. I'm putting it at the back to check if she's read it.

KELLY MCCAUGHRAIN lives in Belfast and has recently completed a degree in English and Creative Writing at Queen's University. She was shortlisted for the 2013 Times/Chicken House Children's Fiction Prize. When she isn't writing, she volunteers with Fighting Words Belfast and takes long holidays in her 1967 classic campervan, Gerda. *Flying Tips for Flightless Birds* is her first novel.

Visit her website at **www.KellyMcCaughrain.com**